Round Up

Round Up

Tony Cheatham

Quiet Storm Publishing • Martinsburg, WV

All Rights Reserved.

Copyright © 2004 Tony Cheatham

No part of this book may be reproduced or transmitted in any form or by any means, graphic, electronic, or mechanical, including photocopying, recording, taping or by any information storage or retrieval system, without the permission in writing from the publisher.

Published by Quiet Storm Publishing
PO BOX 1666
Martinsburg, WV 25402

www.quietstormpublishing.com

Cover by: Clint Gaige

ISBN: 0-9758571-3-4

Library of Congress Control Number: 2005902510

This is a work of fiction. Any resemblance to actual events or persons, living or dead, is entirely coincidental.

Printed in the United States of America

I'm a hustler baby
I just want you to know
It ain't where I been
but where I'm about to go...

-Shawn Carter

Round Up

Chapter One

"Next," said the female voice through the holes of the bulletproof glass. Her voice was polite, but tired, the fatigue stemming from the line of people waiting to do their banking transactions. Vanessa Smith was her name. Richard Anderson couldn't forget it after she was introduced on her first day. He could empathize with her. Hell, he was a teller himself a couple of years ago before he'd been promoted to new accounts. Figured if she could get through the busy payday on Friday she'd stay with the bank for awhile, that was the real test. It was the first Monday after Christmas. Outside was sunny and cool, around 50 degrees, unseasonably warm for the end of December. Perfect for a day of shopping since a lot of people were off of work until after New Years. Richard glanced at the clock. It was a little after one. Customers had been waiting on the other side of the glass doors of the bank before they opened at 9 and had been coming in at a steady clip ever since. More were expected throughout the day to make withdrawals or deposit the checks they got as gifts a couple of days ago. Richard saw the frustration in Vanessa's face. Looked like she was about to cry any second. She was the only teller working since the other two who were scheduled had called in sick. Helen and Jackie. Two older women who were familiar with the heavy after holiday customer traffic. They'd done the same thing to Richard when he was on the front line. It was just apart of the initiation. An elderly man holding a big clear freezer bag full of pennies was next in line. Richard looked at Vanessa's shoulders drop as the man shuffled towards her. Customers behind the old man moaned as the bag of pennies jingled with each step he took. Richard gave Vanessa another couple of days before she quit.

Community National Bank of Baltimore City had a high turnover rate for tellers. And this particular branch was in the southwestern part of the city near Yale Heights considered the red zone, where mostly poor blacks, whites, and latinos lived. If the government hadn't forced the bank to put a location in the neighborhood, the closest branch would've been all they way downtown on Charles Street. Made it easily accessible for the social service recipients to draw money from the ATM with the government card on the first and fifteenth of the month. Richard had seen the routine twice a month, every month since he'd started working at the bank two years ago. He'd seen lots of people come and go because of rude customers, hard work, and low pay. The same reasons why he switched jobs as soon as an opening became available in another department. He was tired of going home every night with a headache, from the combination of stress and frustration in dealing with the public. People were serious when it came to dealing with their money. Found himself wanting to smack a couple of them after they'd been rude to him, thinking he'd short changed them. He kept telling himself not to take it personally, that these people didn't know him, but it was getting harder to listen to his own advice, especially when someone was right there in his face talking down to him like he was stupid. He'd graduated high school, Adam Clayton Powell High and was even taking some courses at Baltimore City Community College. And he had an aptitude for numbers. He could multiply, add, subtract, and divide, in his head without working the problems out on paper like everybody else had to do. Richard considered that his special talent. The school was on a three-week break for the holiday. He wouldn't be back in class until the middle of February. Figured he'd gotten an "A" in college math, his favorite subject. He couldn't wait until grades came back.

 Richard looked at Vanessa counting out the pennies. He knew she was doing it out of courtesy. The bank's policy was to have change–especially pennies–rolled up for deposits. He hoped she'd stay at the bank in spite of her frustration. He wanted to take her out to lunch or something, try to get to know her better. But he didn't even have the funds to take her anywhere impressive to eat. And she didn't look like the type to eat out of a brown bag in the canteen. More like the sit down restaurant kind of woman. Even though she was only two weeks out of training, she looked more like she'd been working there for years. A strand of black hair had come loose from the bun and was hanging in her face. She kept

Round Up

swatting it away as she counted the change. She was a pretty girl, about 5'2", 5' 3". He liked that since he was only 5'7" himself. She probably weighed around 125, 130, had smooth brown skin, the color of coffee mixed with two tablespoons of cream. She dressed nice, mostly in dress suits and slacks, was probably in her early twenties, maybe a year or two younger than his 26 years. Was probably even in college just like he was. He made up his mind to ask her out after work. Figured he'd wait until she had a chance to unwind from the stress. You couldn't talk to a woman when she wasn't calm. She'd blow you off every time.

Richard looked at the top of his cherrywood desk with the smooth and shiny finish, at his nameplate that read Richard J. Anderson, the "J" standing for Joseph, and the title under his name, New Accounts Representative. His space was neat and orderly, two pens in the holder–one blue, one black(nothing in the "in" box, nothing in the "out" box. A picture of his two-year old daughter, R.J. short for Regina James, was in the far corner smiling at him. He hadn't seen his little girl in a week. Richard made a mental note to himself to get over there on the weekend for a visit. He hoped Desiree—R.J's mother—didn't curse him out. He'd missed last months child support payment due to a busted radiator, so he didn't know how she'd act.

Richard perused the rest of his desk. He didn't like papers scattered all over the place. Not that he had a lot of work to do, but an orderly area made him look like he was on top of things. The calm of the music coming from the classical station on the radio on the corner of his desk soothed Richard as he glanced again at the line of people snaking around the black plastic poles connected together by chains. The Marriage of Figaro from the Barber of Seville opera was playing at a low tone on the portable. Sure, it was unusual for somebody Richard's age who was raised up in the city to like classical music, but there was something about the string instruments, the flutes and shit that relaxed him. He even hid his like of it through his teenage years to keep from being called a nerd. Otherwise he would've been whipping somebody's ass every day in the schoolyard. Ever since seeing those Bugs Bunny and Charlie Brown holiday flicks when he was a kid, the ones where they set the cartoons to classical music, he liked it. Been listening to it ever since. But not even Mozart could take away the anxiety he felt in having to deal with the bank crowd this time. If it was really busy, bank policy was to help the tellers, but Richard didn't really feel up to dealing with any rude people who were probably getting more irritable the longer that they had to stand in line. He looked upstairs at the assistant manager, Sara. He could hear her laughing, sounding like a female cat in heat. Watched her fling her blonde shoulder length hair in that way white girls did whenever they were trying to catch a dude's eye. She was standing closely behind one of the two computer guys who were working on the last minute tests for Y2K. She was supposed to be easing customers concerns about the security of their money when the year changed to 2000. Instead Sara had been flirting with the men, particularly the tall one with black hair. Looked like something out of one of those chick magazines, a prettyboy, just her type.

Richard looked at Vanessa again. More strands had come loose from her bun. She looked tired, worn out like she'd been cleaning house all day. Their eyes met for a second, hers begging for him to do something. Richard stood up from his chair, straightened his red silk tie against his blue shirt. He picked up the white bottle of ibuprofen in front of R.J's picture, popped two red and white pills, downed it with a gulp of bottled water to curb the headache he felt was coming.

Richard took a deep breath, said, "I can help someone over here." The line came alive with people turning their heads loudly expressing relief that the teller was finally getting some help. People ran towards Richard's desk like a herd of cattle. He felt a lump in his chest, the same one he used to get when he was a teller.

Three hours later, Richard watched Vanessa close the doors, locking them after the last customer had left. He was tired. She looked exhausted. He pulled off his tie, stuffed it into his pants pocket. Sara came downstairs, her coat in hand, said "good job guys". The words sounded flat, insincere, like it was something she learned in a management training class. One of those textbook phrases that a boss was supposed to say to her subordinates to let them know they were valuable as employees. "Jim's upstairs so if you need anything just call him. I'll lock up behind me. See ya," she said on the way out. Richard realized that he hadn't seen Jim the

Round Up

manager all day. Figured Jim had created some busy work for himself to avoid the crowd.

The orange sun was about to leave the sky for the day. Richard couldn't wait for the warm weather and longer days to come back. He couldn't stand the cold weather months. Especially since it was around this time ten years ago that his father had passed. Richard watched Vanessa pinning the loose strands of her black hair back into the bun. She was quiet as she went to count out her cash drawer, checking to make sure it was in balance. Light jazz playing through the bank's speakers was the only sounds heard in the building. Vanessa didn't talk as she counted the drawer. Richard knew the routine, first the big bills down to the change. He wasn't sure how to approach her so he didn't. Instead he put on his leather coat getting ready to leave. He walked towards the door.

"Lock up behind me," Richard said. She took a deep breath like he was bothering her, started walking towards him, pulling the plug on some blinking Christmas lights that spelled out "Happy Holidays" hanging over the teller counters. Richard watched the teller area go dark as she clicked off the light switch. He still wanted to ask her out, but her face still looked too annoyed. She followed him to the entrance, twisted the key in the lock and swung open the glass door. The cool air outside rushed into the warm building. Richard thought of his '89 Toyota Tercel and hoped it wouldn't give him any problems on the ride home. The phone on his desk rang before he could leave the building. He thought to let it go into the voicemail then changed his mind. Figured coming back in would give him another chance to work up the nerve to talk to Vanessa. She was looking at him, her left arched eyebrow raised, waiting to see if he was going to leave or stay. "Let me get that, might be important," said Richard, in a voice like he was apologizing for holding her up. He trotted across the plush navy blue carpet back to his desk. He heard Vanessa locking the door, standing there to let him back out. He answered the phone in the middle of the third ring, right before the voice mail took a message. He looked over at Vanessa tapping her foot against the soft carpet like she was keeping beat to a song she was listening to in her head. Richard held up one finger signaling that he wouldn't be long. He studied her face. Decided to wait until tomorrow before he said anything to her about going out. He reached for the ibuprofen on his desk for the headache that was coming back.

"Community National, Richard speaking," he answered.

"Richie, y-you gotta come home," a woman's voice said.

Shit, it was his mother. Hearing her caused his stomach to twist in knots. She was heavily into the church scene. And his mother was always on him to get into it with her, which is one of the reasons he moved fifty miles from Colver City to Baltimore. Ma was persistent when it came to religion. As far as Richard was concerned, the church was a hustle. And the preachers he'd seen didn't disprove his theory driving around in their fancy Benzes and living in the luxury homes like they did, while most of the congregation didn't know where next month's rent was coming from. Ma didn't see that though. To her they were messengers of the Lord. Richard grew tired of hearing it. But even with that long stretch of I-95 between them, the distance still didn't seem far enough away sometimes. But this time Richard noticed that she sounded different, her voice was a mixture of shock and pain. Not her usual condescending tone that sounded like he was going straight to hell when he died. "What's wrong Ma?"

She sniffed, pulled the mucus back up her nose. "It's-it's Marky," Ma said.

His mother didn't sound right, didn't sound right at all. Sounded like the time she told him that his father was in the hospital some years back. "What? What about him?" Richard asked. Felt his pressure rising at her reluctance to talk. He could hear another woman crying in the background. Probably Aunt Shelly, Mark's mother. "Tell me what's wrong with Mark!" Richard could hear her voice choking up with tears.

"They-they killed him."

"What? Who killed him? What're you talking about?" Richard asked. He pressed the phone against his ear in silence. Had he heard her right? Did she say his cousin Mark was gone? He wanted her to repeat it, say it again so that he was sure he'd heard the same words. "When did—"

"T-they f-found him this morning."

"What happened?"

"Richie? W-when you coming home? You gotta come."

Round Up

"I'll be there tonight," Richard said. "I just gotta go pack--- " He heard the dial tone. His mother had hung up as soon as she heard that he was coming. Richard stood at his desk, the phone still pressed to his ear. Pictures of his cousin Mark were flashing through his mind like a slideshow. Vanessa's voice bought him back to the bank. She was still waiting by the door.

"You getting ready to leave now? If you are come on so I can close out my drawer," Vanessa said. Her foot was still tapping against the floor.

* * *

Richard drove south on Jackson Avenue, the pain of Mark's death burning his heart. The feeling was familiar. Richard felt the same way after his father died. But this was different. Pop died from natural causes, a heart attack. Mark was taken by a bullet. Violently pulled out of this world into the next one, if there was one. Pop got to live his life. Mark was just beginning his. Richard was heading downtown to the four-story apartment building on Baltimore Street where he lived to pack some clothes for the trip to Colver City. He didn't know how long he was going to be gone. And to be honest, he wasn't all that excited to be going back, especially under the circumstances. It had been four years since Richie had lived there. He only went back once a month to see his mother. He would usually get there in the morning, take Ma out for some food, catch up on each other's lives while they ate, maybe take her shopping for some household things, and then leave before dark. Staying there would have reminded him of his old life, of the things he used to do. A life that he left behind when he moved from Colver. Except for the hum of the heated air blowing through the vents, the cabin of the car was quiet. He didn't want to hear any music, still not believing that Mark was really gone. Richard had just talked to him what, three, four days ago? Even though they weren't as close as when they were kids the two of them still managed to talk on the phone at least twice a week.

During their last conversation Mark had told him that he was planning to get married. He invited Richard over to the apartment where he and his girlfriend Monique lived for a New Years Eve get together with friends and family, since Mark couldn't make it over to Ma's house for Christmas because of a concert he'd set up in Philly. Richard figured Mark was going to drop down on one knee in front of everybody and pop the question. Mark was a romantic. He liked to be the center of attention. Even when they were kids he'd be the one who would put on a show by lip syncing and dancing to a record at family reunions and birthday parties. He liked to be under the spotlight, all eyes on him. Richard wasn't surprised when his little cousin said he wanted to be a promoter. Mark was only twenty-three years old but he had already set up two sellout shows, one of them with R. Kelly as the headlining act. Richard still remembered Mark saying how he was going to start his own promotions company after finishing up at SUCC-State University of Colver City. But now that would never happen. All that potential gone.

Richard pulled up to the curb in front of his building. His head was pounding from another headache. He hoped there was some ibuprofen upstairs in the medicine cabinet. He sat there looking up at the stars with the car idling. He felt the tears coming, the water building up in the ducts of his eyes. If he was going to cry he wanted to get it all out now. He had to be strong for Ma and Aunt Shelly when he saw them. He dropped his forehead against the steering wheel and let the tears fall for his dead cousin.

* * *

Richard walked up the three flights of stairs to his apartment with his mind in a daze. His feet felt heavy like he had on ankle weights. He didn't really want to make the fifty something mile drive to Colver City, especially since he was just there on Christmas. But he had to make sure Ma and Aunt Shelly were okay. He undid the six buttons on his dress shirt, took it off and laid it on the tan couch near the door. Put on a casual light blue sweater that was hanging in the dimly lit hall closet instead. Went to his bedroom and looked at the shoe tree on the back of the door for something comfortable to put on after wearing the hard bottom Italian loafers all day. Wasn't nothing fancy, just something he picked up at one of those retail outlets. Found himself looking for deals nowadays, a big change from the lifestyle he used to know. Didn't have many sneakers, at least none that were in style anyway, exactly the reason that he opted for casual shoes. Back in the day he would've called a dude uptight for wearing shoes like college white boys. But since he got out of the

Round Up

life, copping hundred and two hundred dollar kicks every week was out of the question. Being legitimate definitely had its setbacks.

Richard picked up the phone, heard the beeping sound that signaled there was a message. He entered the code, listened to the lady telling him there were two. The first one was from Desiree wanting to know where this month's child support payment was. Then she threatened to take him back downtown for an increase. Richard deleted it without listening to the rest. He already felt guilty enough for not sending it but he had to get the car fixed. Figured he'd double up on next month's payment. He'd tell her that when he called back to let her know he wouldn't be able to pick up R.J. on the weekend. The second message was from Ma seeing if he had left yet. He went to his bedroom, packed enough for a week's stay and put the bags by the door. He popped two ibuprofen pills from the white bottle on the nightstand next to his bed like they were candy and dry swallowed. Richard's mind was numb. He looked at the glass case by the door holding his model collection, a small light shining on the scale size metal replicas of exotic cars. There were two BMW's, two Mercedes Benz's, a Lamborghini, a Porsche, and a Ferrari. On the top glass shelf was a red Corvette. Mark had bought him that. Said he was going to get Richard the real thing after making it in the promotions business. Richard felt his insides quivering. He remembered the day Mark gave him the present after his first concert was a success. Richard readied himself to leave. He picked up the phone, dialed the bank. Left a brief message that he was going to be out for the rest of the week because of a death in the family. He made another call to Desiree, told her machine what happened to Mark and how long he was going to be out of town. Added that he'd call her later. Richard hoped the news would soften her anger enough to prevent a return trip downtown. He grabbed his bags and headed downstairs to the ride.

CHAPTER TWO

Richard drove the last mile of I-95 north before his exit, seeing the ramp for highway 595 to the northeast side of Colver City where his mother lived. He admired the lighted skyline of the city. Would never think that they shined down on a place that had the highest murder rate in the country. Which was due in part to the fact that Colver also had the highest number of heroin addicts too. Bodies were just casualties of war over profitable corners.

In another few minutes he'd be pulling up in front of his mother's house. It was about an hour before midnight and an unusually warm night for December going into January. The radio was playing some sleepy classics, something by Chopin. He didn't listen to rap as much as he used to. Seemed like he needed to change everything about himself when he stopped hustling. Nowadays most of it was about the same thing anyway. If it wasn't about women and getting some ass, it was about driving the newest whips and truckloads of cash. Felt that he was past that point in this stage of his life.

Richard merged onto Lincoln Avenue after exiting from the highway, drove south for a couple of miles, came to the 3500 block and parked in front of his mother's brick front rowhouse. He found a spot between a red '87 Ford Mustang and an '86 Jetta with faded black paint. The houses on either side of hers were vacant with plywood covering up the windows and doors. Richard wanted Ma to move to a better neighborhood, maybe somewhere in the county. But she was stubborn about staying where she was. After a few arguments, he didn't bother to say anymore about the subject. Richard killed the engine to the Tercel, felt it sputter before shutting down. Looked through the front windshield, saw a corner dealer serve a customer under a street lamp at the end of the block. The dealer did a double take at Richard when he pulled up. Richard averted his eyes and turned away. He wasn't scared but he

Round Up

didn't want to chance getting into a staring match. The days of proving how hard he was were far behind him. Looked to the other end of the block, saw some teenagers were sitting on the steps in front of a vacant row home. He sat behind the wheel, took a deep breath before getting out of the car and making his way up to the house. He could see the living room lights on through the two small windows on the front door. He used his key to get in, stepped into the vestibule, and stopped. Immediately felt the heated air warming his face. Richard could hear Ma comforting his Aunt Shelly. His mother called out his name.

"Richie, that you?"

"Yeah Ma, it's me," Richard answered. He made his way up the long hallway, lit by a dim 15-watt bulb hanging from the ceiling, glancing at the framed pictures on the wall. Some were of Mark and Richard as kids, a couple pictures were of Ma and Aunt Shelly, and one was of Richard, Ma, and Pop in a family picture. That one always made him stop and look at it for a moment. Ma had always said he looked like Pop. He'd never fully believed it until he got older and saw their similarities. They had the same eyes, same nose, and the same deep dimple on the right cheek. He rubbed his hand over the picture and walked into the open area of the living room. The ceiling high Christmas tree with its blinking orange, green, and blue lights looked out of place during the solemn moment. Ma was sitting on the side of the couch dressed in her pink housecoat. Her right arm was wrapped around Aunt Shelly shoulder. Aunt Shelly's eyes were bloodshot red and swollen, a contrast to her light skin. Her hair was tangled and undone and the brown dress she was wearing was wrinkled. She was leaning forward, her hands interlocked in front of her mouth. She was rocking and shaking her head left to right. Seeing her made Mark's death real for him. He was gone.

Richard felt himself choking up but he pushed the feeling away. Remembered he needed to stay strong. He went over and knelt down in front of his aunt. She didn't look at him, her eyes still staring at the floor. He squeezed her wringing hands and looked up at his mother. Watched Ma pat her sister on the shoulder before getting up and walking towards the kitchen. Richard followed her. Once there she hugged him, held him tightly. Richard understood. Although it was painful for Ma to have lost her nephew, her sister's only son, she was happy that it wasn't her child. Behind her Richard could see the two wheeler that he and Mark used to fight over when they were kids. Ma pulled away wiping her eyes.

"You alright?" Richard asked. He spoke in a low tone, not wanting to upset his aunt any further. Ma nodded her head. "When did all this happen? And how come nobody called me sooner?"

"She got the call this morning. They found him and his girlfriend dead inside of Marky's fancy car. Police said somebody had shot both of them. I didn't know anything either, until Shelly called me up in tears talking about come downtown with her to see if Marky was dead. I didn't call you until after she was sure it was him. I didn't want you worrying over nothing," said his mother. Richard leaned against the counter, his arms folded over his chest.

"I can't believe this," said Richard, more to himself than his mother.

"Shelly kept telling that boy not to showboat with that expensive jewelry and fancy car. Somebody probably followed him home after one of them parties he gives, saw where he lived at, and waited for him." Richard thought about the platinum necklace with the diamond studded cross Mark wore and the silver BMW with chrome rims he drove and thought that's probably what happened. "Or it probably had something to do with that girlfriend of his."

"Monique was cool." Richard knew no girl would have been good enough for him or Mark in his mother and Aunt Shelly's eyes. And Ma really didn't like Desiree anymore after she took Richard downtown for child support.

"Hmph," his mother responded. "How's my grandbaby anyway?"

"Bad as ever."

"Leave her alone. She's just being a child."

"Do the cops know anything?" Richard asked.

"If they do they ain't telling Shelly nothing. You know how Colver City police are. Just another shooting to them. The only reason that they're even halfway putting some effort into this is because it was on the news. If this had happened uptown in Roland

Round Up

Springs where most of them live, I bet they would've caught somebody by now."

"Yeah," Richard answered. Even though she was right, he really didn't want to get into a political conversation about Colver's racial injustices with his mother. Once Ma got on her soapbox she could keep going for hours.

"And you know what else?"

"What's that?"

"Shelly ain't even cried yet."

"I saw tears in her eyes when I was in the living room."

"No, not the tears of shock that automatically comes when you hear someone close to you has been hurt. No, I mean the tears that come when a mother loses her child. Her only child."

"Probably hasn't really hit her about Mark being gone."

"I wish she'd hurry up and let it out. She's starting to scare me."

"Just give her some time," Richard said. He noticed his mother look behind him at the front door.

"Where your bags?"

"I left 'em in the car."

"You bring enough for the week?"

"I'm okay."

"The funeral's gonna be on the 31st."

"New Years Eve?" Richard questioned. "That's gonna depress a lot of people."

"Good. Mark got killed two days after Christmas. If somebody thinking more about partying than coming to his funeral then they wasn't his friend anyway."

"I didn't bring a suit."

"You about the same size as your father, wear one of his," his mother said. "Now go get your bags. I'm gonna get back in there with Shelly."

"Alright," Richard replied. He decided to go shopping for a suit before the funeral. He couldn't wear one of his father's. Would have felt like he was disrespecting his old man. Before Ma left she hugged him again. He could see she was trying hard not to let the tears come to her eyes.

"I'm just glad—"

"I know Ma," Richard said. He watched her walk back into the living room with his aunt.

* * *

Richard sat on the twin bed in his old room, looking at the walls plastered with pictures of his favorite exotic cars, the same ones he had in the display case at his apartment. Ma hadn't touched a thing in his room since he moved out. That was Ma's subtle way of saying he could come back home anytime he wanted. He could hear her talking to his aunt through the open vents of the floor of wooden planks. She was reciting a verse from the Bible saying something about Job and the tests of his faith. Richard rose off the bed and went to the window that faced the alley. Under the low lights of the street lamps he could see a pro servicing a john in the backyard of a vacant row house. He wasn't surprised to see nothing had changed. The backyard was like a free hotel. Pros knew it was a quick place to get paid. He watched for a minute before pulling down the shade and going back over to the bed. When Richard was younger he got off on looking at pros doing their business. Remembered jerking his dick many times looking at them. Now looking at the scene made him want to vomit. He clicked on the 13-inch color television in time to see the credits for The Late, Late Show going up the screen. Meant it was about 1:30 in the morning. He turned the tube off, turned on the bookshelf stereo system instead, hearing that song *Loving You* by Minnie Ripperton from back in the day. Reminded him of Monique since it used to be their song. Also reminded him that he hadn't been any kind of relationship since they'd broken up. Sure, he had some one nighters to satisfy his urges, nothing more than getting his rocks off, but he was starting to feel the need to have something deeper. It was hard trying to stay on the right path without some kind of support. Vanessa had been the first decent chick he had seen in months. That's why he hoped something would happen between them. Switched instead to a twenty-four seven classical music station to get out of the lonely mode. He recognized a symphony by Bach and parked.

Richard felt restless, fidgety, like he had to keep himself busy so as not to think about Mark anymore. Ma said him and Monique had been shot to death giving robbery as a possible reason. But that explanation didn't sound right to Richard. Why would the

Round Up

robbers have shot them? Mark was book smart, but he was also street smart. He knew to avoid situations where he could get possibly get set up. He would have given up whatever they were after without a struggle. And Mark knew he had to be extra careful since he was high profile. People assumed that he was well off because of the success of his shows, and the clothes and jewelry he wore. Made him an easy target for stick up kids and jackers. The truth was Mark was in debt. He used most of the money he made to pay for college. Mark told him that during one of their conversations. He also said that he got the nice clothes from record companies as gifts and favors for helping to promote their artist. The diamond studded platinum necklace was given to him after a singer backed out of a concert at the last minute. It was an incentive not to sue for breech of contract. And whatever money was left after paying rent and the lease on his BMW went to helping his mother. After his father left them seven years before, taking all the family money with him, Mark promised he would take care of her. Maybe Monique had something to do with what happened. Besides the fact that she was Mark's girl, what did he really know about her?

Richard grabbed his wallet from the bedside table and looked at the picture of R.J. when she was about a year old. She looked like an even combination of Desiree and Richard, some people saying R.J looked like her, some saying more like him. Richard rubbed his finger over the cute face in the picture, making a mental note to call her in the morning. He couldn't imagine the pain he would feel if something had ever happened to his little girl. Richard closed the wallet and placed it back on the table erasing the thought from his mind. He drifted off to sleep listening to the soft strings of a violin.

CHAPTER THREE

Richard was awakened the next morning by the siren of a fire engine passing through the block on the street. He could hear the AM gospel station that his mother listened to all day every day through the floor. Shirley Caesar was singing something about Jesus being her best friend with that depressing voice of hers, drowning out the music coming from his radio. He clicked it off. Peeked at the clock on the nightstand beside his bed and saw it was ten after seven. Ordinarily he'd be making his way to the bank. But today wasn't ordinary. It was the first full day after Mark was killed. That's when the realism set in that life had to continue. Richard's thoughts drifted to his little girl. Desiree was getting R.J. ready for daycare right about now. He picked up the phone, dialed her digits. The phone rang once before a man answered. It was Antoine, Desiree's son's father. His voice was deep, raspy like he'd been interrupted from a sound sleep.

"Desiree there?" Richard asked. He could hear cartoons on the television in the background. Figured R.J. was lying on the floor watching them just like she used to when he was living there.

"Naw."

"Did she already take my daughter to daycare?"

"How the fuck I'm s'pposed to know?"

Richard took a deep breath. Kept his frustration in check. Didn't want to get into a shouting match if R.J. was sitting right there. "Could you tell her that Richard called?"

"Yeah whatever," Antoine said. Sounded like he was half listening. He hung up before Richard could say anything else. He knew Desiree wouldn't get the message. Decided to call her again around lunchtime. Antoine didn't like Richard. Never had. Richard figured it was because Antoine thought Desiree still wanted to be with him. Antoine didn't have a thing to worry about. Even though Richard and Desiree had talked about

Round Up

reconciling a few times things didn't work out. Decided it was better to be friends. Though Richard was a little hurt when Desiree got pregnant by Antoine a few months after their breakup, Richard kept his thoughts to himself. Thoughts like what role was this man going to play in raising their daughter? Richard was going to mind his own business just as long as nothing happened to his little girl.

Richard got out of bed, hit the head, brushed his teeth, took a quick shower, put on some navy blue sweats, a white tee shirt, and some blue and white Adidas sandals that he used as slippers. He went downstairs to the smell of spiced sausage frying on the stove and muffins cooking in the oven. A plate of scrambled eggs topped with melted cheese was sitting on the counter. Aunt Shelly was sitting at the kitchen table. She looked like she hadn't slept. Ma didn't look much better. Both of them were still dressed in the clothes from the night before, Ma in the pink robe, Aunt Shelly in the wrinkled outfit. Richard kissed his aunt on the cheek. She smiled a little. He sat down at the table to the left of his aunt. It hurt him to see her so depressed.

"Smells good," Richard said.

"I haven't cooked like this since you lived here," Ma said. She turned the sausage over in the frying pan with the metal spatula, the grease popping furiously for a second before settling down. After she finished cooking, Ma put two sausages, some cheese eggs, and a muffin on a plate and sat it front of his aunt. Aunt Shelly looked at the food and leaned back in the chair she was sitting in. Ma put the same thing in front of Richard. The food smelled and looked especially good. A hunger pain reminded him that he hadn't eaten anything since getting off of work the afternoon before. Ma scrubbing the frying pan was the only sound heard in the kitchen. A knock broke the silence. Richard and his mother looked towards the front door. Aunt Shelly continued looking at the plate of food in front of her.

"Who could that be this early in the morning?" Ma asked. Richard got up from the table. Walked towards the vestibule peeking through the small windows to see who was on the other side. Two men were standing out front. The tall brown skin guy was wearing a gray blazer. The short white man next to him was wearing a black one. Strange, since Richard had heard the DJ on the radio, report that it was bitter cold outside. His piecing blue eyes caught Richard's attention. Thought they made the dude appear evil.

"Who is it?" Richard asked. He was looking through the glass.

The black man's voice was muffled as he spoke through the door when he answered. "Colver City Homicide."

"Put your badges up to the window," Richard responded. He'd seen people ask that on television. Figured it was the smart thing to do. The men alternated showing him their credentials. Richard had never seen a detective's badge up close so he didn't know if they were authentic or not. He undid both locks and opened the door, the cool air sinking to the floor at his bare feet.

"Yeah?" Richard answered.

"Is Delores Anderson here?" The brown skinned detective asked.

"What you want with her?"

"Is she here?" The detective asked again. His voice sounded frustrated and bothered.

"And who are you?" The other detective asked.

"I'm her son."

"Well son, we need to follow up on some questions we asked her yesterday at the coroner's office," said the taller man.

"I didn't get your names," Richard said. He was looking at the taller man, but felt the piercing blue eyes of the other man staring intensely at him. The tall detective took a deep breath before responding.

"Ronald Fields."

"Paul Ryan," answered the other man.

"Now can you go get Ms. Anderson please?" Detective Fields asked.

"Hold on," Richard said. He closed the door, left the men out front. His mother was in the living room standing by the stereo. She had turned down the solemn gospel music coming through the speakers.

"Who was that?" Ma asked.

"You talked to some detectives yesterday?"

"Was that them?"

"Yeah, I just wanted to make sure—"

Round Up

"Boy why didn't you let them in?" Ma asked. "I swear you don't use the good sense God gave you sometimes." She ran towards the door. The two detectives entered the living room area a few minutes later, his mother apologizing for Richard leaving them outside. Richard locked eyes with Detective Ryan who was still staring at him. Richard noticed a funny smell coming from the man when he passed by, like garbage that had been sitting all day in the hot summer sun. The detective looked away after a brief staring match. "You want anything to drink?"

"No ma'am," Detective Fields answered. "We just stopped by to ask some more questions. Yesterday wasn't a good time to really get information."

"I'm glad you waited until today anyway. I was so exhausted and I sleep so sound, I probably wouldn't have heard you at the door if you came over."

Richard watched the detective give Ma a fake smile before expressing his contrived sympathy. "I can understand with everything that happened."

Ma motioned him to the plastic slip covered couch that crinkled when he sat down. The other detective remained standing. "It's nothing else to tell you. Like I told you before I don't know much. His mother and me didn't see too much of him because of how busy he was. My son Richie and Mark were close though. They acted more like brothers than cousins. Maybe he could tell you something." Detective Fields turned to Richard. His thick eyebrows sat over his gray eyes like two caterpillars. He was frowning.

"Did Mark have any enemies, someone who didn't like him?"

"I live in Baltimore," Richard said. "So I really couldn't tell you about who liked Mark or not. I talked to him maybe once, twice a week." Richard watched Detective Fields reach into the inside pocket of his blazer pulling out a palm sized white pad and a pen. He wrote something down then asked another question.

"When was the last time you talked to him before yesterday morning?"

"The day after Christmas. He invited me over to his place."

"And before that?"

"Two, three days I guess."

"And he didn't sound worried or concerned about anything?"

"No," Richard responded. The detective turned towards Ma.

"How's the mother doing?" Detective Fields asked. "I'd like to talk to her, ask a few questions."

"I don't think she feels like talking but you can try. Follow me," Ma said. Detective Fields followed Ma into the kitchen. Richard stayed in the living room. He didn't want to see Aunt Shelly break down again. He was surprised when Detective Ryan didn't follow his partner. Instead the detective leaned against the wall near the Christmas tree, the lights blinking in unison. I'm Lost Without You by Be-Be and Ce-Ce Winans was playing low on the radio barely audible through the static. Richard noticed the man was staring at him again. This time the detective didn't turn away when Richard noticed him looking. They engaged in another staring match until Richard said something.

"What?"

"Something wrong?"

Richard knew the detective was trying to play a mind game, find out what he knew. "You're staring at me."

Detective Ryan jolted to attention like he was bought out of a trance. "Oh my fault. I was just imagining how losing your cousin must be painful for you," he said.

"Yeah it is," Richard responded. He watched while the white man walked around the room, studied him as he looked at the pictures on the wall. There were a few minutes of silence before the detective started talking again.

"So you live in Baltimore huh?"

"Yeah."

"You like it?"

"It's alright."

"Never been there myself. Don't like traveling too much. Shame huh? Even though it's only an hour away, I've never thought to take the drive."

"Oh yeah?" Richard asked. His voice was monotone, uninterested. He wanted the man to stop talking to him.

"I figure you seen one city, you seen'em all. They all got crime. I could stay right here in Colver and see that," Detective Ryan said.

Richard was only half listening. Only answered because he heard the man stop talking. "Really?"

"You know about crime right?"

Round Up

"What do you mean by that?" Richard asked.

"Nothing. Just meant that you're probably fed up with it like everybody else who left the city for the suburbs and other cities," Detective Ryan said.

"I guess." Richard could see that the Detective was frustrated by the fact that he wasn't getting anything useful from him. Detective Ryan's demeanor changed. Like he was trying to keep control of his anger.

An outburst from the kitchen interrupted them. Aunt Shelly was crying and shouting about Mark being gone. "She's really torn up," the detective said.

"Yeah."

"So were you born here or in Baltimore?"

"Here."

"Why'd you move?"

"Why all the questions?"

"Just figured I'd shoot the breeze while they're in there talking."

Richard eased the hostility in his voice. "What was your question?"

"Baltimore. Why'd you move to Baltimore if you don't mind me asking?"

"Just wanted a change."

"A change huh?" The detective asked. Richard didn't answer. He asked a question instead, wanting to steer the conversation away from himself.

"So you any closer to finding out who killed my cousin?"

"We're still looking over the crime scene, asking questions."

"So in other words no."

"We've got leads; people we still have to talk to," Detective Ryan said. "You know how it is. Something like this happens, everybody's scared to say anything thinking the same thing is gonna happen to them." He was quiet for a moment like he was thinking of another question to ask. "So—," he started. The detective was interrupted by his partner and Ma coming out of the kitchen into the living room. Richard was happy. Now maybe the cops could get back out to the streets where they belonged. They weren't going to find out who killed Mark sitting in their living room.

"I'm sorry she couldn't tell you anything. She's still so upset," Ma said.

"I understand," Detective Fields said. "You should probably give her something to go to sleep. Might make her feel better."

"I'll try."

"Thanks for your time Ms. Anderson. We'll be in touch as soon as we find out something," Detective Fields said. He started walking up the hallway, his partner close behind him.

"See ya later," Detective Ryan said. He was talking to both of them but was looking at Richard. Richard raised his chin in response.

Richard listened to the front door open and close. He walked towards the vestibule to lock up behind them. Aunt Shelly screamed out loud again about her baby being gone. He watched his mother run into the kitchen to comfort her sister. Richard went upstairs to go back to sleep.

Round Up

CHAPTER FOUR

Richard rolled over to the left side of his twin bed. Lifted his right eyelid to see that it was 12:15 in the afternoon. He'd slept for three hours, though it felt more like he'd been asleep for eight. And he didn't feel refreshed or rested but lackadaisical and sluggish. Richard turned over on his stomach and closed his eyes. He heard three taps on the other side of his bedroom door. Figured it was his mother coming to find out why he was sleeping the day away.

"I'm alright Ma," Richard yelled. His voice was groggy and deep. Caused him to clear his throat.

"It's Shelly," she said. Richard threw his feet over the side of the bed, shuffled to the door. He pulled up the baggy basketball shorts that were hanging off of his ass. He'd changed into them to get back into bed. They were more comfortable than the heavy sweats he had on earlier. His aunt was standing on the other side; her arms crossed over one another like she was hugging herself. "I'm sorry Richie, I didn't mean to bother you."

"You ain't bothering me Shelly. C'mon in," Richard said. She walked in looking around like a visitor to a strange city even though she'd been there countless times over the years. He cupped her by the elbow like she was an old lady crossing the street and walked her to his bed. Aunt Shelly was Ma's baby sister, five behind his mother's fifty years but she could easily pass for thirty, thirty-five. She didn't have any gray hair and her skin still looked as good as a cup of cocoa with two melted marshmallows. Mark used to get into plenty of beefs behind young guys commenting on his mother. He considered himself the man of the house after his father left them, and Mark took his job seriously. And it didn't help that she dressed in tight jeans and skirts that showed off her healthy backside. But looking at her right now, her eyes red and swollen from crying, Richard couldn't tell that she was the carefree Aunt he knew while growing up. "How you feeling?"

"I'm holding on. I've been trying not to think about it. But then I see something that reminds me of him. Then all this pain comes and I," she stopped and took a deep breath. Richard could tell she was about to cry again. But she stopped herself. "Why Marky? He wasn't hustling or nothing! He didn't have no illegitimate babies or nothing! He was putting himself through school, paying his own way! Why him? Why not them knucklehead good for nothings in the street who ain't about shit?" she said. Richard didn't know how to answer the question or what to say to make her feel better.

"The detectives said they still had some people to talk to," Richard said.

"That don't mean shit. You know as well as I do that means they wrote down the names of some junkies that were hanging around the scene to have something to report back to their sergeant. When the next killing makes the news, they'll forget all about Marky," said his aunt. Richard hugged her. He felt the tears rolling down his back. Her sobs sounded dry like her well of tears was empty.

"It's gonna be okay," Richard said. His aunt didn't answer.

* * *

Richard bounded down the steps on his way out the door. An hour after talking to his aunt he got dressed. Threw on some blue jeans and a button down shirt. He wanted his aunt to feel that something was being done to find out who killed Mark. Figured he'd go out into the street and ask around to see if anyone knew anything. He walked into the living room and saw Ma reading the bible on the loveseat. Aunt Shelly was lying on the couch, the left hand resting on her face. The right hand was palm side down on her exposed stomach. Ma peered over the tops of her reading glasses at Richard when she saw him.

"Where you going?" She asked.

"I'm gonna see some old friends real quick. I'll be back soon," Richard said. Ma gave him a worried look.

"Get back here by seven o'clock you here me? You ain't here supper is going back in the refrigerator and the kitchen will be

Round Up

closed for the night," Ma said. She's still the same, Richard was thinking.

Richard stepped out of the door, the cool air chilling his hands. The temperature had dropped since the early morning. He zippered up his almond colored three-quarter length leather jacket and put on his brown wool skull hat. He stood on the front steps watching the cars drive by on the street in front of the house. Reminisced back to the days when him and Mark used to sit there watching the hustlers drive by and fantasizing about owning their fancy rides. Richard remembered when he had his blue BMW. But that was back when....

"Richie!" A voice shouted. "Is that Richie Rich?" Richard looked down the block towards the deep and husky voice. He hadn't been called by his street name in years, since he left Colver City for Baltimore. Richard looked at the 6 foot tall melted caramel colored man walking towards him. Santana Jackson. His lanky frame made him look awkward and clumsy. But his curly black hair and dark eyebrows attracted the women to him. He was wearing baggy blue jeans, a black leather hipster, and some running shoes by Nike. Santana used to swing with him and Mark when Richard lived on the block. Kind of like the stepbrother to Mark and Richard's brother relationship. Even though he was half Hispanic, he didn't know any Spanish. His Puerto Rican mother died when he was two years old, leaving him to be raised by his black father. Santana barely knew his mother's side of the family. His father kept him away from them thinking they were going to kidnap him and take him to Puerto Rico or something. Even though Santana never talked about his mother back then, Richard and Mark could tell that he missed her from the questions he'd ask about Ma and Aunt Shelly. Things like did they read to them at bedtime and if they made them lunches for school.

Santana came up on Richard, gave him a one arm hug around the back, and gave him a soul handshake. Santana pulled back, looked Richard up and down. "Man you been movin' on up like George and Weezie Jefferson and forgot all about a brother," Santana said, referring to the old television show. "How come you didn't come down to my crib to say what's up?"

"I just got here last night," Richard answered. Actually Richard had been back and forth many times since he'd left to come see Ma. He just could never bring himself to pick up a phone to call or go see Santana. When Richard left, he wanted to leave everything behind that reminded him of his old life. And contacting Santana would have been a step in the wrong direction. Noticed the diamond stud in his left ear. Looked like the stone was at least a half carat to a carat. "When'd you get the rock?"

Santana gave a sneaky grin like he'd been caught in the act of doing something wrong and didn't care. "You like?" He turned his head to the right, showcased another rock in his lobe. "I got them a few months ago."

"They real?" Richard asked.

Santana face turned sour, like he had eaten a lemon. "Hell yeah they real! I don't front with no fake stuff!"

"Must have set you back some loot."

Santana gave that sneaky smile again. "Chump change." Santana's attitude changed from happy to sad in the next moment. "Sorry about what happened to Mark man. He was like my brother you know? I couldn't believe that shit when I heard it on the news," Santana said. He took out a pack of Newport's from inside of his jacket, offered one to Richard. Richard shook his head. Wondered when Santana picked up the habit. Santana shrugged, leaned against the Tercel with his feet to the curb, and fired up. Took a deep draw and blew a smoke ring into the air. They both paused to watch a girl walk by in tight black jeans that showcased her bubble shaped ass. Santana shook his head. Had a look on his face that was a window into his mind of the sexual things he could do to her if he had the chance. Looked down at his shoes and frowned. Richard watched Santana lick his thumb then bend down to wipe a smudge off his blinding white left sneaker.

"Where you heading?" Richard asked.

"To Angelo's," Santana responded.

"Angelo's?" A laugh left Richard's mouth. "That place still give out one napkin to wipe your mouth after eating one of them greasy subs?"

"Sure do."

Richard shook his head. "Let's walk," he said. Angelo's sub shop was a few blocks away on Rice Avenue. He hadn't been there in years. He hopped off the steps and started up the pavement.

Round Up

"So how you been? I heard you were working at a bank now. You trying to go white collar now? They paying you good?"

"It's alright," Richard answered.

"I'll bet that chump change you making what is it, every two weeks? I know it ain't nothing like you used to pull in every day," Santana said. Richard was trying to avoid the subject of the old days, back when he used to hustle. That was another one of the main reasons why he moved to Baltimore. He wanted to start over and leave the past behind him. Still, listening to Santana made him reminisce on the loads of money that flowed like water back then. And honestly, the struggle Richard felt in trying to make an honest dollar often made him want to get back into the game. There was many a night after a stressful day of school and work that he held the phone in his hand ready to make that call to one of his old connections. He combated the feelings by making a deal with himself. Figured he would get a good night sleep and if he felt the same way the next morning, he would go back. When the next morning came, he'd feel better. Getting back out there into the streets was a step backwards and he was only looking forward. Richard ignored Santana. Asked a question over his inquiry.

"You know why anybody would do something like this?" Richard asked.

"You know how it is man. You don't need a reason to get a slug in you in Colver. He might've just been a casualty of the streets."

"You know if anybody didn't like him?"

"Couldn't tell you. After you left we stopped hanging out. I mean we were still cool and everything, we spoke whenever we saw each other. But when Marky started making change from his promotion hustle, he barely came around the way anymore."

"You think somebody stuck him up?"

"Naw man. They found him in the Beemer. If that was a car jack they would've left their asses in the street."

"True," Richard answered. "Nothing was missing?"

"I heard the chain was gone but a junkie could have came by and snatched that after he was dead."

"What about Monique?"

"Her? No disrespect to Marky or nothing but that chick was fine as hell!" Santana said. Richard remembered the last time he'd seen her at their apartment. Monique was 5'3", brown like chocolate cocoa, with coal black hair that hung down to the middle of her back. And even though she was wearing an extra large Colver City Comets football jersey that was cut to the middle of her flat stomach, it couldn't hide her breasts that were shaped like two halves of a sliced honeydew melon. Plus the tight designer jeans she was wearing clung to her rounded hips showing off her apple shaped ass that was held up by firm and fit thighs. Santana was right about how good looking she was, but Richard kept his thoughts to himself. Agreeing with Santana would be like disrespecting Mark. Even if Mark was no longer with them. "It's a shame she had to go out like that," continued Santana. "I heard they found her with two bullets through her eyes. That's some crazy shit. Whoever did that had to be psycho or something."

"Yeah," Richard commented. Richard knew that was a message that Monique had seen something she wasn't supposed to have seen. The question was what was it? Maybe Mark was just a casualty to someone who was really looking for her.

"Unless the funeral parlor can work a miracle on her face her peoples are gonna have to keep the casket closed," Santana said. He dropped the square to the sidewalk, extinguished it with the heel of his left shoe. Blew the last of the smoke from his lungs into the air. "Far as I know she was cool though."

"It don't make sense to me."

"Getting killed never does man," answered Santana.

* * *

Angelo's sub shop hadn't changed any since the last time Richard was there four years before. A lighted yellow sign that read Angelo's in cursive letters with a smiling man making pizza hung over the glass double doors. The bulbs had burned out in the "O" on the sign, making it look like Angel's instead of Angelo's. Richard followed Santana into the shop. Heard Frank Sinatra's voice singing My Way, through the speakers in the ceiling. Ever since he could remember Angelo's had never played any black music even though the shop was in an urban neighborhood. The original owners, an Italian couple had bought the place in the sixties back when Colver City was mostly white. Back before the city was considered an urban area. Eventually the owners changed, but the music didn't. Voices like Dean Martin, Tony Bennett,

Round Up

Frank Sinatra, and other singers were heard coming from the speakers from the time that the place opened at nine in the morning until the doors were locked at eleven at night. Richard had never thought it was a problem. Made him have an appreciation for other types of music in the world besides hip-hop.

A man was sitting by the entrance on a wooden bar stool in a brown cotton jacket, khakis, and black army boots. The cheap cologne he was wearing burned Richard's nose when he passed by. Santana slid into one of the two remaining booths close to the front entrance. Richard sat across from him, looked around the joint. He saw a poster advertising something called the millennium sub, which was nothing but a steak and cheese sandwich with extra cheese and onions. Eight of the ten tables were occupied with people. Six people were waiting in line to order food, four males and two females. The lunchtime crowd was mixed with school kids on holiday break and dropouts. Richard saw the owners still put up that faded green artificial tree they used every Christmas. More bulbs were burned out than lit.

Richard watched Santana chin nod to some dudes sitting at a nearby table. Richard glanced at them. He'd never seen them before. People who lived in the neighborhood usually hung in Angelo's so Richard figured the dudes must have moved in after he'd left for Baltimore or they were from somewhere else. Richard didn't figure them to be visitors since Colver City wasn't the kind of place to come to for pleasure. They returned Santana's greeting with a nod before staring at Richard. Richard didn't look away. If he did they would think he was soft, weak. He didn't want to get into anything with them but would if necessary. It had been years since he had to play the hard role. It was the one part about hustling that he didn't miss. Somebody was always waiting in the background to be the next man on top. Richard noticed one of them was staring at him harder than the rest. He was dark skinned, about 5'4" wearing a black leather jacket and matching black Colver City Comets football skull hat. He was wearing diamond studs in both of his ears like Santana. They sparkled under the low lighting in the shop. Richard felt his heart beating faster. He could feel the adrenaline starting to make its way through his body. They locked eyes with each other until Santana got his attention asking something about Mark.

"Huh, what did you say?" Richard inquired. Richard turned to face him.

"I said cops been around yet?"

"Yeah this morning." Richard motioned his head towards the door. "What's up with him?"

"Security. They hired him after a shootout happened here last year."

"Damn, things that bad?" Richard asked. Four years ago, nobody had to worry about catching a bullet just for getting something to eat, Richard thought.

"So what did they say?" Santana asked.

"What?"

"The cops, what did they say?"

"Nothing really. Just a bunch of dumb ass questions. You ask me they're not gonna find who took Mark out."

"You don't think so?"

"Naw. Colver City cops are ass backwards."

"Tell me about it. My cousin Tina fucks with this cop over in the Northern District. Said he told her that there's a five year backlog of bodies that Homicide can't solve."

Richard shook his head. "See what I mean?" They were both distracted by two girls walking into the shop. One was plain with no real style to her. She wore a short hairstyle, cotton jacket, though Richard could see the girl had a nice shape from her tight blue jeans. The other girl stood out like a new Mercedes in a junkyard. Her long brown hair highlighted with blonde streaks hung down to the shoulders of her red leather three quarter length coat. Her black jeans clung to her thighs and were tucked into the tops of the red boots she was wearing. When she took off her sunglasses, Richard could see her arched eyebrows. She looked familiar. "Who's that?" Richard asked.

"Come on man, you ain't been gone that long."

"What?"

"That's Geena," Santana answered.

"Who?"

"Geena Lansing man. Take a closer look," Santana said. Richard looked closer at the fourteen-year old who now looked liked she was in her twenties. The long hair made her look different. More mature. He remembered her as a skinny ten year old little girl who dressed in baggy

Round Up

jeans and big shirts. The two girls walked over to the line of people waiting at the counter. Geena's hip motion was hard and deliberate like a fashion model on the runway. The dude who was staring at Richard called out to her.

"Geena! Come here real quick!" The dude yelled. Geena turned around to face him, clucked her tongue and continued talking to her friend. "Geena you hear me talking to you?" The guy rose out of his seat, pulled up his baggy pants, and walked over to her. He reached for her left arm. "You hear me b---" Before he could touch her, security had hopped off the stool and placed himself between the short guy and Geena grabbing the kid's left arm. The security guy towered over the young dude.

"Problem young brotha?" The guard asked. His voice was firm, commanding.

"Get off me!" The short guy yelled. He pulled away from security reaching towards his dip. Security grabbed him, spun the dude around securing his hands behind his back. He escorted the young guy out through the glass doors. The crew with him left after their leader was gone. Security came back and sat down on the stool. Richard glanced at Geena who was looking up at the menu like nothing happened. Her friend looked shaken. Geena opened up her pocketbook, dropped her sunglasses inside. She looked up and saw Richard. Their eyes met. She smiled and made her way over the table where he was sitting.

"Richie how you been?" Geena asked. Richard stood up, saw a glimpse of the little girl he remembered. He hugged her smelling Tommy Girl perfume. He knew that because he'd bought some for Desiree when they were together. Richard felt her firm breasts against his chest. His discomfort made him pull away. "Hey Santana," she said. Santana responded with a quick nod of his head. Walked over to the line to order some food. Geena sucked her teeth at his dismissive actions. "When'd you get back Richie?"

"Last night," Richard answered. Her attitude turned sullen.

"You here because of Mark?"

"Yeah."

"I can't believe that shit," Geena said. Hearing her curse took Richard by surprise. He couldn't get the thought of the ten year old skinny little girl out of his mind.

"What was up with that young dude?"

"Who Priest?" Geena asked.

"You describing him or is that his name?" Richard asked. Geena giggled like the little girl that she was.

"That's his nickname fool. I don't know his real name," Geena said. She clucked her tongue. "He's just mad because I stopped fucking with him." Richard left it alone. What she did was her own business. "When's the funeral gonna be? I need time to go shopping for an outfit. I got to look good."

"I'll let you know," Richard answered. He didn't want her there. She was acting more like it was a party than a time of mourning.

"Okay," Geena said. She reached into her pocketbook, pulled out a pen, tore off a corner of the food menu on the table and wrote something down. "Here's my cell phone number. Call me when you find out." Geena called out to her friend. Said she wanted to go somewhere else to eat. Then she left. Richard sat down. Watched Santana come back over to the table holding a white bag that was soaked through with grease. He sat down, tore into the sandwich like it had been days since the last time he'd eaten.

"The fuck she want?"

Richard could smell the onions from the bite of sub in Santana's mouth. "What's wrong with you?"

"Chicks a freak man. I wouldn't have even spoken to her if I were you."

"How come?"

"She been with every dude in the neighborhood. You might as well call her a pro. You buy her something you can get that ass."

"How'd she get like that?"

Santana took another bite of the sub, leaned back in the booth and put his hand on his stomach like it was bothering him. Richard wasn't surprised. "You know that dude Calvin up on Lonon Boulevard?"

"Yeah."

"Well she was fucking around with him for a couple of months last year and—"

"Calvin? Ain't he like twenty-eight, twenty-nine?"

"Yeah…then he turned her out and got rid of her ass. She's been like that ever since. Now she won't even talk to a dude unless he's talking about spending money on her," Santana said. Richard shook his head.

"He messed up a good little girl," Richard said. He saw a woman walk into the shop holding a little girl's hand. The little girl's hair was done into two ponytails that hung down to the dimples in her cheeks. Reminded him a little of R.J.. He shook his head thinking how the kids weren't even safe anymore.

CHAPTER FIVE

Richard sat on the beige carpeted floor in Santana's small room playing NBA Live on the Sega Dreamcast video game system. Santana had taken off his jacket, changed into a purple and yellow Lakers jersey with matching shorts. His left bicep showcased a tattoo that read pimp daddy, a drawing of a woman in a short skirt leaning against a street light centered under the words. It was tight, Richard had to admit, but personally he'd never deface his own body like that. Richard wasn't really paying attention to the television screen. It had been a couple of hours since they'd left Angelo's and Richard's mind was still on the drastic change in Geena. He remembered when she didn't even like boys and was still playing with Barbie dolls. Talking to her though, he could see that her mental level hadn't reached the maturity of her body. Santana was sitting on his bed furiously pressing the keys to the game controller.

"Yeah! Yeah!" Santana screamed. He stood up from the bed, held his arms up in the air. "That's how you dunk!" Richard dropped the controller, rubbed his hands together. "What's wrong with you?"

"Can't get my mind off Geena," Richard answered.

"Why you wasting your energy? She's not a little girl anymore. And it's not like she didn't know what Calvin was about. He was messing with a friend of Geena's before her, so she knew the deal."

"Who?"

"Tammy," answered Santana. Richard remembered how close Geena and Tammy were as young kids. How they played with dolls and did cheers when they were little girls. He was also beginning to see a pattern in how Calvin worked. Both girls had absent fathers.

"Why hasn't somebody called the cops on him?"

Round Up

"Tammy's mother did, but they couldn't prove anything was going on between them. Cops investigated him for a couple of weeks then dropped it. Geena started messing with Calvin after that. Caused Geena and Tammy to stop speaking to each other."

"He probably can't handle chicks his own age."

"Why are you so worried about what he's doing? It's not like they're your sisters or nothing."

"It's wrong that's why. That could be my little girl," Richard said. He would give his life before he'd let that happen, he thought.

"That's exactly why I don't have no kids. It's too much crazy shit to worry about out here. I tell you what I would do if some old dude came sniffing around my little girl's pussy. I'd put two bullets in his ass and worry about the cops later."

"That sounds good but then you'd get locked down right when your little girl would need you the most."

"I'm just telling you what I would do."

"I love my shorty to much to do something like that. I'd feel like doing it but I don't know if I would." Richard could see the strange look that Santana was giving him out of the corner of his eye. Like Santana had expected Richard to have responded differently than he did.

"I forgot you had a kid. Wassup with you and the mother? You still together?" Santana asked.

"Naw."

"She's probably killing your pockets with that child support right?" Santana asked.

"I'm taking care of my responsibility, paying what I'm supposed to. Besides, it ain't that much," Richard answered. Not yet anyway, he was thinking. He was sure there was going to be a return trip downtown courtesy of Desiree.

"More power to you. Taking care of myself is hard enough without having to worry about a crumb snatcher," Santana said. Richard looked around the small room that was the size of a jail cell complete with the bars on the two windows. Richard didn't like the fact that there were bars on the windows. Made him feel closed in and cramped. Clothes were scattered all over the floor. And the smell of dirty sweat socks hung in the air. A poster of Shaquille O'Neal from his days in Orlando hung over the bed and a picture of Michael Jordan in his classic red and black sneaks was on the wall behind Richard. There were five trophies from when Santana played high school ball. He got a scholarship to Georgetown to play at the college level and flunked out after his second year. Distracted by too many girls and not enough studying.

"What are you talking about taking care of yourself? You still living with your mother. You ever gonna move out of here?" Richard asked.

"Not as long as she's letting me live here rent free," Santana responded. He pressed the reset button on the computer game. "You wanna play another round?"

"Naw, I'm gonna head back home. I'm kind of hungry, and you know how Ma is."

"You gonna eat dinner already? It's not even three o'clock yet."

"My stomach don't have a watch."

"That's cool. I gotta take a shit anyway. That millenium sub from Angelo's is fucking with my stomach."

"Is that what that bubbling noise was? I thought you were still hungry."

"You lucky you didn't get anything to eat."

"Not the way that food looked," Richard said. "I'll catch you tomorrow." He opened the door to the room to leave. The fresh air was a comfort to his nose.

"Richie, hold on a sec."

"What's up?" Richard asked. He watched Santana rise off of the bed, lifting up the mattress he'd been sitting on. Santana held his stomach for a moment to calm the bubbling before he reached under and pulled out a .9 millimeter. He held the gun gingerly in his right hand like a newborn baby.

"Nice ain't it?" Santana asked.

Richard clucked his tongue. "What you gonna do with that?"

"Somebody fuck with me, they catching a hot one. No offense, but I ain't going out like your cousin."

"You got something like that, sooner or later you gonna have to use it," Richard said. He knew Santana would never pull the trigger on the nine except to shoot cans and bottles. He wasn't a

Round Up

killer. Or at least he wasn't when Richard lived there. From what Richard was seeing he wasn't so sure anymore.

"I'll do what I gotta do Rich."

"It's your world. I'll see you later," Richard said. He eyed the .9 once more before he left.

"It's good having you back around. Like old times," Santana said.

"Except Mark ain't here."

* * *

Richard's temples were starting to throb. The headache was coming back. Richard knew Ma didn't have any ibuprofen in the house. She still thought Tylenol was the cure for everything. He'd have to go the corner store at the end of the block to get what he needed. Richard thought of the nine that Santana had shown him. Both he and Santana used to carry nickel-plated .22 automatics but they were mainly for show. It was necessary in the hustle. Doing business without one was like a soldier going into battle without an M16. Mark had been the only sensible one not to have one. He said he didn't need one to boost his manhood. The only time either of them had used their guns was to shoot into the air on New Year's Eve. When Richard left the business behind and moved to Baltimore, he got rid of his. Hurled it into the Chesapeake the night before he left. Richard didn't want to admit it but a lot of what Mark had been saying was starting to make sense. He decided to give the straight life a try. If it didn't work out, he could always get back into the game. As long as there were junkies willing to get high, there'd be drugs to sell.

A man was sitting on the steps of the house next to the corner store. When Richard got closer he could see that it was the same dude from the night before. Now he was dressed in all black, from the ski cap down to his Timberlands. Richard kept his eyes straight ahead as he passed by the man.

"Richie…Richie Rich! Nice to see you back in the neighborhood," the man said.

Richard stopped. Looked the man straight in his eyes. "I know you?" He didn't want to start trouble, but he wasn't going to act scared either.

"No, but I know you. That's all that counts. The name's Nico."

Richard ignored him, started walking. "Whatever," he said. The man got off the step, stood in Richard's way. "That's messed up what happened to your cousin. I know your aunt and mother are crying their eyes out."

Richard mugged the man. "Unless you a long lost cousin or something, stay outta my family business."

"Ain't nobody in your business. I'm just offering my condolences brother. But I am telling you this. You thinking about coming back, you'd better think again. This is my block now, you hear me Richie Bitch?" The man asked. He lifted up the bottom of his black leather coat, exposed the handle of a .32 to emphasize his point. Richard walked around the man, and walked into the store. He got the red and white bottle of ibuprofen, paid the Korean owner, and left. When Richard came back out, the man was gone. He saw two Colver uniformed officers parked on the corner of where Lincoln Avenue met Jefferson Street and knew why.

* * *

Richard smelled his mother's onion meat loaf as soon as he walked into the house. Didn't think anything more about what had happened outside. There was always somebody trying to play hard out there. Richard wasn't apart of that life anymore so he wasn't worried. He was glad Santana lived within walking distance. For some reason seeing Geena acting the way she was really did a number on his head. Made him think of R.J. and how some smooth talking hustler could talk his way into her life. And R.J. had an absent father, the same as Geena and Tammy did. That made her a potential victim for guys like Calvin. Richard knew Antoine would care more about his own kid than to teach R.J. about respecting herself when it came to dudes. He made a mental note to spend more time with R.J. so that he could teach her himself. No one would love her more than her own daddy, Richard thought. Richard hung up his coat and went to the bottom of the steps. A slow talking deep voice on the radio was talking about upcoming events at area churches. Aunt Shelly was still sleeping on the couch. Richard could hear pots and pans being shuffled around in the kitchen. He knew if Ma was making the meatloaf, her garlic mashed potatoes, and spicy collard greens were the side dishes.

Round Up

"I'm back Ma!" Richard yelled into the kitchen.

"Food will be ready in a little bit," Ma responded. Richard bounded up the steps to his room. Broke the seal on the red and white bottle, and dry swallowed two pills. He picked up the phone. Looked at his watch. Saw it was a little before four thirty. Desiree's workday was winding down. He hated still knowing her schedule even after they had been apart so long. Made him feel like he was still in her life somehow. He dialed the digits.

"Thanks for calling CDG Industries, this is Desiree speaking, how can I help you?" Desiree answered.

"It's me Desi," Richard responded. She hesitated before speaking. That angered Richard. Made him think he was the last person on earth that she wanted to deal with.

"What is it Richie?" Desiree asked. Her voice sounded annoyed.

"Did you get my message this morning?"

"No," Desiree answered. Richard wasn't surprised. "What do you want? I have to get ready to pick R.J. up from the babysitters."

"You get my message about Mark on the voice mail?"

"Yeah, I got it," Desiree answered. Richard expected an I'm sorry or How did it happen? But she didn't say either one.

"What time you getting home with R.J.?" Richard asked. "I wanna talk to her." He knew what time Desiree would be home. For some reason he just wanted to keep her on the phone. She ignored his question.

"Look Richie, I'm gonna give you a heads up. I wasn't gonna tell you at first but I'm taking you back down for an increase. What I'm getting just ain't enough. Plus you're irregular with the payments or I don't get them at all. I think this is the best way to solve the problem. You should be getting served with the papers sometime this week."

"Why it gotta be like that?" Richard asked. The last place he wanted to go was back to court. The judge took his manhood with the looks he gave and the derogatory things that he said. And it wasn't just to him, it was to all the fathers who came into that courtroom. As far as Richard was concerned he was just a name on paper followed by a set of numbers…social security and how much was going to be paying.

"I just told you why. I'm not getting enough."

Richard knew she wasn't getting enough money because she hadn't taken her second child's father downtown. Richard found out from R.J. by mistake that the dude didn't have a job. He'd also found out that they argued all the time and that he had hit Desi once. When R.J. told him that, Richard found himself grilling her for more information until she started crying. He stopped himself, gave her a big hug, and told her that he loved her. Richard would have bought up some of the things that he had found out, but it would've only made things worse. Besides, it was none of his business. Now if the dude ever put his hands on R.J., that was a different story. "Desi, I'm sorry about the last payment. The car broke down and I needed the money for—"

"I also asked that they take the money right out of your check. That way I don't have to worry about getting it."

"You're serious."

"And don't call me Desi. I hate when you call me that. My name is Desiree."

"I don't believe this shit."

"If you wanna talk to R.J. you can call her later, okay?" Desiree asked. Richard didn't answer. "Okay Richie?" She asked again. My name ain't Richie, its Richard, he was thinking.

"Alright," he said.

"I'll talk to you later, bye," Desiree said. Then she hung up. The dial tone echoed though his head like an alarm clock waking him up out of a sound sleep. Richard looked at the phone, then placed it in the cradle. Desiree had distanced herself from him. Most likely because Antoine told her to. He wasn't supposed to be bothered by anything she did anymore, but for some reason he was. He laid back on the bed, left arm draped over his eyes.

Richard woke up a few hours later. Ma's voice was telling him dinner was ready from downstairs. He looked at the digital clock on the side table, saw that the yellow digits read 6:55. He hadn't meant to drift off, but with so much on his mind, he wasn't surprised that it had happened. He got out of bed feeling the depressed state of the house when he went downstairs. A choir was singing about the gates of heaven on the radio. He went into the kitchen and saw his aunt sitting at the table. She looked better. Ma was mixing some red juice in a glass pitcher on the counter. The heat from the stove warmed him from the cool of the rest of

Round Up

the house. Richard sat down in front of his aunt. He spoke. She smiled weakly. Ma put a plate of food in front of Aunt Shelly, him, and then herself. They ate in silence as the solemn gospel music played from the radio in the living room.

After dinner Richard went back to his room. He looked at the clock. It was seven thirty now. If Desiree still did things the way she did when they were together, she was cooking dinner right now. R.J. would be watching a cartoon on the kids cable channel until it was time to eat. Richard looked at the phone. Picked up the receiver and dialed the digits. His heart pumped hard with anticipation of talking to his little girl.

Antoine answered. "Yeah?"

"Can I speak to R.J.?"

"Who's this?"

"It's her father."

"She's sleep," Antoine answered.

Richard heard the cartoons on the tube in the background. "Then let me speak to her mother."

"She's busy."

Richard tried to keep his anger under control. It was bad enough Antoine had turned Desiree against him. Now he was trying to take away his little girl too. He gritted his teeth. "Tell her to call me back at my mother's house."

"She don't wanna talk to you! And don't call my motherfucking house no more either!" Antoine yelled before the line went dead. Richard called right back. No one answered. Richard hung up, called back again. Still no answer. The rush of adrenaline made him hang up and call again. The way Richard felt, he was going to dial all night until someone answered.

Antoine answered. "What!"

"I wanna talk to my daughter!" Richard yelled.

"If you don't stop calling my house like you crazy, I'm gonna beat your ass in front of your goddamn kid!" Antoine yelled. The line went dead again. Richard stopped himself from calling again. Not because he was scared, but because he felt himself losing control. His heart was hurting. But things weren't going to get settled tonight. He hung up the phone, turned on the radio with the remote, and cut the light.

Tony Cheatham

CHAPTER SIX

Detective Paul Ryan sat in the faded blue velvet recliner, watching the blonde haired chick riding the black guy's horse cock on the 25-inch tube in front of him. Her fake tits didn't move even though she was hopping up and down like a goddamn rabbit. Usually he got a rise from watching that kind of shit. But now he didn't feel so much as a tingle in his dick. It had been two hours since his shift was over. The sun was high in the sky. Usually he was asleep by the time the morning news went off at nine o'clock. Ryan glanced at the digital clock in the VCR, saw it was going on ten. All night long he'd been telling his partner Fields that he couldn't wait to get home and hit the sheets. But he wasn't tired anymore. As a matter of fact he felt rested and relaxed, like he'd gotten eight hours sleep.

Sometimes working graveyard played tricks with your mind like that. And Ryan had been coming in early on twilight for the overtime coming up on a year now, so he was really wired. It was easy money so why not? He hated working the night though. It wasn't normal to be working when you were supposed to be asleep. But he endured it. Partly because the money was good, but mostly because he was tired of the shit from his coworkers on day and twilight. Sure, Ryan knew he had a b.o. problem. Had the same problem since he was a kid. His grandmother—who he lived with—had taken him to the doctor plenty of times, said it was something wrong with his glands. The doc gave him medicine but the stuff made him throw up and gave him a hell of a case of diarrhea. Ryan chose to deal with the smell over the medicine. At least the smell didn't make him sick. So he dealt with the wisecracks. When Ryan grew up he decided to be a cop. The badge gave him the power to stop the insults. Except it didn't stop it from other cops. So he switched to graveyard. There the guys didn't give a damn. They just wanted to do their eight hours and

Round Up

go home to bed after shift was over. And that's where Ryan had been ever since. And the overtime from going to court got him an extra twenty-five grand a year to his base of thirty six. And he didn't have to give any of it away for alimony or child support like some other schmucks in the precinct. No, marriage wasn't for him. Not that he could find a chick that could deal with his b.o. anyway. He simply couldn't imagine the thought of waking up to the same chick for the rest of his life. He'd rather rent the pussy and kick the broad out after he was done with her. And for times when he didn't feel like being bothered, he could go to his library of porno, pop a tape into the VCR, and yank his dick until he was satisfied. And kids definitely weren't for him. They were too messy and bothersome, always asking for a handout. That's why he had himself fixed. He didn't want to be bothered with the hassle.

Ryan banked his most of his money after paying bills and stocking up on food. The only other expense he had was paying for the nursing home where his grandmother stayed. And that really wasn't an expense since the hustlers were inadvertently footing the bill. Sure, Ryan made good money from the overtime but it wasn't enough to give his grandmother the care she needed after her stoke. Naw, the real dough came from shaking down the low lifes peddling that shit adding to the city's already notorious reputation for being the drug capital of the nation. But that was a problem for the mayor to worry about, not his. He was just capitalizing on what was already a booming business. Still, it hurt like hell to have to put Granny in a home. She had always been a feisty and independent woman. Figured that was where he got his character. But with his schedule, Ryan just didn't have time to give the care that she needed. Ryan searched for days trying to find the right place. Then he came across a joint that looked perfect. When Ryan found out how much the place was a month, he knew what he had to do. Word had gone around the city a couple of years back about a group of rogue cops over in Eastern District had been shaking down dealers. Eventually the cops got pinched by internal affairs and were fired from the force. But Ryan was different. Their problem was that they got greedy. Ryan took just enough to pay for room and board at the nursing home.

Ryan thought about going into work later that night. No doubt his partner Fields was going to exert all his energy to try and close the Anderson case as soon as possible. But Ryan just wasn't feeling the duties of the job the way he used to. Years of working the streets had worn him down. And his shift, the graveyard shift was getting to be a hassle to the point of where he hated the people that he was supposed to protect. To Ryan it seemed like every kind of low life in the streets of Colver City came out when it got dark. To Ryan, the freaks really did come out at night. And he really hated the hustlers. Especially the corner hustlers who hung out day and night on the street corners peddling that shit. He liked how they scattered like roaches when he and Fields drove by their blocks in the blue unmarked Crown Victoria even though they were homicide cops. Knew to the hustlers, it didn't make a difference. Cops were cops. Truth was, Ryan wouldn't have helped narcotics even if his job depended on it. He hated those narcissistic assholes along with every other cop in the precinct.

Ryan chuckled when he thought about the dealers. Seemed like every young kid who got his first fancy ride with chrome wheels and tinted windows thought he was a kingpin. In actuality they were the low rungs on the ladder. The bottom feeders of the drug game. Of course the cops had to be at the top of the game, to keep things even; to give things a balance. Ryan liked the power and respect that his authority afforded him on the streets. Nothing could beat the high he got when he arrested one of the punks and they began to whine about getting busted. Then there were the smart asses that wanted to resist arrest and put up a fight. Then they turned to little girls once they were getting booked. But to hear the low lifes tell it, they were the top dogs—untouchable—at least until they were caught. Then they were the first ones trying to make deals with the States Attorney for lesser time to bring down the real moneymakers. They did it every time.

Ryan looked at the tube again and saw the young guy getting ready for the money shot on the blonde broad's plastic tits. She was squeezing them together puckering her lips trying to look seductive. When the young guy blew his load, Ryan clicked off the television. Ryan slid out of the easy chair and walked over to his bookcase. He liked crime novels. They were the only kind that he read. Couldn't stand those corny romance novels that broads liked. Men like the ones in those books, who treated their women like queens were bullshit. And he couldn't stand that all women's

Round Up

network either. Chicks in those movies were always being victimized by some lunatic guy. To Ryan chicks were far more conniving and devious than men could ever be. Ryan ran his fingers over the books on the shelf. He liked books by Elmore Leonard and Micheal Connelly, but his favorite writer was George Pelecanos. Ryan liked the later books where the writing had a harder edge than the earlier stuff. Pelecanos wrote the way it really was in the streets as if he'd been a cop before. He pulled out Pelecanos' last one, The Sweet Forever, and sat back down in the recliner. He read the first page feeling his eyelids getting heavy. By the middle of page two, Ryan was asleep.

* * *

The phone rang jarring Ryan from a sound sleep. He sat up from the chair he was in and looked towards the phone in the kitchen. He stumbled towards it picking it up in the middle of the next ring.

"Yeah," Ryan answered.

"You still sleep?"

Ryan knew the voice. It was his partner. "Goddammit Fields, why you calling me this early? Didn't I just leave your ugly mug?"

"Good morning to you too."

"C'mon what is it?"

"I wanna go back over the crime scene again," Fields said.

"Can't this wait until we go on shift?"

"No. We might see something in the daytime that we missed that night."

"Shit Fields, I was just getting ready to get some serious shuteye," Ryan answered. "Ain't nothing gonna change at the scene between now and when we come on." He could hear Fields' kids, a boy, Brian who was twelve, and a girl, Jennifer, who was ten, laughing in the background. Then he heard their mother telling them to quiet down. Their laughter was turning his stomach. Ryan thought of how Fields' family looked like something off of an episode of the Cosby Show. Fields was a good guy though. His wife was cute too. Had a nice round ass on her five-foot brown frame. Figured that was why Fields worked all the overtime he did. A chick like that wanted to be taken care of and Fields was doing a good job of that by putting her up in that big house in that expensive part of town. Ryan had met them all over Thanksgiving when Fields invited him over. Ryan figured what the hell? It was better than watching the Gilligan's Island marathon on the tube. Fields invited him over for Christmas dinner too, but Ryan declined. Ryan's in-laws were coming over to see the grandkids. And he didn't want to sit there feeling like a third wheel. So Ryan made up an excuse that he was going to see his mother. Wound up spending the holidays with a bottle of brown Barcardi and a porno.

"Why didn't you go to sleep when you got home? You complained all night about how tired you were. Jacking off over those flicks again weren't you?"

"Mind your goddamn business."

"Solving this case is my business. I'm gonna be there at three-thirty," Fields said before the line went dead.

"Fuck!" Ryan yelled. He couldn't have cared less if the case was ever solved. It was probably just another drug territory beef that got settled with a bullet. Before the night was out Ryan was sure there would be more bodies. There always were. Those people never learned. He glanced at the VCR. The numbers were blinking 12:00. Figured the power must have cut out while he was sleep. He went into the small kitchen that was only big enough to hold a sink, one of those compact refrigerators, a counter, and a window. He kept the drapes drawn. Didn't like the thought of anybody being able to look into his life whenever they goddamn well felt like it. He looked at the battery operated clock on the wall, saw it was one-thirty. Damn that Fields making him come in before shift. By the time he showered and dressed Ryan figured there'd be just enough time to make his weekly stop before Fields got there.

* * *

Ryan drove down Williams Road, took a left onto Stevens Boulevard, and made a hard right onto Landon Avenue, en route to Washington Projects. He was listening to Mick Jagger singing over a Keith Richards guitar riff blasting through the back speakers. The Stones were tough in their prime. Ryan couldn't count on two hands how many broads he'd paid to screw while one of their tunes was on. Now the stones just looked like a bunch of old guys clinging to a shell of their former selves.

Driving the strip was like being transformed to another world. One where poverty was the norm, and hustling was like working an

Round Up

entry level position of a fortune 500 company; a promise of financial success in the future. He drove his 1991 mud brown colored Mercury Sable steadily at forty miles per hour slowing down to a creep at fifteen when his eyes caught sight of who he was looking for. The short kid was dressed in true thug fashion wearing unlaced butter Timberland boots, baggy black jeans, a Baltimore Ravens Jersey, and a purple ski hat pulled to the tops of his eyebrows. He was puffing on a Black and Mild cigar like he was goddamn Donald Trump himself. The kid was laughing loudly like he didn't have a care in the world until he saw Ryan pulled up to the curb. The kid's happy face froze and twisted into a scowl. Ryan could hear the kid telling the five guys standing around him to go make him some money. They looked confused by his change. But they scattered without question. The kid hiked up his jeans and took a pull from the thin cigar before making his way over to Ryan's car. The kid leaned into the driver's side window.

"What's up?" The kid asked. He smiled showing his yellow teeth. Ryan pushed his head back out with force causing the kid to fall to the pavement. Ryan peeked out of the window in time to see the kid scrambling to get up. "What the fuck is wrong with you?" The kid yelled.

"Get in the car," Ryan answered. The kid pulled his pants up and made his way around to the passenger side door. He opened the door, sat in the seat pouting like a four year old. The smell of the Black and Mild was making Ryan dizzy.

"What the hell is this, fuck with Priest day?" The kid asked. "People keep putting their mothafucking hands on me, I'm gonna start popping some shots. I already had to go home and change once today because of some punk in the sub shop wrinkling my clothes. I'm gonna get his ass though."

Ryan didn't acknowledge whatever nonsense the kid was talking about. "Where is it?"

"Gotta go get it from one of my people," the kid said. "Drive down to Rockway Park."

"What the fuck I look like, a chauffeur to you?" Ryan asked. He'd had enough of the game playing. He wouldn't have even driven over if he didn't need the money. Had the feeling he was going to want to take his frustrations out on some pussy later on. Maybe even with more than one chick. And he still had to make a payment to the home for his granny. He pulled over to the curb with a sharp right turn of the steering wheel. Made the kid fly to the other side of the car. Ryan grabbed the front of the kid's shirt with his left hand, pulled his department issued .9 and pushed it into the kid's right cheek. He noticed the kid's eyes grow wide like those black actors in those old time minstrel movies. "Stop fucking around with me kid! Give me my cut or I'll have Narcotics all over your black ass so fast you'll think it's raining cops! You don't get me what I want right now, I'm gonna snatch those fake ass diamonds outta both your ears!" Ryan shouted. He moved the gun into his mouth until the kid started searching in his pockets for some cash. He pulled out a knot of money bound tightly by a rubber band. Ryan glanced at the hundred on the top and snatched the rest. He pulled the nine from the kid's parted lips. Wiped the spit off on the kid's shirt. "I'd better not have the same problem when I come back next week, understand?" The kid nodded his head. "Get the hell outta my car."

The kid opened the door and stepped out on the pavement. He got a sudden burst of courage and shouted, "You owe me change you smelly mothafucka! That's enough money for two weeks of payments!"

Ryan slammed the door, screeched the tires on the Sable back up Landon in the direction of his apartment. Thought they lived in fucked up times when a guy could wear earrings and it was considered cool.

CHAPTER SEVEN

Detective Ronald Fields stood in the doorway of his kitchen after hanging up with Ryan. He was watching his wife Charlene stirring cake powder in a steel bowl for dessert to serve after dinner. Her hips shook vigorously as she mixed the batter. His eyes probed her ass cheeks wiggling when she moved. Long brown legs extended from the jean skirt she was wearing which stopped in the middle of her thighs. He knew without seeing them that her toes were polished to a high red gloss. Fields knew she wasn't wearing a bra because he couldn't see any strap lines through the tee shirt she had on. Excited him even more. The wire whisk she was using constantly scraped against the side of the bowl, metal against metal. They'd been having problems but he figured he'd give another try at making things better between them. He walked up and slid his hands under her shirt, cupping her breasts from behind with both hands. Damn they were soft! Fields was thinking. Felt good in his grip like warm water balloons. He squeezed them and pushed his groin into her backside so that she could feel him. Charlene stopped moving. Put the bowl down on the counter in a huff, removed his hands from her breasts. Pushed her backside out bumping him off of her.

"Stop it, the kids are here," Charlene said. Her tone wasn't playful but serious and annoyed. She didn't give promises of any pleasures later on because there wouldn't be any. She would get into bed, roll over and sleep. Fields moved away from his wife. He wasn't one to argue. If she didn't want him to touch her, he wouldn't. Leaving the kitchen he could hear his wife starting to stir the mix again.

Fields walked into the living room. Saw his son and daughter parked in front of the big screen, their heads nesting on palms supported by perched elbows. They were watching one of those new types of cartoons where farts and burps were supposed to be funny. Fields found them disgusting. What happened to Bugs Bunny and Daffy Duck, cartoons like that? Fields never expressed his thoughts on anything involving happenings in the house. The kids had the run of the place. And their mother let them. Whenever he tried to administer any discipline, she always backpedaled him, reversed whatever decision he had made. Still, he didn't protest. Charlene was the one raising them. She was the one who took them to school. She was the one who went to the PTA meetings and extracurricular activities. She was the one who cooked their dinner and tucked them in at night. So that gave her the right, he rationalized. And that was the way it should have been. A mother belonged at home with the kids. And he was obliged to take care of them. Be the provider to make sure food was on the table, that the house had heat in the winter and air conditioning in the summer. Fields paid for camp. Paid for Charlene to get her hair done every week. Paid for the clothes they had on. Fields did all that to make sure his family was comfortable. Yet these people...his family...made him feel like a goddamn stranger in his own house. Sure, he put in a lot of time at the job, but that was part of being a cop. Hell, Charlene knew his buying the four bedroom, three bathroom house in Rockdale, one of Colver's best neighborhoods wouldn't come without sacrifice. He'd have to work as many doubles and get as much court time as possible to be able to afford that standard of living. That's where the money was, in the overtime. Then right after they got into the house and the excitement wore off, and he started to put in the extra time, Charlene started acting distant. Sex dwindled down to nothing. No kisses, no hugs. Nothing. Fields kept his pain and feelings of neglect inward like a man was supposed to do. So what that days would go by without her saying anything to him. She was happy in the house. The kids were happy too, long as he kept the cable on and got them whatever new video game system was currently out.

Fields sat down in the black leather recliner and kicked his feet up on the matching ottoman. The kids were staring blankly into the 55-inch big screen. A talking sponge drank something and burped out loud. Fields laughed out loud thinking the children were going to join in with him. They didn't. As a matter of fact, Fields thought he noticed them exchanging annoyed looks at each

Round Up

other. Fields got up and went into the bedroom he and his wife shared. He closed the door behind him and sat down on the side of the queen-size bed. Fields hated the huge bed. He liked feeling her warm body next to him when he came off shift. It was Charlene's idea to get it. The few times he and Charlene slept together she stayed so far on her side Fields felt like he was sleeping alone. Fields clicked the remote to the CD player in the corner of the room and parked his head on the pillow. The sound of Najee's trumpet doing a cover of Anita Baker's song Sweet Love floated into the room. Put him at instant ease.

Fields' head wandered to that space in his heart that was starting to consume him. Filled his head with doubts and crazy thoughts of leaving them. Sometimes he thought so much he'd get dizzy thinking of the way things were. First it started out as a sharp pain like a pin prick when he thought about his home situation. But the pain was getting unbearable now. Only forgot about it when he was in the streets, part of the reason why he stayed away from the house. Ryan had the right idea. Living a life of solitude, being bothered only when he felt the need to. The family put on a good act when Ryan came over for Thanksgiving. Charlene couldn't keep her hands off of him. Even the kids acted like he was a doting father. Like they all knew the role they were supposed to play of a loving family whenever guests came over. Fields tried to keep Ryan there as long as he could, knowing it would go back to normal when he left. The minute Ryan left, the show was over. Fields went to bed thinking he could continue the magic he felt when Charlene acted like when they first got married. When he slid his hand up her nightgown, she moved it away, told him to go to sleep. Fields wanted to get an encore performance from his family for Christmas last week but Ryan didn't want to come over. Said something about going to see his mother. Fields wound up finishing some paperwork to avoid dealing with the loneliness. Yet as miserable as Fields was he wasn't going to leave. A father belonged with his family no matter how rough things got. He had a real family, his family, and he loved them. There'd be no way in hell he could bear coming to pick up his kids for visitation and seeing Charlene with another man, giving him the happiness and love she used to give him. And he wouldn't have his kids looking to another man as a role model besides himself. So he stayed. Sure he had affairs here and there. A man still had to satisfy his urges, but they were empty feelings of lust. Nowhere near the love he felt for his wife.

Fields needed to clear his head. He was glad to have to go into the street today. Figured working on the murder case would get his mind straight and put some more money in his pocket. He was glad Ryan was going to be there. He was a good partner. Sure Ryan was a rough around the edges—the odor problem he had for one, damn he stunk sometimes, and the hint of prejudice he had against minorities—but that made for good backup. Someone who wouldn't hesitate to shoot when the time came, no matter what consequences he'd have to face after the fact. Ryan was raw and hard and that was a valuable asset to have in someone who was watching your back. First Fields had a stop to make though. Charlene hadn't slept with him in months but he still had someone taking care of his physical. Fields picked up the phone, dialed a pager number, waited for the lady's prompt, and entered their special code. Meant for his friend to meet him at The Timberlake, a small motel on the outskirts of town where Colver's city limits met the county line, in an hour. It was one-forty five now. That would give him just enough time to meet her, then get down to the crime scene in time to meet Ryan. Fields hung up and dialed the weather to cover his tracks in case Charlene checked up on him. Even though he knew the chances of that were damn near nonexistent.

* * *

Fields stroked like he'd just gotten out of jail from a 20 year stretch. The woman screamed his name like he was filling every crevice in her body with pleasure. Threw in some calls to God and Jesus too. Monica Wilson. They met six months ago at the courthouse. He saw her typing a letter at her desk in the clerk's office and spoke to her. There was an instant attraction between them. Didn't take long for them to end up between the sheets, even after he told her was married. Hell, she was married too. But her husband had forgotten that he was, and was screwing every woman that gave him a second look. Fields got with Monica whenever they had a free moment, which wasn't much. She never questioned or declined him. Wherever he said to be that's where she was. This was the third time they had gone at it within the

Round Up

half-hour they'd been together. The first time Fields lost control. It was over in a minute. He wasted no time in going for round two, which lasted longer. But round three was a marathon. Fields was sweating over the top of the woman like he was coming to the finish line of a ten-mile race. Partially from his exhaustive activity but mostly from the broken heater that was continuously spitting out 90 degree heat with no way to turn it down. Fields didn't worry about it since they weren't going to be there that long. The feeling was beginning to rise up from his groin, making its way into his chest, and that was it. Fields collapsed on top of the woman who was blowing woos like a train coming into the station. Neither spoke. Fields rolled over to the left side of the hard mattress and controlled his breathing. He heard the sound of a match striking across granite before smelling cigarette smoke. A crow was talking to his friends outside the room.

"Damn Ronny!" Monica said. She was still breathing heavy. "You were really backed up weren't you?" She took a drag from the smoke and blew it into the air. "She still holding out?"

"Yeah," Fields said. He liked talking after sex. Figured he was one of the few men who did. It was a relief to be with somebody who wanted to be with him. He thought of Charlene's reaction when he said he was leaving. No be careful, no I'll miss you, no I love you, just alright.

"Maybe there's somebody else. I can't see her missing out on good loving like that for no reason," she said. Fields didn't want to believe that was the reason, though he thought of it himself many times. He took a deep breath. The room smelled like a mix of cigarette smoke and stale sex from their session along with the many others before theirs. "The kids acting any better?"

"Nope."

"I dunno, why you just don't ship their ungrateful asses off to a boarding school somewhere," Monica said. She took another draw on the smoke and set it down in the V of the black ashtray on her side of the bed. Fields chuckled softly. Only a woman with no children would say something like that. Remembered how they virtually ignored him when he said bye and left out. It wasn't like he hadn't considered the idea himself, though never seriously. Indifferent as they acted they were still his babies. Ungrateful monsters that they were.

59

"So did Santa get you what you wanted for Christmas?" Fields asked.

"He sure did," Monica responded, grabbing his sore bone. He felt it move a little before limping again from exhaustion. It was the most he'd used it in such a short time since the last time he saw Monica a month and a half before. She got up to go to the bathroom. Fields watched her firm ass as she walked across the carpeted floor. He loved how comfortable she was being naked around him. Not like Charlene who always went into another room to dress and undress. He could hear Monica's stream hitting the water before the flush. Then she came back out and slid beside him in the bed. Her body was soft and warm. Fields hated to get up but he had to make it over to Ryan's house. If Ryan didn't see him, he wouldn't hesitate to turn around and go somewhere else, claiming he didn't see Fields. He picked up his watch from the bedside table.

Monica got the message. "Yeah you'd better get out of here," she said. She picked up the smoke, took the last draw before extinguishing it.

Fields smiled. He was glad she understood without him having to explain. He got out of bed, got dressed. "Why couldn't I have married you?" Fields joked.

Monica smiled, said, "happy New Year if I don't see you. Remember the signal if you want to hook up or something," she said.

"I know, two rings on the cell." Fields kissed her hard reminiscent of the way he used to do Charlene. He walked out of the room, got into the blue Crown Vic, and gunned the engine ready to meet with his partner.

Round Up

CHAPTER EIGHT

Detective Ryan watched the streets from the passenger side of the unmarked as Fields drove. Colver City was a hellhole. He was thinking about quitting the force. Maybe work for another department in the suburbs somewhere. Ryan figured after they finished this case he'd take a little vacation time to make sure that's what he wanted to do. He decided that when he came back if he felt the same, he'd start the wheels rolling. He had a friend in one of the York, Pennsylvania precincts. York would be a good place, just over the Maryland line. Not too far from home, but far enough away from the bullshit in this city. Figured he'd give the guy a call, visit the place to see if small town life was what he was looking for. Ryan felt the bulge of money that he'd snatched from the dealer in his left front pocket. He didn't have the chance to hide it. Fields was waiting for Ryan when he got back to his place. He got into the car and they left. Glanced at his watch, noticed it was going on four o'clock. It would be dark in an hour. Ryan wanted to be finished and out of Berwyn Heights, the crime scene, by then. It was well known that the area of the city hated cops. Especially white ones. Ryan wasn't crazy about the "Murder Heights" residents—the nickname the cops gave the area—either.

"Quit driving like an old lady. I wanna be in there and out. Bad enough you got me out before shift as it is," Ryan said.

"We will be," Fields responded.

A sweet fragrance filled Ryan's nose. He'd smelled it before, knew where it came from and who. "I see you're still not getting any at home," Ryan chuckled.

"Better than not getting any at all."

"Fuck you," Ryan responded. He thought about the women he was going to pick up later. Remembered that a couple of pro's owed him a favor after talking to a partner who worked in vice to let them loose after pinching them on a solicitation sweep. Ryan screwed one of them for free and said the other two owed him. Figured tonight was a good time to cash in on his favor. He'd get them to do each other then do him. Ryan smiled at the thought of the lesbo action. The car stopped in the middle of the block on Martin Luther King Boulevard. Ryan spotted a corner dweller evacuating his post upon seeing the unmarked vehicle. They both got out. Ryan looked around feeling trapped between the line of connected buildings on both sides of the street. No trees or greenery was in sight. He looked up using the yellowing sky from the setting sun as an escape. Fields was already bent down at the spot where the male vic was. The female vic was found in the car. He was riddled with a full clip, while she had two slugs in the eyes. It was vicious. The city hadn't even bothered to wash away the blood from the street yet. Ryan pulled out a pack of smokes—Malboro's—tapped the pack against his palm, slid one out, and put it between his lips. He fired up the smoke and walked over to where his partner was kneeling. Ryan saw the blood still on the asphalt and shook his head. "This is a piss poor city." Fields moved some pieces of crushed glass with a pencil. He looked up towards Ryan before locking his eyes on something across the street. Ryan turned around and saw a man sitting on the steps of an abandoned row house. He was at the scene the night of the murders sitting in the same spot. He stuck out in Ryan's head because of his unibrow and frog eyes. Looked like something out of a circus to Ryan. Apparently Fields remembered him too. Ryan watched him trot across the street. He touched the handle of the 9 millimeter Glock on his hip and followed his partner.

Ryan extinguished his smoke under the rubber heel of his left walking shoe once he was on the other side of the street. Fields walked up to the guy who was holding a brown bag with the long neck of a bottle peeking through the top in his right hand. The cap was still on. Ryan noticed he was fiddling with something in his right, curling his fingers around something in the palm of his hands. Fields stood in front of the guy with one foot on the house steps. Ryan could smell the alcohol emitting from the man's clothes. The man's lazy red eyes confirmed his high. Ryan looked the man over. He was still wearing the dirty hip length denim jacket and blue jeans he had on the other day. He was also wearing a faded gray ski hat. The man smiled upon seeing the detectives.

Round Up

Fields started right in without hesitation. "Weren't you here the night that couple got killed?"

"Maybe. What's it to you?" The man answered.

Ryan couldn't stand back talk. He came from behind his partner and got directly into the man's face. Grabbed him by his collar with both hands. "What the fuck you say to me?" Fields pulled Ryan away from him.

The man didn't even blink. "Feel better?"

"Just answer the fucking question, were you here or not?" Ryan said.

"Yeah…yeah I was here. So what? I didn't do nothing."

"Didn't say you did. I was just wondering if you happened to see anything," Fields said.

"I see things everyday. I'm out here damn near twenty four seven."

"Getting a job would take care of that you know," Ryan said. Fields shot him a look.

"So if you're out here why didn't you see who shot that couple?" Fields asked.

"I make it a point to mind my own damn business. All I noticed was that the ride pulled up and stopped on the other side of the street. After that I went into the alley and took a piss." He held up the brown bag. "This cheap shit runs right through you."

Ryan chuckled sarcastically. "I can imagine chugging a whole 40 ounce in one sitting would do that to you."

Fields talked over Ryan. "Okay tell me this, did you hear anything?"

"I might've."

"What did you hear?"

The man looked to his left and right. "Man if people see me talking to you they gonna know I said something."

Ryan snatched the object that the man was palming in his fingers and threw it on the ground. Saw that it was a diamond stud as it bounced against the sidewalk. He dismissed it as fake without another thought. "I could give a fuck what people think!"

"You don't have to live around here," the man responded.

Ryan chuckled again. "I wonder what I would find if I frisked you right now. Maybe crack rocks or some blunts or something right?" Ryan asked. He was getting tired of the question for question session. They were losing daylight messing around this clown. Fields shot him another look. His left eyebrow was raised this time.

"Hey man I ain't no pipehead. All I do is drink."

Fields picked up the sparkling trinket from the sidewalk and handed it back to the man. "Did you hear anything?" Fields asked again.

The man closed his eyes like he was thinking long and hard about the subject. His dirty brow was wrinkled. "Yeah...I heard something. A bunch of shots, I heard a bunch of shots. I can't remember exactly how many."

"I'll bet you'll remember if I cuff your ass," Ryan said. He moved closer to the man.

"For what?"

"Open container."

The man lifted up the brown-bagged bottle, smiled, said, "It's not open."

Ryan snatched the bag, twisted off the screw top, and started pouring it on the steps where the man was sitting, beer splashing on the three men's feet. "It is now." Fields snatched the bag. Ryan walked over to the curb, fired up another smoke hearing Fields apologizing to the low life. Fields was better with his own kind, thought Ryan. The decision to leave Colver was making itself clearer. Ryan felt his anger making him want to pull his gun and put it against temple of the bastard until he talked. And if Fields had not been there, that's exactly what he would have done.

One of those gigantic SUV's drove by on King Boulevard with rap music blaring out of an open window, the driver nodding his head to the beat. Ryan thought of it as noise. Just hearing it gave him a headache. If Ryan were still in the traffic division, he would have pulled them over just to fuck with them. All the talk about racial profiling was just that, talk. It was only common sense that when you saw a young black kid driving a ride worth fifty grand that something wasn't right. Those suits in the state legislature didn't know what it was like out there. Cops needed some kind of edge against the corner dwellers. But those bastards in Annapolis, they just didn't understand, thought Ryan. Ryan killed the smoke and turned around in time to see Fields walking towards him shoving his note pad into the inside of his jacket.

Round Up

"Did you get anything?" Ryan asked.

Fields ignored his question. "You need to keep that in check."

"What the hell you talking about?"

"You know what I'm talking about," Fields answered. He stopped walking and looked Ryan directly in his eyes. "Before we go anywhere, you're gonna cut that shit out. That guy almost didn't wanna talk to me! I told you before, we work with these people not against them! So whatever hangups you've got, you'd better get rid of them now!" Fields yelled. Ryan watched his partner walk back across the street to the unmarked. Ryan flicked the still lit smoke near a dumpster. With any luck it would catch to the trash and burn the place down. Ryan walked, looking at the orange sky turning dark. He couldn't wait to see the pro's later. He had a lot of stress to work off.

* * *

Ryan took a swig of the single from the six-pack that he bought with him to the hotel. The room was near dark with the exception of a dimly lit lamp. He glanced at the digital clock on the side table. Saw it was a quarter after one in the morning. The whores had just left after putting on a show with each other for him. One of the girls sucked Ryan off but he couldn't bring himself to screw either of them. After they were done, he threw fifty at them, told them to split it. They left without a word. He kept his eye on them through the hotel blinds to make sure they didn't do anything stupid like key his Sable. Ryan watched them until they were out of sight.

Ryan had a lot on his mind. The liquor would do a better job of helping him to cope with his problems than the whores could. He still couldn't believe Fields talked to him like he did. They were partners. That ranked Fields right up there with being a blood brother as far as Ryan was concerned. Ryan thought Fields' duty as a cop and as a partner came before any cultural thing he might have felt. Ryan was bothered so much by what happened that he told Fields he needed to knock off early because he was feeling ill.

The situation reminded Ryan of when he was seventeen when another guy, a kid named David, turned against him. He was the only black guy on the football team, a running back. He made all the big plays, was breaking all kinds of school records and was being recruited by all the top colleges in the country. He was so good that he overshadowed all the other players on the team. Personally Ryan didn't care. He had already made up his mind he was going to join the force once he graduated. But with the other guys, football was their life. They wanted all the exposure that David was getting. So it wasn't long before their jealousy made them want to put him out of action. They made up a plan to jump David after school one day, hoping he would transfer or be too scared to play anymore. Ryan had nothing against David. They had hung out a few times, had a few beers, and Ryan considered him okay. Ryan heard the plan in the locker room and initially he was going to mind his own business. But when Ryan saw six guys circling David about to pounce on him, Ryan couldn't stand by and let it happen. It was an unfair advantage. If they were going to fight, Ryan was going to make sure it was an even match. Ryan got some other members of the team on his side to help him. When it came down to a one on one, none of the guys wanted to fight David. David said thanks and walked away.

A couple of years later Ryan was a rookie beat cop on the force. He was assigned one of the worst crime neighborhoods to patrol. Ryan saw a kid running out of a convenience store and chased him. He caught up to him and pushed him down on the street to find out what he had done for him to be running. When the kid fell he scraped his face up pretty bad. Blood was pouring from his left cheek like sweat. Some neighborhood folks gathered around and started yelling about police brutality. Ryan called for backup as they crowd started closing in on him. Then he saw David right in the front of the mob of people. Ryan was slightly surprised to see him. The last Ryan had heard David had been kicked out of school for accusations of rape a year before. Ryan called out to him hoping David could get the crowd to calm down. David ignored him, started pounding on him with everybody else. Ryan made sure David was one of the first one to get thrown in the wagon when backup came. He wanted to know why David didn't do anything to help diffuse the situation but he didn't ask. As far as Ryan was concerned he should have let the team kick David's ass when he had the chance. Over the years Ryan developed tunnel vision when it concerned how he thought about blacks. In his eyes they didn't want anything more out of life but to drink, get high, and have a bunch of kids. Sure, there were exceptions to the

Round Up

rule, like Fields, but the majority was what he saw and dealt with on a daily basis. And now Ryan felt Fields was turning on him too.

Ryan swallowed the last of the liquor and crushed the can. He tossed the empty at a trashcan on the other side of the room and missed. The tin bounced off the wall to the mirrored dresser before hitting the floor. He pulled the cover over his nude body and shut his eyes. He hadn't planned on staying all night at the run down joint but then figured why not? He'd paid his forty-five bucks for the room. Figured he might as well make good use of it.

The next morning, Ryan woke up with a splitting headache. He got up, showered, put back on the dirty clothes from the day before. Could still smell the cheap perfume from those pros in them. Ryan felt a buzzing in his pants pocket. Knew that it was the department issued pager. He clicked the button to see what time the call had come in. Saw that it was two-fifteen in the a.m. Fields was going to raise hell for not calling him right back. He dialed the number in the pager to hear Fields had left a voice message. Said the guy on the step had given them a dead end, to some address in Branton Hills, a middle class suburb of mostly well to do minorities. Said it was for some teenage girl who would know anything there was to know about any hustlers in the city. Fields said that he went to see the girl, but didn't get anything useful. She put on the innocent act for her mother. Said she didn't know anything. But Ryan knew her type. One of those money hungry chicks that latched on to whoever had the flashiest clothes and the fanciest cars. The kind who moved her hips when she walked, like she was used to putting her goods on display. And with the maturity of a woman's body mixed with her youth, she wouldn't have a problem getting what she wanted. And in a few years after she was all used up, she would be cast aside for a newer and fresher girl. Ryan had seen that story too many times over the years to count. Fields said that after a few more questions the kid's mother intervened and wouldn't let her say anything else. If Fields had let Ryan handle things, he would have got a good lead. The guy knew more than what he was saying. All Ryan needed was a chance to prove it.

CHAPTER NINE

Detective Fields sipped decaffeinated coffee from his favorite mug at the breakfast table in the kitchen. He sat it down on the glass top, looked at the words Colver City's Finest framing the state seal of Maryland and smiled. Yeah, he was a cop and he loved it. And lately that was starting to mean more to him than his own family did. It was close to four-thirty in the morning but he wasn't tired. After Ryan played sick and knocked off early, Fields went to talk to the name he'd been given, found out it was nothing, came back to the station, did some paperwork, and walked out of the precinct's doors at four o'clock. Fields was still reeling from the dead end lead. But with the girl being a minor and her mother's intimidating presence, he wouldn't be able to talk to her anymore to find out if she really knew anything. He made a mental note to find a way around dealing with the girl's mother. She probably hung out at Angelo's sub shop over on Rice Avenue like the rest of the kids in the area did. He'd stake out the place, talk to her then.

Fields thought about Ryan and the way he had talked to the guy on the steps. Sure, Ryan had his problems, but he was a good partner. They had been working together for ten years. Their partnership was the closest thing that Fields had to family since he didn't have any siblings. Fields knew his partner felt the same way without Ryan ever having to express the words. Fields hoped Ryan didn't take offense to how Fields had talked to him but they were too close to getting a hit. Even though it was a dead end, the guy still gave up something. He just as easily could have dummied up and said nothing. Besides, they might have to go back to they guy to see what else he knew. Fields knew Ryan. He could see that Ryan was getting tired of the streets. The fire that used to be in his eyes was starting to dimmer. He was probably even thinking about opting out for the early retirement the force was offering, transferring to another precinct, or maybe even quitting altogether.

Round Up

Fields hoped that Ryan wasn't going to go the extreme of quitting. He was too good a cop for that. Fields figured Ryan just needed to relieve his stress. With Ryan that meant getting a six pack, a woman or two, and a night to sleep off whatever was bothering him. That's why Fields didn't say anything when Ryan claimed he was sick. When they saw each other on shift that night, Fields knew Ryan would be okay.

Fields gulped the last of the lukewarm coffee and put the mug in the sink. He looked at it for a moment, and put it in the dishwasher. Charlene had told him too many times not to put dishes in any empty sink. Made him feel like one of the kids instead of the man of the house. Figured he didn't need to give her one more reason to hold out on making love with him. Just thinking of Charlene made his dick hard. He wanted to call Monica to relieve his lust but her husband was home from a business trip. And anyway, being with Monica didn't completely comfort him the way he wanted and needed. Sure, she solved his immediate need for physical satisfaction, but the feeling he needed to make the lovemaking completely satisfying was with his wife. But he knew Charlene wouldn't do anything except push him away when he tried to slide his hands under her cotton pajama top or down into her panties.

Fields killed the lights in the kitchen and walked into the bedroom. The light from the hallway shadowed the room. Charlene was sleeping on top of the thick royal blue comforter. She was lying on her side. The white satin pajama top she was wearing had risen to the middle of her stomach. Showed off the satin white bikini cut panties that hugged her hips. Made her legs look extra long. Fields stared at her for a moment. He knew that if Charlene had any idea that he was coming home early, she would have worn the red and black flannel nightgown that came down to her ankles to bed instead. He undressed, looked at his hard dick, and walked over to the bed. Even though Fields knew that his wife didn't desire him, knew how she was going to reject him, at least he'd be touching her.

CHAPTER TEN

Richard drove southbound down Martin Luther King Boulevard in his Tercel. Santana was sitting in the passenger seat. He had called Richard earlier that morning. Said he knew somebody that maybe able to help them find out who shot Mark. Richard showered, dressed in some blue jeans, a sweater, and his casual soft bottom shoes. He ate breakfast and left. Put on his lightweight leather hipster on the way out of the door. Ma was praying in the living room with his aunt, so he didn't disturb her to say that he was leaving. Richard got into the cold car, hit the engine. It stalled. He turned the key back, hit the engine again. Prayed it would turn over. When it started he drove the block to Santana's house. Sure, he could have walked, but the car needed the activity to assure that it would keep working. Santana was sitting on the steps when he pulled up. He looked like an apache from the old western flicks with the red bandana tied around his head. The wrap was perfectly coordinated with the red sweatsuit Santana was wearing. There was a bulge in his dip when he rose from the step. When he got into the car, Richard asked where they were headed. Santana told him to get on the boulevard. The soft music caught Santana's attention. He looked at Richard then back at the radio in the dash where violins and flutes were playing a symphony. Santana shook his head and chuckled.

Richard looked over at him. "What?"
"You still listen to this classical shit?" Santana asked.
"Yeah, so?"
"Figured moving to Baltimore was gonna change your tastes."
"It's good music. You should check it out sometime."
"Naw, this is good music." Santana shoved his right hand into the pocket of his jacket. Pulled out a tape and shoved it into the deck. Big Pimpin, one of Jay-Z's joints blasted through the

Round Up

speakers. Santana started nodding his head in time to the beat of the music filling the car's cabin.

"So who are we gonna talk to?" Richard asked. He turned the music down to hear Santana.

"You don't know him. Just some dude."

"How you figure he knows something?"

"That cat is out here twenty four seven minding everybody else's business. He has to know something," answered Santana. He turned the music back up, threw his hands in the air like he was at a party. "This is the shit!"

Richard looked at the city as he drove; thinking Colver would never change. When Richard lived there, he remembered the Mayor saying how he was going to open up new drug programs to get the prostitutes and the addicts off the street. Said how he was going to create jobs to lower the unemployment rate that was the highest it had been in twenty years. Promised he was going to overhaul the police force changing the city's reputation of having the most lackadaisical and incompetent law enforcement agency in the state. Even started some joke of an anti drug campaign by printing TRUST in big black letters against a red background on a bumper sticker and plastering them all over the city. Richard laughed when he saw it for the first time, thinking the citizens didn't need another Nancy Reagan "Just Say No" slogan. They needed some real help, like more drug treatment centers and programs. But the Mayor hadn't done a damn thing so far. Violent crime was worse than ever and the city was on course to pass the number of killings from the year before. Richard remembered his mother saying how the Mayor wasn't doing anything but using Colver City as a steppingstone to a higher office. Richard hoped that wasn't the case. The people in the less than prosperous areas of the city didn't deserve to be used and tossed aside like trash, forgotten about like last year's toys at Christmas. But in the years since the Mayor took office that's exactly what it seemed like he was doing. He spent more time making himself look good on the national level while letting his own city continue it's downward spiral due to high crime and an over abundance of drugs. Richard remembered when he hustled. At the time, it didn't seem like all that big of a deal. Besides the fact that he couldn't buy the flashy jewelry and clothes like everybody else because of Ma, he was happy with the money he was making. But when he saw a brand new navy blue BMW at the dealership, he couldn't help himself. He bought it and kept it in a garage a few blocks away. Ma thought he was still riding the bus and he never told her different. He had always told himself that he was simply providing a service that had a high demand. That he was doing it to help take the burden of bills off of Ma. The rationalization appeased his conscience, that is, until he saw the effect of what he was doing was having on the community. Women sold their bodies. Men robbed and killed. And it was all to get that money for the next hit.

Richard hit rock bottom when he got robbed for his car by one of his customers. The junkie came at him like he was ready to buy. Next thing Richard knew, he was staring at the nose of a shaking .38. The junkie was so nervous he couldn't keep the gun straight. Richard's heart was pumping like he'd just finished running a mile, thinking the junkie was going to pull the trigger by mistake. The nervous man kept the gun on him while a couple of his friends searched Richard for the keys and the money. After they took the car and sped off, he let out a deep breath. Richard had lost it all in that one moment. He didn't get mad about the car because it was material. Ma had taught him that. And the money was dirty; it never really was his. But he thanked God for allowing him to have his life. After that, Richard walked away from the game.

Richard looked at the streets around him and wondered how much worse things had gotten since he left. He stopped at a light where Peterson Avenue crossed over the Boulevard. A white pro on the corner lifted up her black leather skirt, pointed at the patch of trimmed blonde hair between her legs. Richard looked at her then looked away. When the light flashed to green, Richard pulled off. He noticed the mayor's re-election signs posted over the plywood of abandoned buildings. Richard hoped the people would step up to the polls to get the man out of office. But that was a stretch. As long as the blacks in the city voted Democrat and whites voted Republican, the mayor would stay in the office for another four years. Even though he had just eaten, Richard could feel the tightness in his stomach signaling he was hungry. He felt around his pockets for some money and came up empty. Meant he'd have to stop by a bank machine if he wanted some cash. He

Round Up

knew finding an empty machine would be next to impossible since it was close to the end of the month. Independence card users were lined up to make their monthly necessity withdrawals for milk and cheese. Richard made a mental note to hit Santana up for some money after they were finished.

* * *

"Pull over here," Santana said. Richard pulled up the curb across the street from some vacant rowhomes. Noticed Santana was looking out of the driver's side window. Richard followed his eyes to a man sitting on the steps of one of the buildings with a brown bag.

"What's up?" Richard asked.

"This is where it went down. That cat over there is always out here. I'll bet he could tell us who did it."

Richard looked at Santana then back at the man, thinking that the drunk probably couldn't even remember what happened a few hours ago. How was he gonna remember details from something that happened a few days before? "You sure?"

"Hey ain't no harm in trying right?" Santana answered, stepping out of the car.

"You say so," Richard said. He started to open his door, but Santana stopped him.

"I'll go over and talk to him. Just sit tight." Richard watched Santana trot across the street fumbling with his waist. Richard turned off the music Santana was listening to. The thumping bass was stirring his headache. Figured maybe it was time to see a doctor about the pain. Something had to be wrong with him. He turned to a jazz station. Recognized Najee doing an instrumental cover of Anita Baker's Sweet Love. Richard leaned back, kept his eyes on Santana and the drunk cat across the street. Santana was talking to the dude. Richard moved his eyes over to a kid of about fifteen or sixteen standing on the corner with his hands in the pockets of his leather bomber jacket with Avirex in big white letters across the back. Junkies—black, white, latino—were standing around him waiting to be served. Richard remembered those times when he had to act like a drill sergeant to a platoon of lost souls when he was low level. The dope heads would roam around the street like zombies waiting for the store to open up. He'd yell to get them to line up. Scream at them to shut up while he worked. Berate them to keep them begging for more drugs making promises to suck his dick if he gave them a dose. He hated doing it, but it came with the job. It was what they expected. They didn't seem to care how he treated them just as long as they got their next hit. There was this feeling of power that he couldn't forget. A feeling, that for a moment, he was God to these people. People who were under his complete control for as long as he wanted them to be. He had their short term destiny's in his hands. That feeling was addictive…and misleading. In reality, Richard knew that he was lower than these people; a squashed bug under their shoes.

Richard couldn't deny that he wasn't a junkie himself, but for the adrenaline rush. Much as Richard's conscience bothered him sometimes about what he was doing, he kept coming back. And sometimes when the higher ups shitted on him about turning over a bigger profit…getting more for less and making him feel like less than a man in the process, he passed those negative feelings onto the fiends he serviced. When Richard got to feeling like that, he volunteered to serve the dope heads. That's when he really got to cursing and ordering them around. Needed to bring himself back up to where he needed to feel like a whole man again rather than half a man. The worse part was that he never got to see the man in charge who was fucking with his manhood. He worked for a nameless, faceless dude who gave orders to another dude who gave orders to another dude who gave orders to the guy Richard worked for direct, a dude who went by the name of Jerome. Told himself that one day he wouldn't be taking orders anymore. He'd be giving them. That was probably the lowest point in Richard's life.

Richard looked on the other side of the street and saw another kid, about ten or eleven years old. Knew he was watching out for a roundup. That was when a whole crew of Colver's Narcotics did a surprise sweep and arrested everybody in the immediate area, slapping them a distribution or solicitation of a CDS charge, or if they couldn't come up with anything else, a loitering beef. The chaos looked like a bunch of cowboys herding together a bunch of cattle. Richard had thankfully never got caught in a roundup. He could see the kid was a vet from the experienced way that he paced back and forth across the sidewalk like a caged tiger, keeping his eyes on all the corners. Richard looked back over across the street. Saw a street light on the corner.

Round Up

The trunk was decorated with shiny balloons, flowers sat on the ground at the base. A makeshift memorial; meant somebody had caught a hot one and got a first class ticket to see the man upstairs. Richard cut his eyes over to Santana who was standing in front of the drunk man now. Looked like he was yelling. Then he saw Santana grab the man's coat, pushing him away in the next moment. Richard lurched forward when Santana went into his dip and pulled out the nine millimeter he had shown Richard in his room. Santana put the nose of the gun against the dude's head. Richard could see that the man was scared. Tears rolled down the man's eyes as his mouth moved nervously. Richard's attention was drawn back to the crowd of junkies who began scattering. The lookout must have signaled that the cops were coming.

"Roundup!" A kid shouted before running off down an alley.

Richard rolled down the window and yelled across the street. "C'mon man!" He watched Santana smile at the man before putting the nine into his dip. He ran back across the street and got into the car. Santana was huffing and puffing with a twisted smile on his face. Richard pulled off just as six cop cars blocked off all the corners. "What was that all about?" Richard asked. Santana pushed the tape back into the deck making the speakers thump with the bass from the music.

"Punk didn't wanna give up a name."

"Why did you have to pull on him though?"

"Made him talk didn't it?"

"What did he say?"

A looping rhythm and bass came through the speakers making Santana have a lapse in the conversation. "Man this is the shit!"

Richard clicked the music off. "What did he say?" He asked again.

"Geena."

"What?"

"He gave me the name of that freak Geena."

CHAPTER ELEVEN

Richard sipped his orange soda still not believing what Santana had said. They stopped at a Kentucky Fried Chicken on Pinewood Avenue—a few blocks from where Mark was killed—to get something to eat. With the exception of two elderly women, the place was empty. It would be another half-hour before the lunchtime crowd started coming in. Richard wanted to be gone before the rush started. Santana was chewing on a leg from a three piece and biscuit. Richard had lost his appetite upon hearing Geena's name. He had barely touched the two piece dinner he had ordered. Elevator music was being piped in through the ceiling speakers.

"I told you she wasn't no good," Santana said. He popped the plastic lid off of his soda, took a swig, and crunched on some cubes of ice from the drink. "She probably set him up."

"But why would Mark be involved with her?" Richard asked.

"C'mon Richie, Mark wasn't a saint. He was probably screwing that freak behind Monique's back. Makes sense to me."

"No it don't. I know my cousin."

"A man is gonna be a man."

"She's a kid! Probably just got her damn titties!" Shouted Richard. He noticed the elderly women in the other booth looking at their table and shaking their heads.

"You've been gone a long time. Things changed around here. Geena might be young but she knows how to use her body to get what she wants. She thinks like a twenty-five year old."

"She hangs out at Angelo's right?"

"Like her home away from home. She knows that's where all the money is."

"Hurry up and finish eating. We're going over there."

"I'm almost done," Santana said. He looked over at Richard's tray. "You gonna eat that?"

Round Up

* * *

Detective Fields drove south on Remington Street. Made a right onto Oliver Avenue, then a sharp right onto Rice Avenue. He was on his way to stake out Angelo's to see if the girl would show up. He just wanted to talk with her. Ask her a few questions away from that hawk of a mother of hers. Fields was up early that morning. He'd been thinking about his wife. When Fields got into bed, he tried kissing Charlene on her neck. She told him to leave her alone. He pushed his groin against her ass. She scooted to the edge of the bed. In frustration, Fields yelled out, what the fuck is wrong with you? Charlene got up, put on her robe, and left the room. He heard the door to the guest bedroom down the hall slam shut. Fields went back to sleep, awoke a couple of hours later. He showered and dressed. Put on some light brown khacki's and a button down shirt, slid into his soft bottom loafers. He walked past the closed door of the guestroom and started to knock then changed his mind. He went downstairs towards the kitchen.

The kids were already up, eating cereal and watching television. One of those irritating cartoons was on. Fields spoke, they didn't respond. He spoke again in a louder tone. They acknowledged him with a low hello like he was bothering them. He grabbed his blue jacket and went out the door. Slid into the leather seats of Crown Vic and sped out of the driveway. The frustration he felt was eating at his insides like heartburn, but he refused to believe it was due to the stress from his home life. He put the blame elsewhere. The case. Yeah, it was the case that was stressing him. He pulled out his cell phone ready to call Ryan, then changed his mind. If Fields knew Ryan he was still recovering from whatever dealings he had involved himself with in the middle of the night. Besides, Ryan was lacking in his dedication to solve this murder. Fields was beginning to feel like he was carrying his partner. But that's what good partners did; picked up the slack when the other's life was spinning out of control.

Fields parked a block away from Angelo's. He wanted to keep the car out of sight. An undercover ride stuck out like a white tiger in a zoo. Made his way over to an Ethiopian restaurant across the street. Fields walked in, sat at one of the empty tables by a window so that he could watch out for the girl. Even though it was near lunch, the place was barren. He wondered whose bright idea it was to put an ethnic restaurant in an all black area. A place like this would do well in Plesson or Jameston, the more diverse areas of Colver where the college crowds hung out. But here, he guessed the place would be out of business by the end of the year. A waitress, her jet black fine textured hair tied up in a bun to the back of head, asked him if he wanted anything. Fields looked at the one page menu laying on the wooden tabletop. Saw the one thing that looked safe to consume.

"Let me get some coffee please," Fields said. The waitress smiled, spun around and walked toward the kitchen. He focused his attention back to Angelo's. People were hanging out in front and walking inside. The place looked more like a nightclub about to open its doors. Fields saw familiar faces that he had busted when he walked the beat. They were juveniles back then. Now they were in their twenties ready to go to the next level of their criminal careers. The waitress bought the coffee back, put it on the table and smiled at him. She had pretty skin. That smooth coffee color that those kinds of people had. He looked back across the street. Saw a Gold Maxima with chrome wheels pull up in front of the joint. A short guy, his red ski hat pulled down nearly over his eyes, stepped out on the driver's side. Then the girl he was looking for stepped out on the passenger side. Fields looked at the girl. Knew her mother couldn't possibly have known where she was and who she was with. He got up from the table, left four for the dollar cup of coffee and walked out the door.

* * *

Richard pulled into the parking lot next to Angelo's. He saw the short dude that Geena had been arguing with the day before getting out of a gold Maxima. Santana was the first to see her. "There she is right there." Richard looked at Geena stepping out of the passenger side of the car.

"She was just arguing with that dude yesterday and now she's right back with him," Richard said.

"Shorty must have some money or she would've been dropped his ass," responded Santana. Richard opened the door to the Tercel. He was about to get out of the car when he saw that detective who had come over his house. He closed the door. Watched the man go into Angelo's.

"Oh shit," Richard said.

Round Up

"What's wrong?"

"That cop, the one who was over my house asking questions about Mark?"

"What about him?"

"He just went in there."

"Probably wants to talk to that freak too."

"Let's wait out here until he comes out," said Richard, "then we'll go in and see what she's gotta say."

* * *

Detective Fields walked into Angelo's. A hand stopped him at the door. Fields looked to his left. Saw a man sitting on a wooden stool. Recognized him as Jeff Winslow, a former cop from the Eastern District. He was kicked off the force a couple years back after shooting the man that was sleeping with his wife. Winslow got ten years probation. The defense worked it so that it sounded as if Winslow had feared for his life and was justified for the shooting so he didn't do any jail time.

"Fields how've you been?" Winslow asked. "What the hell you doing here?"

"Checking some things out," Fields answered. "You're looking good."

"I've been okay. Trying to find work where I can. It ain't easy for an ex-cop with a background like mine. This is the best job that I've had since that thing happened, and the news made me look like I was crazy."

Fields looked away at some kids laughing by the door. He couldn't look Winslow in the eyes after that statement. Truth was, Winslow wasn't a clean cop. Fields had heard more than enough stories about how Winslow was on several dealer's payrolls to mind his business when it came to their activities. A few more months and Internal Affairs would have caught him in a sting anyway. Fields changed the subject. "I was wondering if you could help me out a little."

Winslow moved to attention. "Sure, which one of these hoods you want me to grab for you?"

Fields chuckled. "None. I just wanna lay low for right now. Just keep an eye on things outside. You know, make sure everything's cool while I'm in here."

Winslow's body language softened. The hard cop stare in his eyes was replaced by a look of disappointment. His shoulders dropped like he'd just been given some bad news. "No problem. Let me know if you need me," Winslow answered. He sat back down on the stool and crossed his arms. Fields walked towards the counter. He heard Winslow giving the third degree to a kid coming in through the doors. Figured that was to make Winslow feel like a cop again. Fields walked over to the booth where the girl was sitting. The guy she was with had his left arm draped over her shoulder. She sat cuddled up under him. Fields noticed the guy's hard eyes looking at him the closer he got to them.

"I'm Detective Fields," he said to the girl, "I stopped by your house yesterday to ask you some questions."

"I remember," she responded. Fields could hear the attitude in her voice. Knew she was putting on the tough act for her boyfriend's benefit. Cooperating with the police would break the code of the street. "My mother told you I didn't know anything."

"I just thought of some questions that you might know the answer to. Can I speak with you…alone please?" Fields asked. Looked at the boyfriend. She put on the whole show of huffing and puffing before unlocking her body from her boyfriend's grip. When she got up, he stood up too. A boy with a missing left front tooth stood up when the boyfriend got up too. A platinum chain hung to the center of the short man's black long sleeve shirt had the word "thug" on the front in white block style letters. "I said I wanted to speak with her." Fields gave the boyfriend the once over with his eyes. He was about five feet, maybe even four eleven, had a stocky body, and an old face. Was probably in his middle to late twenties. Fields shifted his eyes over to the girl. She was tall and curvy. Had the short man by at least five inches. Her pants were skin tight on her hips. She had a youthful look to her in spite of all the makeup that was painted on. When he last saw her, she looked to be about fourteen, maybe fifteen. Now the girl looked like she was damn near in her twenties. Fields thought they looked like an odd couple, her height and youth to his lack of stature and maturity. One thing was clear to Fields though. The short dude was too old to be dealing with the kid.

"She ain't talking to you without no lawyer," said her boyfriend.

Round Up

"I'm glad you never miss an episode of Law and Order genius but she doesn't need one. She's not under arrest. Now can you get the fuck away from here please?" Fields said. Priest walked away to another table giving Fields the hard look again before he left.

"My mother told you I didn't see nothing," the girl blurted.

"Exactly...your mother told me. I need you to tell me...umm—"

"Geena and I didn't see nothing."

"Okay Geena, were you anywhere near the eight hundred block of Martin Luther King Boulevard the day before yesterday?"

"No."

"Did you know Mark Anderson?"

"No."

"How about Monique Booker?"

"Nope," answered Geena quickly. Fields knew he hit something, but she wasn't going to give up any information willingly. Not today anyway.

"Here," Fields said. He reached into his pants pocket, pulled out his wallet, and gave her one of his cards. "Call me if you happen to remember anything." The boyfriend came back over, snatched the card out of her hand.

"She sure will."

Fields smiled, walked towards the door, chin nodded to Winslow and left.

* * *

"The cop's rolling out," Santana said. Richard followed Santana's eyes out of the window. Watched the detective get into his car.

"'Bout time. Seems like he was in there forever," Richard answered. They got out of the car, trotted across the street to the restaurant. They walked in, saw Geena and Priest lip locking at the order counter. Richard walked over to Geena feeling the dude giving him the hard stare.

"Geena can I talk to you for a minute?" Richard asked.

"The fuck you need to talk to her for?" Priest yelled.

"Mind your business man, I said I wanna talk to her!" Richard answered, reaching for her arm. Priest smacked it away. Richard turned around like he was walking away, then launched his fist into Priest's jaw. Priest fell back into the counter. Geena screamed. Two of Priest's boys jumped out of the booth. A dude with a missing front tooth grabbed Richard around the neck while the other one picked Priest off the floor. Santana snatched the boy from Richard's neck tossing him into a booth. The two teenage girls sitting there screamed and ran towards the door. Richard watched the stocky guard put Santana in an L hold yelling for everybody to clear out. Richard looked over at Priest who was going into his dip. Richard made his way through the crowd of people rushing towards the entrance. He caught sight of Priest pointing the .45 automatic towards him. Richard ran behind the guard who was still holding Santana. The guard turned around trying to reach for Richard. Two shots rang out. Richard heard the guard yell out as one of the slugs caught him in his broad back. He released Santana who ran behind Richard to the door. Santana pushed three teenage girls and a teenage boy aside, grabbing Richard on the way out of the door. Richard saw the black detective making his way across the street as they hit the corner on the way back to the Tercel.

* * *

Detective Fields got into the Crown Vic. Hit the dashboard out of frustration. He was jumping through hoops to talk to this girl Geena. Maybe she didn't even know anything. Fields scratched that thought. A girl like her knew something. Fields knew she wouldn't use the card he had given her until she was in a situation where she had no other recourse but to call him. In the fast life that she was living, that time would come sooner or later. Young girls that age thought they knew everything. That the good times lasted forever or as long as the money flowed like water, and the boyfriends were willing to take care of them. But the girls never realized that they were expendable. Could be replaced as easy as old shoes. Fields was thinking this as he fired up the ignition. Then he heard the two shots from inside Angelo's. He knew without thinking that the big mouth short dude had something to do with what was going on in there. Fields opened the door, trotted back across the street, holding the .9 millimeter towards the door. Kids were screaming and scattering out the entrance. Caught Mark Anderson's cousin running away out of the corner of his eye. He waited for the door to clear and made his way up the steps. Fields saw Winslow on the floor bleeding as a white man and woman, probably the owners, tended to him. They told him that the shooter had run out the back door of the store with a girl and that an ambulance had been called. Fields looked down at Winslow who was looking up at him. Winslow's eyes expressed the immense pain he was in.

"You're gonna be okay Winslow, just hang tight," Fields said. Heard an ambulance siren about a block away. Fields knew that Geena would be calling him soon. She was going to be looking for some protection.

CHAPTER TWELVE

Richard floored it down Martin Luther King. Hooked a sharp right on Statesman Heights towards the suburbs where Statesman Heights crossed over the county line and turned into Statesman Road. Richard couldn't believe what just happened. He was just glad Santana had been there. Otherwise Richard would have been a blurb in the Colver Star's obituary pages.

"You okay?" Santana asked.

"Yeah," Richard answered. He knew the next day or even that night would be a different story. His body was already starting to ache in the spots where he'd been punched. Richard caught a glimpse of Santana's fair skin starting to redden. "You'd better put some ice on that mark on your face."

Santana rubbed the sore spot, "so what now?"

"I dunno," Richard responded. Santana turned up the tape and leaned back in the seat, his left arm resting over his face. Richard just drove in silence. Drove until the abandoned city buildings and treeless skies made way to residential homes and green lawns. In the county, liquor stores weren't situated at the end of the block. They sat in between bookstores and supermarkets in strip malls and were called taverns. Richard kept straight on Statesman until it changed into Route 26. He was heading towards Monmouth Lake, a quiet place he'd found by accident when he'd gotten lost going to a job interview some years back. When he discovered the spot, Richard came back often to get away from the fast pace of city life.

The lake was a manmade attraction that served as the center of a planned community. The water's edge was surrounded by posh restaurants, trendy clothing stores, and a pavilion where jazz bands played music during community events. When Richard found the place he couldn't believe someplace so perfect existed. He kept the place a secret. Had never even told Mark. He wouldn't have

Round Up

bought Santana here either, but it was one of those times that Richard needed to clear his head. Richard had always came when it was warm and sunny out. Today was cool, the place near desolate. The overcast clouds gave the place a different feeling, drab and dreary. With the exception of a man walking his dog, and a young couple taking an afternoon walk, the place was empty. A huge lighted Christmas tree stood in the middle of the square. Richard parked and killed the engine. It sputtered two times before cutting. Santana sat up when the music stopped. He looked around trying to assess his surroundings.

"What the---?" Santana questioned. Richard got out of the car without answering. Walked towards the lake where benches sat on the water's edge. He sat down, felt the chill wind blowing across his face. Bing Crosby singing about a white Christmas was being pumped into the air though outside speakers planted into the ground. Santana joined him a few moments later. Neither of them spoke right away. Richard watched Santana looking side to side taking in the tranquility of the place. "Richie where the hell we at?"

"My spot. You should feel special. I didn't even bring Mark out here," Richard said.

"It's too quiet for me," Santana answered. He leaned back on the bench and shoved his hands into his jacket pockets.

"That's how I like it."

"You say so." Santana surveyed the surroundings again. "How you find this place?"

"By mistake."

"How many times you been out here?"

"A lot."

"Cops ever bother you?"

"No. Why would they? I'm just sitting here."

"When did a brother ever need a reason?"

"Don't bring that negative energy out here."

"I'm just being real. You coming out here dreaming about some fantasy place where you ain't wanted. People like us belong back in town," Santana said.

"You ever been outside of Colver?"

"For what? Why I gotta go a hundred miles to see the same thing I can see in my own backyard? It's a waste of time."

Richard didn't bother continuing the discussion. Santana's world was back within the city limits, like a dog trapped behind an electric fence. "There's other things out here man."

"I'm sick of this church boy shit! You gonna sit there and tell me that you don't miss the money? You made a name for yourself! Remember how we used to look up to Nikki Barnes and how he used to run Harlem? And James "Bianco" Thompson, the way he ran Colver City?"

Richard remembered the stories he'd heard about Bianco Thompson. How he set up his best friend by giving him to the mob. And how he tried to kill his own son. The Colver Star reported that Bianco had died of a heart attack, alone in his condo back in June. Richard wondered what was worse for the old man, living with the memories of the way he lived his life or dying alone the way he did. "Yeah, I remember."

"People knew you as Ritchie Rich on the street! You used to drive a Beemer! Now look at your ass. Working in some bank for some chump change, driving that piece of shit ride you got."

"That piece of shit keeps me from getting pulled over by the cops every five minutes."

Santana laughed. "You think that just because you wearing a tie and button down shirt that you different? That the cops not gonna fuck with you anymore? I got news for you my man. Your hands are dirty. And they're always gonna be dirty." The man walking his dog walked past them. He locked eyes with Richard before giving Santana the once over then looked away. "The fuck you looking at?" Santana yelled. He stood up and lifted the bottom of his jacket. Revealed the 9 millimeter in his waistband. The dog barked at him. "Shut that mutt up before I put him in the pet cemetery!" The man shook his head and hurriedly walked away. Richard stood up. Walked back towards the car. Maybe Santana was right—no, he wasn't right. There was no reason to think that he'd made a mistake. He walked away from the game for a reason. Richard decided it was time for him and Santana to part ways for right now. A dull pain was making its way up Richard's neck. Figured it was the conversation with Santana that triggered it. He still had to go shopping for a suit for Mark's funeral. And it would be better if he were alone.

Round Up

A half-hour later Richard was driving north on Front Street. He had dropped Santana off about a half-hour before. It was close to four o'clock in the afternoon now. Richard glanced at the sky. Knew darkness was about an hour away. Traffic would be picking up soon when rush hour started. Richard wanted to be in and out before he found himself sitting in a sea of automobiles. Front Street was the fashion district of downtown Colver. Clothing stores—men's and women's—were sandwiched together for three blocks. He went to Bowman's, the same store Pop shopped in when he was alive. Richard remembered holding his father's huge hand as a six-year old kid as he walked through the store looking up at the racks of suits. The same white man always helped Pop. Called his father Mr. Anderson and called Richard little Anderson. A white man, probably in his mid 40's came out from the back. He was dressed in a blue suit with a matching blue pin striped shirt. Coordinated it with a yellow tie. Richard glanced at the comb over on his balding hear. Wondered why white men did stuff like that when it was clearly obvious they were trying to hide something. The salesman was nice though. Helped Richard pick out a nice suit—a black double breasted Kenneth Cole number—and got him on his way just as the downtown traffic started to pick up. Street smarts made him put it in the back trunk. He ignitioned the ride. Sputtered once before starting. The throbbing in his neck was worse now. Checked the glove compartment of the Tercel, found two empty medicine bottles. Pulled into the lot of the CVS on Grantley Avenue to restock on ibuprofen. He walked in through the automatic doors, saw the young security guard glance at him before going back to the book he was reading. Richard looked at the ceiling directory to guide him to the aspirin aisle. Why couldn't every CVS be set up the same way so that he didn't have to search for what he was looking for? This store had the stuff in aisle 3. Go into another one, it would be in aisle 6. It seemed like that to him anyway, Richard was thinking. He went to the back for a soda to wash the pills down. Opened the plastic fridge hitting a woman next to him with the door.

She yelled, "watch it!"

"My fault," Richard said. He took a closer look at the woman. He never forgot a face. It was April Brown, a girl who used to like him. They got together twice before going their separate ways. "Long time April."

April did a double take at him and yelled, "hey Richie!" They hugged. He felt her mounds against his chest, remembered how soft they were. "Sorry to hear about your cousin. I saw it on the news." Richard had forgotten that she had met Mark. They'd done a double, Mark and Monique, him and April to the movies.

Richard looked her over. She looked good. Her coal black hair had grown to her shoulders. She'd put on some weight in the right places. Her eyes were a different color though. He remembered dark brown, now they were a weird colored hazel with that weird looking black dot in the pupil. Contacts. "Yeah," he said.

"When's the funeral?"

"Thirty-first."

"New Years Eve?"

"Yeah. It's going to be more like a home going celebration than a funeral," Richard said. He wanted to ask if she was going, but didn't. Would've sounded too much like he was asking for a date.

"That's a shame what they did to Monique," said April. She shook her head. "I figured something like that would happen sooner or later."

"Why?"

"The people she hung around with."

"What people?"

"I don't like to talk bad about the dead."

"I don't think she'd mind," Richard said.

April smiled and started talking. "I saw her with this guy at the movies a couple months back. I thought her and Mark had broken up. Then I saw Monique and some girl she used to hang out with grinding with this other guy at the Paradox Club on Franklin Boulevard a little while after that."

"What did the girl with Monique look like?"

"Short, long brown hair to her shoulders."

That sounded like Janell Rogers to Richard. She stripped at the Nightlite Club on St. Marks Avenue. Mark had never liked Monique hanging out with her. Said Janell knew too many guys and was a bad influence on Monique. From what Richard was

Round Up

hearing about Monique, maybe Mark was right. "Forreal?" Richard questioned.

April nodded her head. "Then when the Comets had a home game against the Lakers, a friend of mine saw her with that guard Mike Davis at one of the after parties," said April. Richard couldn't believe what he'd just heard. If Monique had been hanging around with one of the Colver City Comets, the city's NBA team, she'd been under the sheets. Especially messing with Mike Davis. He was known for the number of women he slept with. Richard's head was pounding from the discovery. "What's wrong? You look sick."

"A little headache that's all."

* * *

Richard drove south on Echart Boulevard thinking of what April had said. This thing with Mark and Monique confused him. If Mark was really having the kinds of problems that April said he was having, why didn't Mark call to talk about it? Had they grown apart so much that they couldn't even discuss their problems anymore? He had to dig deeper into this thing, find out what was really happening. He'd stop by the Nightlite Club later to talk to Janell, see what and how much she knew. Richard clicked on the radio to cover the knocking and pinging from the Tercel's engine. Beethoven was performing his fifth symphony on the classical station. Leaned back against the headrest and looked at the city. Richard's mind felt clouded with thoughts that were beginning to overwhelm him. Head felt like a pot of water on the stove about to boil over. Richard stopped at a red light, looked over at the bus stop to see what cuties might be over there. It was an old habit that he picked up from the days when he, Santana, and Mark would cruise the streets. He did a double take at a girl coming out of a bookstore on the corner. It was Vanessa. He was surprised to see her here in Colver City, especially on a workday. Richard pulled over to the curb. He was intent on not missing another chance to talk to her. If she turned him down, at least he would know where he stood. Richard leaned over to the other side of the car, rolled down the window.

"Vanessa!" Richard watched her turn around, looking at the direction of the voice. She saw the car and kept walking. Richard called out to her again. "Vanessa, it's Richard, from Community

National!" Richard stepped out of the car, his arms outstretched from his sides like he was a bird ready to take flight. He felt the eyes of the people at the bus stop staring at him. Vanessa looked at him and smiled. The gesture caught Richard off guard considering the way she acted last time he'd seen her.

She started walking towards the car. "Hey Richard? What you doin' here?"

Richard returned her smile. Noticed she looked even prettier than she did in the bank and much more relaxed. Had thoughts on making another play to ask her out. Figured he'd talk to her to find out where her head was at first. "I used to live here. I'm staying at my mother's for a little bit. You need a ride somewhere?"

She shook her head. "That's okay. My car's right around the corner."

"Could I talk to you for a minute before you go?" Richard asked.

"I was about to go to Starbucks for something to drink. You wanna come with me?"

Richard's insides jumped. "Yeah, hold on a sec." Richard killed the engine, locked up the car, and followed Vanessa. "So what are you doin' here on a workday? You quit already?" He chuckled.

"Sure did."

"For real? Damn, I was just joking," Richard said. He had thought she would at least last another week. They walked into the shop. Richard heard Vanessa order some fancy drink, a café la tait or something. Asked if he wanted something. Richard had never been in the place before. Until now, he thought the joint was for those Wall Street type cats that made lots of money from investments and the Internet.

"Umm, just order me something," Richard answered. Watched her order the same thing that she had. She paid with a twenty, got back five and some change. They waited in silence while the drinks were being made. When they were ready, Richard grabbed his and followed Vanessa to a nearby table. "So why'd you quit?"

Vanessa took a cautious sip from the lip of the plastic lid. Left a trace of her red lipstick on the top, answered, "I couldn't take it anymore. The day after you left, we had another crowded day.

Round Up

There was only me and another teller handling all those people. Neither Sara nor Jim helped us out. Sara was still upstairs flirting with the technicians and Jim was hiding away in one of the offices acting like he was doing paperwork. I went on my lunch break and kept right on going."

Richard pulled himself from looking at her ample cleavage when she stopped talking. Hoped she didn't notice. Felt his dick hardening at the thought of her undressing in front of him. Did his best to keep eye contact with her. "I thought you lived in Baltimore," he said.

"No I just got me a little place downtown while I'm working my way through school. My father lives over in Hampstead."

Hampstead was in the Northwest side of town where the well to do blacks lived. Richard knew she came from money. She had a rich look to her. "Which school you go to? Maryland State or Logan College?" Richard asked. They were the only two local colleges she could've gone to.

"Maryland State," Vanessa answered. Richard noticed the way her eyes demonstrated an interest in him. He knew how to differentiate between a chick who was only interested in who he was and somebody who really wanted to get to know him from his days as a hustler.

They talked for about an hour. Richard told Vanessa about R.J., about school, his love for exotic cars. Vanessa told Richard about her two older sisters who were married with children and their doctor husbands. He held back on telling her about Mark. Felt that would be divulging too much about himself, too soon. Besides, Richard didn't want to mess up the moment with such depressing talk. She also told Richard how she wanted to try to make it on her own, and only going to her father for help of necessary. Now that she had quit her job, this was one of those necessary times. When Richard saw her look at her watch, he knew they were about to go their separate ways. But not before Richard had gotten her number and given her a promise that he was going to call her the next day. He walked Vanessa to her car and watched her drive off before going back to his own ride. Richard remembered that he needed to go to the Nightlite club and lost a little of his happiness.

CHAPTER THIRTEEN

Detective Ryan looked at the undesirables who were hanging out in the doorways of the liquor stores and on the corners as he drove south on MLK. Nine o'clock in the morning and they were already staking claim to the areas where they would be for the rest of the day. Ryan's head was still splitting with pain. He knew it was from the beer. He was getting old. No longer in his prime. When he was a rookie at the young age of twenty-one, he could put away a case of suds, lay the pipe to a couple of chicks, get a couple of hours sleep, and still put in a whole shift plus a couple hours of OT. Now at 42, a simple six pack was giving him a hangover. Felt like somebody was pounding his head with a jackhammer. And his body felt sluggish. Heavy like there were hundred pound weights attached to his legs. What he needed was some coffee and a couple hours of shut-eye in his own soft bed. Figured he'd be fine after that.

Ryan drove past Remington Street and looked at the red brick building on the corner. It was the home where granny was staying. Ryan's first thought was to keep driving. Then guilt took his heart hostage. He hadn't been to see the old lady in a month. Ryan didn't think he could take seeing her hooked up to all those tubes and shit again. But he decided to give it a try. After all, she did raise him. Ryan still remembered when his mom left him with granny. Said she was going out for a pack of smokes and would be back in a half-hour. That half-hour turned into the rest of his childhood. Ryan did a U in the middle of the street and parked on the side of the building.

The sterile smell of the place hit Ryan's nose as soon as he walked through the sliding glass doors. He walked up the receptionist—a cute chick that looked to be in her early twenties—and asked if Rebecca Owens was available. The cutie smiled, said the orderlies were changing the sheets and that they'd be done in a

Round Up

minute. Ryan walked over to the waiting area and sat down. An instrumental tune filled the air that was irritating him. Sounded like the theme song to Happy Days, the old television show about those kids from the '50's. Ryan looked in the direction of his grandmother's room. Saw the door open up with two black men dressed in white coming out laughing. Ryan could feel his temper rising at their nonchalance. How the fuck could they laugh when was probably a step away from dying? Ryan continued looking at them as they walked down the hall. One was carrying a bundled sheet with a large brown stain showing. Ryan got up and walked out. As much as he loved his grandmother and everything that she had done for him, Ryan knew he wouldn't be back to see her again. Whoever that sick old woman was in that room wasn't the same woman Ryan had known growing up.

Ryan opened the door to his apartment and was hit in the face by the smell of his garbage. Made him feel like throwing up. And even though the hangover was still attacking his head, his stomach was grumbling for something to eat. It was close to lunch so Ryan figured he'd grab a bite, hoping it would stay down. He took the bag from the plastic can, knotted it and sat it outside the front door. Sprayed rose fragrance air freshener to cover up the smell. Ryan picked up the phone. Didn't hear the three beeps that let him know he had a message. He was glad. Didn't need any more distractions to make his hangover worse.

Ryan draped his jacket on the hook on the back of the door and peeled off his shirt. The place was warm. He left the heat on 75 when he wasn't at home. Hated like hell coming home to a chilly place. Ryan clicked on the tube and went into the kitchen for something to eat. He opened the fridge. Didn't see anything except some leftover Chinese food from Danny Chengs on 32nd Street in Chinatown from a couple of nights ago and some condiments. Inspected the freezer and saw a couple of frozen steaks and a pack of hot dogs. Ryan heard the three chimes indicating a breaking news event coming from the television. He came out of the kitchen and stared at the tube when the newscaster said something about a shooting in Angelo's over on Rice. Ryan knew the place. The joint where all the black kids hung out. The lady didn't give any details about the shooting citing that details were still sketchy and shit like that. Ryan knew they didn't give a damn about what happened. They just wanted the credit for being the first news channel at the scene. To Ryan it was just another case on his already filled plate.

* * *

Ryan was awakened by hard raps at his apartment door. He fluttered his lids, adjusted his pupils to the sun coming in through the window. Stumbled to the front door and looked through the peephole. Saw it was Fields standing in the hallway. He glanced at the clock on the VCR. Saw it was three quarters past two. Ryan opened the door a crack so that only his left eye was showing.

"What do you want? Shift ain't for another hour and a half."

"Thought I'd come by and pick you up," answered Fields. "What, you got company?"

"Maybe."

Fields pushed his way into the apartment. "Ain't nothing in here except your collection of porno's. Who you got in your imagination today?" Fields asked. He looked at the scattered boxes of naked women on the carpet. Fields walked towards Ryan's chair, looked at it, thought twice about what might be on the fabric and sat on the couch instead. "This place looks like shit," said Fields, lifting his nose in the air, "and it stinks in here. Smells like rose flavored garbage."

"It was your mother's day off."

Fields chuckled. "I see you're picking up some skills from the street."

"Whatever. Look I could've made it in on my own power."

"Calm down. I was in the neighborhood and saw your Sable in the parking lot. Just wanted to make sure you were okay after you knocked off early last night is all."

Ryan scratched his nuts through the hole in his boxers. "I'm fine." He noticed Fields looking around the room. Saw Fields gingerly picking up the crime novel Ryan was reading on the floor.

"You and your books. Why you wanna read about this stuff when we live it everyday?"

"Keeps me motivated."

Fields examined the book, flipping it over to the back then again to the front cover. "George Pelecanos. Never heard of him."

"He's the best."

Round Up

"I'll take your word for it," responded Fields. He dropped the book back onto the floor. "Look, I wanted to get back into the Anderson case. We lost a lot of time with that dead end. Didn't even get anything out of that young girl. I went to talk to her at that place where the kids hangout, that joint Angelo's, but didn't get much more than what I got when she was in front of her mother."

Ryan picked up a pair of wrinkled jeans from the floor. Slid them on. "Speaking of which, I saw on the tube that somebody was playing cowboy over there."

"I know. I had just left out. Witnesses pointed the finger at some guy they call Priest. Some short guy."

Ryan raised his eyebrow. Stopped fiddling with the button on his pants. "Yeah? Anybody we know?"

"Never heard of him before this. Kid sure has a big mouth though. And he's fucking around with the girl we need to talk to. I gave her my card so I'm expecting that she'll be calling me."

"Yeah?"

"Yeah, I hope it's soon. I really want that Priest kid."

"I heard narcotics say something about doing a sweep, maybe they got him already," Ryan said. He hated the street name for a sting. Round up. Sounded like he was a cowboy in the old west and shit. Though with all the gunplay in the streets it damn near felt like the OK corral sometimes.

"Maybe. I'll check it out later. Just in case, I took out a warrant on him. I'm gonna spread the word that the cops are looking for him. Kid's gonna start getting real nervous, real quick. Wannabe thugs like him always do. They're only about as brave as the gun in their hands."

"So what about the girl? You think she's gonna lead us to him?"

"Sure do. And once we get him, I'll bet he knows something about what happened to the vics."

Ryan knew he'd have to get to the kid first. Talk to him to make sure the little spade didn't give up Ryan's name in some kind of deal the States Attorney might offer. "Sounds good to me."

"You know something else?" Fields asked.

"What?"

"It's probably nothing but I saw Mark Anderson's cousin, the one we interviewed with his mother, running out of the sub shop too. Now I know it's the neighborhood hangout and all but why would he be there so soon after his cousin's murder? You'd think the guy would be watching his back, you know, just in case someone wanted to off him too."

"There might be something more to it. I meant to run him past you after we went over there that day. I saw the kid before."

"Where?"

"Three, four years ago when I worked in the Northern District. He was a dealer, went by the name Richie Rich or something."

"How come I never heard of him?"

"He was good. Stayed low profile, never made a blip on the radar screen. The flashiest thing he had was a blue Beemer, but it was regular. No fancy wheels or anything. Looked respectable like all the other cars on the street. Then one day he was gone. Of course somebody picked up right where he left off."

"You think he's here for some type of retaliation?" Fields asked..

"Maybe he's trying to play junior detective or something. Find out what happened to his cuuuz." Ryan heard his partner take a deep breath, like the comment had irritated him. Ryan was only trying to be funny saying cousin the way he said it; the way he thought black people sounded.

"I dunno, maybe. Like I said, it's probably nothing. If there is something going on, it'll come out sooner or later."

"At this point I don't give a fuck. The faster we get this one done, the better," Ryan said. He walked into the kitchen. Grabbed an open carton of milk sitting on the counter. Killed the rest of it in one swallow. "You ready?"

"Aren't you gonna shower?" Fields asked.

"I already did. Damn, how many showers does a guy need to take in one day?"

Round Up

CHAPTER FOURTEEN

    Terrell "Priest" Adams gassed the Gold Maxima down MLK Boulevard, hooked a sharp right onto Kelly Avenue towards Banneker Homes. Terrell popped a tape into the deck by Craig Mack, the Flavor In Ya Ear Remix by Puff Daddy to calm him. The song was a classic. It was an old jam from back in '94 but it was still one of his favorites. Ranked it right up there with Live in Hollis by Run DMC. No one had thought to put five rappers with different styles into the same song. Terrell had to give it to Puff, he knew how make a tight joint. Terrell began to feel safe when he saw the high rise building project a few blocks away with the afternoon sun sitting in the sky behind it. He hoped the chrome rims on the Max were catching the rays so that they would gleam as they spun down the street. The cops who worked in the projects didn't give a damn about the people who lived there. Too much happened over there for the police to keep any kind of control. They only came around when something newsworthy that would make people shake their heads went down. Shit like killings and high profile drug busts. Otherwise, crime was part of the daily events of life in the neighborhood just like waking up, eating, and going to sleep. There wasn't time to be scared of what might happen in the streets. You just lived life and hoped for the best, Priest was thinking.
    The funny thing about it all was that Priest didn't start out on the wrong side of the tracks. He grew up in the suburbs out in the county. Had a good childhood, the best of everything. His mother made sure that he and his older brother Shawn had everything that kids in two parent households had since their old man didn't do shit for them. Even worked three jobs to make sure her sons kept full stomachs. Thanksgiving always had a table full of food and Christmas always had a big tree that touched the ceiling of their two bedroom apartment and a bunch of toys to open up.

But having those things came with a price. The material things didn't make up for her not being there with him and Shawn. His brother took on the responsibility of acting like a father even though he was only older than Terrell by a couple of years. Shawn was a good role model.

Still, having all the things that Mama gave to them, it didn't make up for a father being around the house. And the older Terrell got, the less control Ma had over him, especially with her being at work most of the time. And Shawn was too busy trying to make something out of himself to give a developing young Terrell the guidance he needed to stay on the positive side. Terrell spent a lot of time in the house alone watching black shoot'em up flicks from back in the day like Shaft, and Foxy Brown, when black people wore afros and those funny looking clothes. His favorite flick of them all was Superfly. Terrell even took the name of the lead character Priest from the movie. It sounded cool and Terrell liked the way the character handled himself in the flick.

After graduating high school, Shawn went straight to college. Picked up a part time job to help pay his way through school. Got so that Shawn was hardly at home anymore. Ma tried to get Terrell into something positive too. Enrolled him into community college at first. Terrell hated it. Dropped out after the first couple of weeks. Well, kicked out was more like it. He could have sworn some white dude had called him stupid or something. And it didn't take much to get Terrell's temper to click. Terrell asked the dude to repeat what he said. Before the kid had a chance to say anything, Terrell punched him in the mouth. Then Ma got him into one of those technical schools. It was more interesting than community college. Terrell liked tinkering with machines and shit like that. But the teachers still made him do some book learning. He stopped going after a month. With so much free time on his hands Terrell found it hard to stay out of petty trouble, shit like assaults and car thefts, but Ma was always there with a high priced lawyer to get him off. Terrell's luck ran out after he was arrested for assaulting Tammy, his son's mother. Rumor was going around that she was cheating on him with some cat from over on Broadway Avenue. Terrell went over to her house, asked if it was true. She started stuttering and shit. Looked like she was lying, so he choked her until she passed out. The States Attorney tried to

Round Up

give him attempted murder. Later they dropped it to second degree assault. The judge gave him an eighteen-month bid and called it a gift. Terrell got out in a little under a year.

Even though Terrell didn't talk to Shawn much anymore, he wasn't mad at his brother. Shawn was doing his own thing. He'd graduated college, got a job working for a computer company that paid good honest money. Shawn was doing all right for himself. Shawn even seemed to meet the right girls. He married a nice chick named Brenda that he met at the company. Terrell only met her once but he could see from her proper mannerisms that she was a good woman. Nothing like this money hungry freak Geena sitting next to him. Shawn and Brenda had two kids and a house now. Terrell wanted to find a girl to settle down with too. Try to build a life together. Seemed like whenever he met one that had the potential to be his wife, things always messed up, especially after he had a kid with them. He had three kids by three different women and they all acted the same way. Always asking for money for diapers and shit. Since when did diapers cost three hundred dollars? Geena put a scare into him twice claiming she was knocked up. Terrell wouldn't have minded if she did have his kid. Might make her settle down, turn her into the woman he thought she could be. Sure she was young and all, but she was mature for her age. Acted more grown that some of the older women he had dated who wanted to tie him down. One of them was even talking about marriage! No, Geena wasn't like anybody he'd ever met. She never asked what he was doing when he wasn't with her like the others did. She gave him his freedom, even though Terrell wished she would show more concern for him sometimes.

When Terrell thought about his brother he was envious. Yeah, Shawn had it all. Would trade lives with his brother in a minute. But Terrell? Shit, his life was nothing close to a fairy tale like Shawn's. What was he going to do, cry about it? Hell no. People might take you for bad. Treat you like a punk. A man had to handle his business. Take somebody out if they disrespected you. Like that Detective Ryan's smelly ass. Man smelled like rotten chitt'lins. Ryan had the upper hand now making Terrell pay like he was doing just to be in the neighborhood, but that was going to stop soon. There were plenty of young fearless dudes who would put a slug into a cop to get down with Terrell. And like that toy cop in Angelo's who grabbed him and wrinkled up his clothes the day before. Who the hell did that dude think he was jacking him up in front of his crew like that? And everybody in the shop saw what went down too. Terrell had to redeem himself. He hadn't planned on doing anything to the security guard until next week, but since he got into Terrell's business, Terrell figured it was better to deal with the situation now. Terrell hoped the man didn't die, but if he did, oh well. If the man croaked, Terrell would send some flowers to the funeral. That way if he got caught Terrell could say he felt at least some sense of remorse. Judges liked shit like that. But the main one Terrell wanted was that dude who grabbed Geena by her arm. That cat not only disrespected Geena by grabbing her like he did, but he disrespected Terrell, and that was definitely something that had to be made right. Nobody touched what belonged to him, Terrell thought.

Terrell looked over at Geena in the passenger seat. She hadn't said a word since they left the sub shop. She looked scared. Those cops asking her those questions bothered him. She may have acted mature but the fact was Geena was still a kid. Terrell looked at her face while that cop gave her the third degree. Looked liked she was about to cry at any minute. They were going to come after Geena sooner or later. And Terrell couldn't have her tagging along behind him while he was trying to hide out in the projects. An acquaintance of Terrell's mother would hide him out for three hundred a week. Terrell had heard another guy do the same thing after he shot a dude. He hid out in Roosevelt Houses until things cooled down. Terrell knew that he'd have to cut Geena loose, let her go back home to her mother. But once the cops got to her she'd make the case for the State's Attorney against him. Especially when they were in Geena's face threatening to charge her with the shooting. She'd turn on Terrell faster than a streetlight changing from yellow to red. Sounded like an episode of Law and Order that he'd seen just last week. Terrell turned down the thumping bass coming from the speakers.

"You okay?" Terrell asked. His voice was soothing.

"Why'd you h-have to do that?"

"Baby it was an accident. I only meant to scare the dude I was fighting with. The security guard just got in the way."

Round Up

"I wanna go home," Geena said. Sounded like the little girl that she was.

"I can't do that right now baby. We gotta let things cool down a little, then I'll take you home." Terrell could hear the weakness in her voice. She'd probably run to the cops before they had the chance to find her. "Don't worry about it. I'll take care of this all right?" Terrell watched her nervously nod her head. He leaned over, pecked her cheek with his chapped lips. He was going to have to figure out what to do with her before the day was over. "Let's get something to eat, you'll feel better. After that I'll take you shopping at that outlet in Hagerstown," said Terrell. Geena smiled a weak smile. He pulled into a KFC lot and cut the engine. The fried chicken smell seeping into the cracked window of the car was making him nauseous.

CHAPTER FIFTEEN

Richard prayed that the car wasn't going to cut out on him as he drove down St. Vincent's Avenue. Felt like the Tercel was close to its final resting place in the junkyard. Didn't matter though. He was still on an emotional high from seeing Vanessa. He hoped a tune up would fix whatever was going on under the hood. Figured he'd stop by Al's garage on Berkeley Street before he left to go back to Baltimore. Paul Lawson, a friend from high school, took over the business from his father, Al Lawson after the old man retired. Richard had always thought that Mr. Al was a nice man. Used to give the most candy at Halloween, and even gave Paul's friend's presents at Christmas. Ma had told him that Paul was following in his old man's footsteps by doing the same things.

Richard saw the bright yellow sign that read The Nitelite over the doors of the club a block away on St. Thomas Avenue. It was one'o'clock in the afternoon so the club was open for business. Richard parked across the street feeling the car sputter three times before cutting off. He took a deep breath missing the days of driving the reliable Beemer. He stepped out of the car, leaned back on the doors to avoid getting hit by oncoming traffic. Richard trotted across St. Marks Avenue to the doors of the Nitelite. A dude with skin the color of freshly laid tar wearing a three-quarter length leather coat was standing out front. He smiled showing three gold teeth, two on top, one on the bottom.

"Got some hot pussy in the club today man," said the man.

"Cool," Richard answered. The man stepped aside and opened the door. Richard walked in, opened another door to a dimly lit open room. The room was hot. Felt like the heat was pumped up to ninety. Pony, a jam by that pretty boy singer Ginuwine was coming through the system speakers. The one where he was singing about some chick riding him during sex. Two men were sitting at the counter. One dragged on a cigarette. The other was

Round Up

nursing a near empty glass of beer. A skinny woman with some small ass titties and an ass to match gyrated her nude body in the stage in front of them. A light glaze of sweat covered her thin body. Both men looked disinterested. So did the girl that was dancing. Looked like she had emotionally transplanted herself to another world to escape the reality of what she was doing. Richard looked around the near desolate place. No one was at the bar and the DJ looked bored leaning against his turntables. Richard took a closer look at the dude. Saw it was this guy named Glenn Henry. Used to make mix tapes for five dollars around the neighborhood. Called himself "Little G", like that made him harder or something. Richard made his way over to the booth, put himself in Glenn's line of vision. Glenn looked in Richard's direction, did a double take and threw up his hands.

"Yo! Look who's in the house! Richie Rich!" Glenn yelled.

Richard smiled, said, "What's up "G" ?" They slapped hands, hugged.

"Glad to see you back in town man. Wish it was under better conditions."

"I hear you," Richard responded.

"Sorry to hear about Mark."

"Thanks," Richard answered. He appreciated the sympathy but he was tired of hearing about Mark's death.

"When's the funeral?" Glenn asked.

"New Years Eve."

"You know I'm there. Mark was my boy," Glenn said.

Richard changed the subject. He looked around. "So you like working here?"

"To be honest man. I get tired of looking at this shit. At the end of the day all it smells like is pussy and ass around here. Some days I don't even want to come in. It's a dead end gig. I'm only working here until I hear something from the police department. You know I took the test."

"No, I didn't know. You wanna be a cop?" Richard wondered what kind of policeman Glenn would make. Glen didn't have any heart. He'd been picked on by everybody in the neighborhood since Richard could remember. The only thing that made Glenn popular was his skill as a DJ. He also made a lot of giveaways to keep his ass from getting kicked.

"I gotta eat. Mix tapes aren't enough to put food on the table and get the rent paid."

"You don't have to explain anything to me."

"So what are you doing in here? I know these ain't your type of girls. Least I hope not."

"Naw. I'm looking for this chick. You know a girl named Janell works here?"

"Nicknamed Sweet and Low?"

"Yeah."

"Yeah she works here. Why?"

"I wanna talk to her real quick."

"You and a lot of other dudes. You not thinking about trying to get with her are you? Cause if you are you might as well stand in line brotha. She's---" The song the stripper on stage was dancing to had ended. Janell came out from behind a curtain. She was wearing a thong wedged in between swollen brown sugar colored cheeks, pasties on the nipples of her ample breasts, and red high heels on her pretty feet. Her solid frame stood at only five one or two so she was thick. Bigger than the kinds of girls Richard liked but he still would've bedded her if it came down to it.

"Glenn where's my mothafuckin' music?" Janell yelled. Richard could see a small gap in between her teeth when she spoke.

"It's "G" not Glenn!"

"I don't give a damn what your name is, just put on my damn song!" Glenn scrambled over to the turntable. He put on Carl Thomas' Emotional. It was a romantic ballad. Slow and smooth led by the melody. Richard sat down on one of the stools and watched Janell start to dance. She was prettier than Richard had remembered for years ago when Mark begged him to double with him and Monique. Hell, if she had looked like this back then he wouldn't have said no. Her body was nowhere near as curvy as it was now and she used to have a bad case of acne. Face looked like she had a bad case of chicken pox. Richard looked her up and down. Her body was luscious like melted chocolate. And her face was smooth now. No scars or scratches. She looked like one of those naked statues he'd seen at the art museum downtown on Third Avenue. Richard wondered how much money contributed to her transformation. Janell moved like a ballerina. Not nasty or provocative. No, she was more artistic.

Round Up

After the song went off, Richard went over to Glenn. "Is she coming back out?"

"Yeah, she should be coming out in a few minutes to work the crowd for a lap dance," answered Glenn. Richard looked around the near empty room, thinking she wasn't going to have much luck. Richard stood there, talked to Glenn for ten minutes, not really listening to what he was saying, constantly watching out for Janell. Finally Janell came walking out fully dressed in tight blue jeans and some black boots that matched her leather coat. Looked like she was ready to leave. Richard was kind of disappointed. He might have bought Janell the high priced drink she required for some of her time. She was walking past Richard when he put his arm out. Janell glanced at him, her left arched eyebrow raised. She looked annoyed and bothered. A bouncer looked in their direction, started making his way over to where they were.

"Can I talk to you for a minute Janell?"

"I'm getting ready to go...and who are you?" Janell responded. She looked Richard up and down.

"Mark's cousin." He decided not to bring up when they had gone out. Thought it better to leave it in the past.

"Who?"

"Richie Rich...I mean they used to call me Richie Rich." The bouncer reached them, grabbed Richard's arm.

"It's okay Mo," Janell said. Mo walked away as fast as he had come over. She sat down on a barstool beside Richard. "I heard of you. You were a serious baller 'round here. Then you just up and disappeared. I didn't know you and my girl's man were cousins though."

"Yeah, that's what I'm here to talk about."

"Well make it quick."

Richard looked at Janell. Her face was hard, detached from the moment. He guessed she had to be like that to get through a bunch of strangers groping her body all the time. "You know what happened to my cousin and Monique right?"

"Yeah, and it was fucked up. I hoped they catch who did it. Monique was my homegirl."

"Did she dog somebody or something? Why would somebody do her and my cousin like that?"

"I don't know. Dudes just do shit for crazy reasons sometimes. You tell them no and they act like they don't hear you."

"Did something happen at one of the parties you went to or something?"

"We went to a bunch of parties."

"I mean did somebody ever disrespect you or try to push up on you?"

"Of course they did. Happened all the time. We were two fine sista's. Everybody was trying to fuck us."

"Did she?"

"Did she what?"

"Ever lay down with one of the dudes that was trying to get at her?"

"I don't know! We wasn't connected at the hip!" Janell opened her purse, took out a pack of Newports, fired one up without offering Richard one and blew a line of smoke into the air. Richard didn't like chicks that smoked. Made them look trashy, but Janell still looked good, even with the cancer stick between her lips. "Look, all I know is that her and your cousin wasn't getting along too good. She wanted to hang out with me, take her mind off of her problems, and I did. Now if she decided to give up that ass to somebody else then that's her business. Your cousin should've treated her better."

"How you know how he treated her?" Richard asked. Janell blew a line of smoke into his face. "'Cause all of ya'll are dogs. But to answer your question, she told me how he was fucking with a little girl, some underaged chick who probably just got some hair on her pussy. I told her she didn't have to take that shit. She looked too good for that. There's too many dudes out here who would treat her right."

Richard couldn't believe his ears. He hoped that Mark hadn't been messing with Geena, or any young girl for that matter. He got up from the stool. "Thanks," he said. Made his way towards the door. Richard chin nodded to Glenn who was smiling as he passed the DJ's booth.

Janell killed the square in the black ashtray on the counter. Got up and followed him. "Oh yeah, she did tell me about this dude she'd met that she was digging."

Round Up

"Yeah? How'd he treat her?"

"I dunno, never met him. She just called him a pretty boy. Said he drove a chromed out black Benz. " Richard walked. Felt the eyes of the bouncer on him. The bright light outside hurt Richard's eyes until they adjusted. Janell walked beside him. The guy outside the front door made a kissing sound when they exited the building.

"When you gonna let me get some of that Sweet and Low?" He asked. Chuckled a phlegm filled laugh.

Janell ignored him. Looked up and down St. Marks Avenue. "Dammit! I told his ass to be out here!"

Richard was getting ready to make his way across the street. "You need a ride?"

"Thanks, where's your car?"

Richard pointed across the street at the Tercel. "Over there." He saw Janell look at it.

Her face soured. "That's okay," answered Janell, "I'll catch a cab."

* * *

Richard pulled up in front of his mother's house. Shifted the automatic into park and cut the engine. The Tercel only kicked once before shutting off. His head was still killing him. And it was made worse by all the shit he was hearing about Mark. The throbbing pain started at the base of his neck to his temples. Even though Richard had already taken two pills, he popped two more and dry swallowed them. Thought briefly of the warning that medicines said on the bottle about not exceeding the recommended dosage. Fuck it, Richard was thinking. The people who wrote that probably never had a headache like the one he had. Richard looked down the block through his windshield. Nico was parked on a stoop dragging on a square. Richard shielded his eyes from the setting sun seeing Nico looking towards the car. He popped the switch on the hatch and stepped out onto the street. Richard pulled the suit out of the back controlling the blowing plastic with his right hand, shutting the hatch with his left. Richard walked onto the sidewalk feeling the dealer's eyes burrowing into him. The old Richard would've asked the dude what the hell was he looking at. Would've held up his hands inviting the punk for a beat down. But that was a time when money ran Richard's life.

Still, that didn't mean Richard didn't feel like punching the punk in his mouth.

"What's up Richie Bitch...my fault Richie Rich?" Nico yelled. His voice echoed through the block. Richard gritted his teeth and went into the house. He heard Nico call him a pussy after the door closed. The heat of the house and the smell of ham seasoned with glaze greeted him like an old friend in the vestibule. Yolanda Adams was singing about leaving life's battles to the Lord on the radio.

"Richie?" Ma called out.

"Yeah---" Richard answered. Before he could finish, she ran into the living room, hugged him. Took him a second to catch his breath.

"The news was talking about some shooting at that place you kids hang out at! I thought oh my God please let my son be okay!"

"I'm fine Ma, I wasn't nowhere near there," Richard lied. He didn't want to but it made her feel better. Her face calmed instantly. She hugged him again.

"I can't even think straight anymore. Whenever I hear a pop I think you're somewhere bleeding in the street. I could barely even cook."

"I'm fine Ma," Richard repeated. They walked into the living room, Richard saw that the couch was unoccupied. "Where's Aunt Shelly?"

"Upstairs sleep."

"She any better?"

"A little. Good as can be expected under the circumstances," said Ma, looking at the suit slung over Richard's left shoulder. "I see you bought a suit."

"Yeah."

"Looks nice."

"It's alright." Richard was looking at the floor. Ma lifted his chin with her index finger. "Have a seat," she said, pointing to the couch where his aunt had been sleeping. A yellow blanket was crumpled up on the center of the three cushions.

"C'mon Ma ain't nothing wrong."

"Sit!" Ma said. Her voice was stern now. Understanding was gone for the moment. Ma didn't like to be disobeyed. Richard dropped to the cushion. Knew it would irritate his mother. She

Round Up

didn't like bouncing on the furniture. Remembered that from when he and Mark were kids. Huffed his dissatisfaction. Ma took a deep breath before talking. "I know all of this bothers you Richie. But you walking around here acting like you have to be the rock for everybody to cry on. You were the same when your father died. Everybody crying at the funeral except you. You remember that?"

"Yeah Ma, I remember."

"You didn't know I heard you crying your eyes out that night did you? You and Mark were like brothers. Close as close could get. Richie, I know you're hurting. You don't have to hide it from me."

"I'm alright. Just got some other stuff on my mind," Richard responded. His insides had melted from her words. Memories of the two of them playing right there in the living room flooded his head. Richard could almost hear Mark calling him a cheater like he always did when they played cops and robbers. Richard was the robber that couldn't die. Mark could shoot him a hundred times and Richard would claim that Mark had missed. Richard cracked a smile at the memory. The show of emotion must have been good enough for his mother to leave him alone. She gave him a hug and rose off the couch. "Mark is in a better place now."

Richard went upstairs to his room.

* * *

Richard was lying in bed. He'd taken a cold shower, slid into some blue cotton pajama bottoms and a blue wife beater. He liked the way cotton felt against his skin on cold nights like this one. The temperature had dropped from cool in the afternoon to cold. It was early, around seven o'clock, but the night made it feel later. Funny how the same time felt totally different in winter and summer. Richard couldn't wait for the warm weather to come back.

Richard looked at the phone. He picked up and started dialing R.J. without thinking about it. It had been too long since the last time he talked to his little girl. The phone rang twice. Someone answered in the middle of the third. A brief moment gave Richard the chance to hope that it was Desiree on the other end. A deep voice spoke instead. Antoine.

"Let me speak to R.J.," Richard said. He could hear The Rugrats cartoon theme song in the background.

"She's eating."

"Then let me talk to Desiree."

"What you wanna talk to her for? She ain't got nothing to say to you!"

Richard was silent. He could hear Desiree in the background asking who was on the phone. Richard felt his frustration giving way to anger. His heart was thumping hard. Felt like it was about to explode like a balloon that had been pumped with too much air. "Let me talk to my daughter," Richard said again.

"Fuck you!" Antoine shouted. A dial tone came a second later. Richard held the phone to his ear until the recorded voice gave an order to hang up and dial again if he wanted to make a call. This man was trying to push him out of his child's life. This man, who wasn't there to see Richard helping the doctors to bring his child into the world. This man, who wasn't there to get up three times a night when R.J. was screaming for a bottle. This man who did nothing but put the pipe to Desiree good enough to let him move in with her was trying to separate Richard from his kid. Richard pushed down the receiver, reset the dial tone, and hit redial. The phone was answered on the first ring this time.

"Who is it?"

"Let me speak to my daughter," Richard said. His tone was even, restrained.

"I told you punk that she's eating! You call my house again, I'm gonna fuck you up!"

"Yeah? Yeah? Bring it then punk!" Richard yelled. His mouth was working on its own, his brain having lost control. "You fuck with me you dead you hear me mothafucka?" The recording answered saying to hang up and dial again. Richard hit redial again. Another recording answered telling him that the party he was trying to reach was not taking calls. Richard slammed the phone down. His heart was hurting like it had been pricked a thousand times with a toothpick. Richard missed his little girl. Could almost hear her little voice asking about her daddy. He wondered how Desiree responded. What was she saying to those sad brown eyes? What kind of woman would let some dude come in and take over

Round Up

her life like that? Richard hoped that punk was jealous. Not even he could stop his little girl from missing her father.

Richard hit redial once more, got the recording. He slammed the phone down again, and rubbed both hands over his face. Felt the moisture between his fingers from his eyes. The pricks to his heart came faster and more frequent. Made the tear ducts in the corners of his eyes flood with water like it was monsoon season. Richard didn't even hear his mother come into his room. All he felt was the comfort of her arms wrapping around him, pulling Richard close to her warm body. He didn't even mind that she didn't knock before entering like he complained about when he was a kid. The water came harder but the weight in his chest was becoming lighter. She held Richard just like that for what felt like a lifetime. And it felt good.

CHAPTER SIXTEEN

Detective Fields pulled up in front of the red brick building on 55 Register Lane, the 13 Precinct; Northwestern District. There were ten districts in the city, one for each direction on a compass. Fields and Detective Ryan rarely checked in preferring to be out in the field investigating whatever case they were working on, but some days going into the precinct couldn't be avoided. Like every two weeks when time sheets were turned in. Their captain wanted every minute of overtime accounted for, how it was spent, and what work was done for it to be claimed. Ryan blamed the new rules on a nosey ass reporter from the Colver Star who did a story the year before on why the city was paying so much overtime to the cops without a drop in crime. Sargent Ronald Faith was in charge of enforcing the honesty of the time cards. Ryan hated the Sargent. Faith was a hard-edged cop who worked his way up from walking the beat to the important position behind the pine desk in the big office in the rear of the building. Faith knew color kept men down, since he'd fought all the prejudices that come along with being a black cop in crime infested Colver City. Faith was called a sell out by the black citizens for doing his job and incompetent by his white superiors for not keeping the statistics down in his district. Fields thought Faith was a fair man. Ryan thought he was dick head, drunk on the power of his position. Fields had seen his share of the two men bumping heads on everything from Ryan being a minute late to shift to why Sargent Faith seemingly treated the black officers better than the white ones.

The two men walked up the steps of the building, through the glass doors into the arena of desks and cops. The area where their desks were was near the back of the building in front of a window view of the street. Ryan didn't like sitting near anyone. Shift was changing over. The day shift people were making their way home.

Round Up

Twilight was getting settled. A few from day stayed over into twilight. A lot of cases were on the table to be solved so the extra help was gladly appreciated. Just so long as OT could be proven per Sargent Fields. Ryan walked into the arena, eyes locked straight ahead to the area where he they sat. Fields spoke to a few of his coworkers, some who'd been working with since rookie year. Fields copped two sodas—a root beer him, an orange for Ryan— from the machine in the corner of the room. Tossed Ryan his when he reached the desk. Ryan chin nodded his thanks. Fields sat down. Did an eye sweep of the organization on his desk. In contrast, Ryan's desk was scattered with papers and case files folders.

"Let's hurry up and get the time in so we can get back into the street," Ryan said. "I hate this fucking place." He popped the tab, took a swig from the opening of the can without wiping off the rim. Fields looked towards Faith's office. The door was closed. Figured he was in there giving the third degree to someone about fudging the time card. Fields booted up his computer, hit the ion for the timecard he had saved on the desktop. Heard Ryan's machine beep its hello across from him. After the Microsoft intro was finished, a tone invited Fields to open his email. Heard Ryan's machine make the same noise across the desk. Fields clicked on the envelope icon, read that Faith wanted to see him in the office when he got in.

"Aw shit, what the hell does that asshole want now? I haven't even turned in my goddamn time card yet so what's he bitching about?" Ryan asked.

"Faith wants to see you too?" Fields asked. without looking up.

"Too? The bastard wants you in there?"

"Sure does." Fields wondered what it had to do with. Ryan got pulled in every two weeks like clockwork. But Fields never got the call unless it was to say he'd done a good job or something. Faith's office door opened. He looked out into the arena, saw the two of them, and waved them over. Fields got up, made his way over to the other side of the room and into the office. He sat down in one of the wooden chairs in front of the pinewood desk. Watched the Sargent go back and forth between his desk and a file cabinet. The man looked better than most guys of about 47. No gut. Defined arms that could be seen through his button down shirt. Faith

Fields asked. about his family. Fields replied they were fine. Ryan took his time coming to the meeting. By the time Ryan came, Faith was seated in the leather chair behind the desk. His dark eyes followed Ryan into the room until Ryan sat down.

"Glad you could make it," Faith said. His voice was monotone and sarcastic. Fields glanced at Ryan. Knew the words fuck you were floating around in Ryan's head. Faith got to the point quickly. "What's happening with the Anderson-Wilson case?" Faith was talking to them both, but he was looking at Fields to answer.

"We followed some leads, talked to both families. Still not clear why this happened," Fields answered.

"The media is playing this one up. People don't want that kind of senseless violence in their neighborhoods. From what I hear, Mark Anderson was some kind of promoter who put together some high profile shows at the Pavilion. He was pretty well known around town. A young guy trying to do something with his life."

"I've heard," Fields said.

"And the girl was his fiance. That makes it sound like two people with the whole world ahead of them were killed for no reason."

"Shame," Ryan said. Fields could hear the insincerity in Ryan's tone."

"It is a shame. That makes people nervous, angry that this type of thing keeps happening in the city. We've got more killings than Baltimore and D.C. combined. And the arrest rate is ridiculous. Sounds like we're giving the citizens a message that the criminals run this city now."

Ryan spoke up like Fields knew he would do eventually. "So what do you want us to do? We can't help it if the killers aren't participating in the money for guns programs. If you ask me that whole thing was a joke." Fields thought the same thing as Ryan did. Any kid could find a rod and turn it in to get the hundred dollars they were giving away for each one collected. The people who were doing the shooting weren't lining up to give away their hardware.

"Well I don't recall asking you Ryan now did I?" The Sargent asked. "Did I?"

"No you didn't...sir."

Round Up

"I consider overtime an investment and I don't see the city's investment paying off. I want this done soon." Faith sat on the edge of his desk, placed the palms of his hands on both knees. Fields could see the outline of his toned arms through the blue dress shirt. "The shooter is out there," said Faith, pointing to the window behind his desk. "I want him here," he pointed to the floor, "standing on the front steps of this building...with me behind him telling the cameras that he's off the street. Am I clear?"

Fields answered, "Yes sir." Ryan nodded his head.

"That's all gentleman." Ryan and Fields stood up to leave. "Ryan?"

"Yeah?"

"Bring your time card in here. I want to get this over with." Fields heard Ryan take a breath before leaving the office ahead of him.

CHAPTER SEVENTEEN

Richard chuckled at an old Sanford & Son rerun on the tube. The argument with Antoine had happened over two hours ago and Richard could finally feel the stress from the heated conversation starting to subside. Clicked off the television after the credits rolled up the screen to the theme song that Quincy Jones had put together for the show. Gas made it's way up from Richard's stomach and out of his mouth. The ham with the side dish of homemade macaroni and cheese, and green beans seasoned with bacon that Ma had made for dinner made him feel better. That and Ma talking to him. She said Desiree was going to pay for the hurt she was causing him. Said God was going to take care of everything. After she left, Richard said a prayer asking God to let him be around when he did whatever he was going to do. The dinner reminded Richard of the old days when Ma cooked big meals on Sundays when Mark and Aunt Shelly would come over. Mark and Richard would look at whatever sport was in season in Richard room. Football in the winter, basketball in the spring and baseball in the summer. They loved sports more so to argue with each other than the sport itself. Ma and Aunt Shelly would be downstairs in the kitchen while Aunt Shelly bragged about all the young dudes who tried to talk to her. These were times Richard definitely was going to miss.

When the phone rang, Richard looked at it for a second. Knew it wasn't for Ma. Her life pretty much stopped after 8'clock when she went to bed. And with the exception of people from the church, no one called her anyway. Richard picked it up in the middle of the second ring wanting to stop the noise before it disturbed his mother.

"Hello?" Richard answered.

Round Up

It was Santana. "You trying to go to a party tonight?" He was nearly shouting, trying to talk over the music in the background. Sounded like he was in a car.

"Could you turn that shit down?" Richard said. He could hear the volume decrease from the loud bass.

"You happy?" Santana asked.

"Now I can hear your ass. What party you talking about?"

"Pick one, it's a whole bunch of them happening around town."

"I'm gonna pass. I'm not too much in the partying mood."

Santana huffed. "No disrespect or nothing Richie but you gonna let this thing keep fucking with you like this? Marky wouldn't want you to just be sitting around crying your eyes out man."

Richard though about what Santana said. He was right. Mark didn't let things bother him. His philosophy was You can't change the past. What's done is done. Still, Richard didn't feel like dealing with the dudes who would be looking for trouble and the stuck up chicks who dressed like freaks but didn't dance with anybody except other chicks. No, he could do without that tonight. "Naw man, I'm just gonna chill."

"Take it easy then, I'll talk to you later."

"Later," responded Richie. He hung up the phone, picked up the remote from the foot of the bed, pointed it at the CD player. Scanned through the radio stations, heard about a few pre New Years parties that were happening around town. The station mentioned some spot called Retro's on Liberty Avenue. Promised they would have the hottest girls and the best drinks. Wondered if he'd made the right decision. Richard clicked off the radio after a few more minutes of scanning. He glanced at the clock on the bedside table. Saw the yellow digital letters read nine-thirty. It was still fairly early, too early for him to be bedding down for the night. Sleep was becoming more of an enemy to him lately. He'd close his eyes and keep seeing Mark lying in a pool of his own blood with spent bullet casings around his body. And lately the vision was even coming to Richard when he was awake. Felt like his thoughts were being held hostage by the tragedy. Richard knew he needed to get out, do something to take his mind off things, at least for a few hours anyway. Richard started to pick up the phone then figured it would be too much trouble trying to find some gear to wear to go out. He rolled over on his side instead. The phone rang again. Richard sat up, looked at it, and picked it up before the second ring echoed through the house.

"Who is it?" Richard asked.

It was Santana again. "I'm out front, you ready to go?"

Richard huffed out of frustration. Though inside, Richard was secretly happy that Santana made the decision for him to go out. "I'll be down in minute."

* * *

Richard sat in the soft leather seats of the '98 ivory colored Audi A6. Richard thought Santana was smart to cop a ride that was low profile. Most dudes had Benzes and Beemers with chrome wheels and spoiler kits. Even when Richard had his blue Beemer, it was the sedan model with the factory wheels, no extras. Just a regular ride that any average Joe would have who went to work everyday. Richard thought some cars were too showy even if the money to buy them came from honest means. Mark had never learned that lesson. His car was done up to look like a hustler's ride even though he was a legitimate businessman. You name it, Mark had it. TV's in the headrest, eighteen-inch chrome wheels, tinted windows, leather seats. Mark's philosophy was that if he had it, he was going to show it off. Richard felt that was stupid for a young black man to be driving around in something that looked so showy. He might as well have had bolted a neon sign to the roof that read Hey look at me! I'm a hustler! Cops automatically looked at the car and thought a young drug dealer was behind the wheel and nine times out of ten they were right. Showiness attracted too much attention, plain made you look just like everybody else, Richard was thinking. The question on Richard's mind though was where did Santana get thirty-five grand to buy the car? When Richard left five years ago, Santana was small time, didn't have enough heart to go to the big time. Richard figured that when he got out and left town, Santana was going to do the same. In seeing the car when Santana pulled up, Richard guessed that he was wrong.

"Nice ride," said Richard when he slid into the seat. "I guess you doing okay."

"Just a car, something to get around in."

Round Up

"I guess you wouldn't mind switching then." Richard chuckled.

Santana laughed back. "I guess you do miss the cars then huh? That Tercel you riding around in ain't nothing like the Beemer is it?"

"No it's not, but it's one thing about the Tercel though."

"What?"

"I don't have to check my rear view at every stop light to see if the cops are following me." Richard was looking over at Santana who was staring straight ahead. Santana didn't respond. Richard changed the subject. "So where we going?"

"To Fountain's on Lambert Street."

"On Lambert? The only club I know on Lambert is The Moxy."

"Same place, different name."

"Oh." Richard had forgotten how often clubs closed and reopened under different names, different management. Didn't matter how many times they changed names though, the same violence kept happening. Particularly The Moxy which had the reputation of being one of the most dangerous clubs to go to back when Richard lived in Colver. He had the feeling that the same type of clientele from the old club would be at the new one. "I heard about this other place on the radio, some joint called Retro's over on Liberty."

"I heard about that joint. Heard some nice looking girls are in there. You wanna check it out?"

"Sounds cool," Richard said.

"Hold on." Santana made a U turn in the middle of the street, headed north towards Liberty.

CHAPTER NINETEEN

Priest drove north on Route 307 trying to keep his cool. Nothing but darkness and trees outside the car. The digital clock on the dash read 8:30 though it felt much later than that to Priest. It was cold outside but the car had automatically heated to a comfortable temperature, the digital thermostat on the ceiling reading 78 degrees. He'd gotten Geena something to eat then she started talking about going home again. Priest tried to be nice but she wouldn't stop talking about it. Even got to crying after he kept saying no. He offered to drop a grand on the shopping spree if she stayed with him. Geena still didn't stop the tears, talking about she wanted her mother and shit. Finally told her what she wanted to hear to shut her up. She immediately quieted down. Priest realized at that moment how young this girl really was. Sure she had the body of a grown woman, but she still had the mind of a kid.

Priest drove in silence. Listened to the Eric B. and Rakim classic Paid in Full that he'd just copped on CD from Buy'em Back record shop, a used record store on Grantley Street over in Little Jamaica. These new rap tunes just didn't have that same flavor as old school. Most of the stuff now was only about money, cars, and chicks anyway. Didn't take any real originality to talk about that stuff. Besides, he lived the life that those dreamers were talking about. Priest had a safe house in the sticks where he kept his money and jewels. It was a room in one of those run down side of the road hotels that rented out rooms by the month as well as by the night. He took the one at the far end of the complex near the woods between two empty rooms where signs hung on both doors that read "Under Renovation". Priest had been back and forth to the motel for over seven months and had never seen anybody working on the places. Priest paid for six months up front and gave the elderly old black man who ran the place an extra $500 to give him all the keys to the room and another $500 to mind his

Round Up

business. Priest had too much money to lock away in a bank. Besides he didn't trust banks. Not with all that S&L shit going on. Executives were bigger crooks than the stick up cats in the street. And businessmen were much more dangerous. Stick up men didn't smile at you wearing a suit while they robbed you blind. And Priest had so much jewelry he could open up a store. He couldn't take the chance of somebody robbing him when he was in the city. That's why he only wore one chain at a time when he was out. He kept the rest of his chains and rings locked up in a safe in the room. His favorite chain was nothing big or extravagant, just a platinum link with a cross hanging at the end of it. The room was the size of a studio with a television that didn't work, one window, and a bathtub.

Priest glanced over at Geena. She looked scared and in disbelief, like the pigs he'd seen on this documentary show a couple weeks ago right before they got smashed on the head with a sledgehammer. "You okay now?"

"Where we going? You said you was gonna take me home after we ate," Geena said. Her eyes were scanning the woods outside of the car window.

"I'm gonna take you home after we go shopping."

"I don't wanna go shopping! I wanna go home!" Geena shouted.

Priest felt his anger rising. He tried hard to control his temper. "I said I was gonna take you home after we went shopping! Now shut the fuck up!" Geena stopped talking but Priest could still hear her sniffles. "I'm sorry baby. I just wanna do this for you to make up for earlier." Geena didn't say anything. After a half-hour more of driving, they pulled up to the motel room. Priest explained before Geena could ask another question. "I just need to pick up some money. Come on in with me. I don't wanna leave you out here in the dark." Geena reluctantly got out of car. "I keep my money in here. It's safer than banks. He chuckled to make Geena feel more comfortable. Priest opened the door, stepped to the side to let Geena follow him into the dark room. He closed the door, clicked on the light and saw Geena standing in the middle of the room with her arms folded up to her chest of the red leather jacket she was wearing. "What's wrong?"

"You know what's wrong."

"I told you I'm gonna take you back when I'm finished," Priest responded. He went to the closet behind the twin bed. Priest kept a .45 in there in case someone ever followed him to his spot. Pulled some handcuffs he bought from a cop supply store in Virginia from a shoebox on the top shelf. Priest readied himself for the tears he knew were going to come. But he didn't have any other choice. The cops were going to be looking for Geena, and after the way she acted, he didn't have any confidence that she wouldn't run her mouth. Priest turned around with the .45 at his side. Geena didn't react. She'd seen him with guns before.

"Why do you need that?" Geena asked.

"Take off your clothes."

"What?" Geena asked. Her voice was quivering. Eyes were big as a child who was about to get a spanking.

"Undress." The tears started to fall. Priest didn't want to point the gun at her. Hoped she'd do what he wanted without him having to do that.

"Please don't do this! I just wanna go home! I'm not gonna say nothing!"

"Strip!" Terrell yelled. Geena jumped at the sound of his voice. She started undressing like Priest said. Priest felt sorry for Geena but he kept himself hard on the inside. Fought the voice in his head that kept telling him to take her home; that this whole thing was wrong. When she was down to her red bra and matching panties, Priest handcuffed her to the metal bar at the head of the twin bed. Priest couldn't tell if she was shivering from her fear or from the cool temperature in the room. He turned up the thermostat to 75 degrees. Put a stale smelling blanket over her.

"Priest h-how long are you keeping me here?" Asked Geena. Priest got up from beside her. Opened the side drawer, took out a roll of silver duct tape. Ripped off a strip long enough to wrap around her head and covered her mouth. "I'll be back tomorrow with some food." Priest didn't answer Geena's question because honestly, he didn't know the answer himself.

* * *

Priest knew he'd stepped over the line now. Kidnapping. That was some serious business. The kind of shit that made the Feds get involved. And it all happened because some dude wanted to disrespect him by fucking with his girl. Priest still needed a place to

Round Up

go until things calmed down. His apartment was definitely off limits. He lived downtown on Frederick Avenue and was sure the cops were staking his place out waiting for him to come around. He drove a few miles listening to the radio playing the same bullshit songs. Got so Priest hated when a new jam came out since the stations would keep the song in rotation until people got sick of hearing it. They were hyping some new club over on Liberty Avenue. Felt that was a waste of time. One club was just like the next, Priest was thinking. Noting but a bunch of freaks and wannabe hustlers hung out in them wanting to be noticed. That was one scene that Priest was truly tired of. Sure it was fun to get the VIP room and all the freaks he could ask for when he first started making money, but it got old real quick. Couldn't tell who was real and who was phony, so Priest gave up hanging out in those joints altogether a few months ago.

Priest dug his cell out of his jacket, called the only person he knew he could count on, a childhood friend named Thomas Langston. Went by the name Torrio in the street. Thomas wasn't at home. Got the voice on the answering machine. Figured he was out partying someplace. That was Thomas' main problem. He never took life seriously, always looking for the next good time. Priest tried the cell next. Thomas picked up on the first ring. Hard bass was booming in the background.

"Hello!" Thomas yelled.
"Thomas it's me! Priest!"
"Who?"
"Priest you dumb muthafucka!"
"Speak up I can't hear you!" Thomas shouted.
"It's Priest man!"
"Oh what's up! Hold on let me go to a quieter place!" Priest heard the volume of the music go down enough to be able to hear Thomas without screaming. "What's up Priest! How you been?"
"I'm cool. Look, I need a favor."
"What's up?"
"I need to crash at your spot."
"I heard they looking for you. The news flashed a picture of your mug on the tube."

Damn, they worked fast, Priest thought to himself. "Oh yeah?"

"Yeah. I told you that temper of yours was gonna get you fucked up one of these days."

"I don't need the lecture."

"And I ain't giving you one. Look, I'm staying with my girl for a couple of weeks. You can go ahead to my place. I'm not going to be there anyway."

"Thanks. You gonna meet me there?"

"Can't. My girl's got my ride."

"So how am I gonna get in?"

"I got another set of keys on my ring."

"Where you at?"

"At The Retro club on Liberty Avenue."

"I gotta come over there?" Priest asked. It was still too hot to go anywhere near the city. But Torrio lived in Colver County just outside the city. Torrio's place would be a good place to lay his head. So Priest needed to get the keys. He'd just have to be careful going back into town.

"You do if you want to crash at my crib."

"I guess I don't have a choice."

"Call me on the cell when you get down here. I'll come outside."

"Make sure you're somewhere where you can hear me."

"Don't worry about it man, I'll be around."

"Just make sure you are," Priest said. He clicked the end button on the cell and put it in his pocket.

CHAPTERN TWENTY

Richard could hear the booming bass coming from the club a block before they got to Liberty. The street in front of the building was full of cars and the sidewalk was swarming with people like ants near an anthill. There was a roped off section of the sidewalk leading to the front door of The Retro Club. A line of people stood on the other side of the red rope. Music was booming from the speakers of almost every parked car on the street, with people leaning against their rides. Richard noticed Santana's eyes widen with excitement looking at the display of scantily dressed women standing outside in the cold air to get into the club. Santana turned up the car CD player, hit the button on the driver's side for the automatic window's to go down. The cold winter air from outside sucked all of the heat out of the ride. Allowed the deep bass of You Gots To Chill, an EPMD cut that sampled Kool and the Gangs Open Sesame to fill the air. Made people look towards the car to see who was blasting the old school song.

Santana front end parked the car across the street from the crowded building. Got out, hand waved Richard to join him. Richard felt the resurgence of excitement, reminiscent of his old days when he, Mark, and Santana hung out on the block. Then Richard remembered that Mark was no longer with them, and the excitement died just as fast as it had been born. Santana reached inside of his leather jacket, pulled out a pack of Newports. He tapped the bottom against the palm of his hand, extracted a square, put it to his lips and fired up. Santana tilted the pack towards Richard who declined the offer. Santana hopped up on the rear of the car. Richard leaned against the rear side panel, watching the people waiting in line. A female's scream made Richard turn his head in the opposite direction. Saw two girls walking towards them.

"Hey baby!" One of the girls screamed. Richard looked at her open jacket noticing her huge breasts heaving through the top of her shirt. Thought for a moment that she was one of the many women he knew from his past, back in the days when money lined his pocket. Richard watched her, bracing himself for a hug, until she walked over to Santana. Her friend stayed back on the sidewalk. "I haven't seen you around, where you been?"
Santana smiled. "Keeping busy, you know how it is."
"You could have at least called me."
Richard heard Santana cluck his tongue, turn towards Richard. "Don't start that shit Rhonda. I'm out here trying to show my boy Richie a good time."
"Hey," said the girl. Gave Richard the once over before focusing on Santana again. Richard knew that was to assess what type of gear that he was wearing. "So when we going out again?" She Santana asked.
Santana ignored her question. "Who's your friend?"
Rhonda looked over her left shoulder like she had forgotten that somebody was with her. "Alicia."
Santana said, "She shy or something? Tell her to come over here and talk to my man." Rhonda clucked her tongue, waved the girl named Alicia over to the car. Richard looked at her. Saw that she might be a cute girl. The white go-go boots with the matching mini skirt was a good start. He wanted to get a better look at her. Since the streetlight where they were standing was broken, Richard wanted her to come closer out from the dark to the light of the car. Richard didn't appreciate having the girl as a hand off. Eventually he would have made a move on her, Richard was thinking. While the girl made her way over to them, Richard noticed the Gold Maxima with the chrome wheels pass by on the street. Even with the tinted windows, Richard knew who was inside. Richard glanced over at Santana who was too involved with Rhonda to notice. The ride went up the block did a U turn, creeping back down the street towards them.

* * *

Priest didn't like crowds. But at least with so many people around, the chance of the cops catching him was slim. He could hear the noise from the club on Liberty a block before he got there. The traffic grew more congested the closer he got, causing him to

Round Up

slow down to a creep. He was glad that he got the car washed that morning. The chrome wheels should really be catching the streetlights. He saw the women dressed in next to nothing and remembered when chicks like that wouldn't give him the time of day. Amazing what driving a certain kind of car and wearing the latest fashion could do for you in a girl's mind. Made him think briefly of Geena sitting in the dimly lit room out in the sticks. He'd have to get her a radio or portable television, anything to make her stay there a little more comfortable. Especially since she'd be there for awhile. Or at least until the cops stopped sniffing around her, asking all types of questions and shit. Sure, he knew Geena's mother was worried, but hey, that wasn't his problem to worry about. Besides, he was going to send her home after things cooled down anyway.

Priest scanned the crowd, looking for an alley to park in. Then he could call Thomas, get the key and get out to the county. Priest was glad he didn't have to take the hike back out to the country where Geena was until the morning. He'd bring her some breakfast, uncuff her for awhile, talk to ease her mind, make her—what did they say that prisoners did when they were held captive for a long time—identify with her captor, that's it. At least he learned something from watching that kidnapping documentary on the Public Television Station a few weeks back. Anyway, Geena would be cool after spending a couple of days with him. Priest dug the cell out of its cradle on his hip. Dialed Thomas' cell. The phone rang one time then went into the voicemail. Priest huffed from frustration, hit the redial button. One ring, voicemail again. Dammit, thought Priest. One ring before voicemail meant Thomas had his cell turned off. Priest put the phone back in the cradle on his belt. Priest figured he'd take a drive through the block, see if Thomas was hanging around anywhere out front of the club. A girl wearing a leather jacket with big titties caught Priest's attention on the side of the street. She was standing in the front of some dude. Another cat was behind them. When the girl moved away to wave her hand at some other chick Priest looked harder. He couldn't believe it! The dude from Angelo's! And the other dude who was with him. But the streetlight over them was broken. Maybe it wasn't who Priest thought it was. He drove further up the block did a U and came back down. Hell yeah! It was the two of them!

* * *

Richard saw the Max coming towards them. He jumped off the rear trunk of the car. Pushed the girl standing between Santana's legs out of the way.

"Don't touch me!" Yelled Rhonda.

Santana threw his arms up in the air. "What's wrong with you man?"

"The dude who shot the security guard in Angelo's just drove by! Geena's boyfriend!" Richard yelled.

Santana was still paying attention to Rhonda. "So?"

"We'd better roll."

"What?"

"Let's go!"

"Fuck that man! I ain't running just because some punk drove by!"

Richard saw the Maxima getting closer to them. His stomach was flipping like he was on a roller coaster ride. One of the tinted windows lowered slightly. Richard started running towards the back of the ride when four popping sounds filled the air. He tripped on an empty 40-ounce beer bottle on the street, recovered from his fall and got behind the car. The people in the street and on the sidewalk scattered in all directions. Rhonda and Alicia screamed and ran towards the crowd. Richard called for the girls to come where he was but they kept running. Sounded like female cats in heat. Santana ran to where Richard was crouching behind the car. Crouching, he opened the driver's side door, pulled a .38 from under the driver's seat. Shoved it in Richard's hand. Richard palmed the grip of the weapon tightly. Felt the handle slipping from his sweaty palms. Didn't even point the damn thing. Just held the weapon, shook it like it was his dick after taking a leak. Sure he had held and carried a gun before. But except for dry firing one a few times in his room when Ma wasn't home, he'd never pulled the trigger. Then again, he never needed to. Richard had always been respected by everyone he'd dealt with in the game. Never doubled crossed anybody and never set anybody up. Besides, once you pulled, the next step was to use it. There was no turning back from that without looking like a punk. Richard

Round Up

wanted to stand up but a weight inside his gut made him stay low to the ground. Richard couldn't believe he was sitting in the middle of a battleground. His mind was flooded with thoughts of his little girl, how he wanted to see her again. Prayed that he would get another chance to. Thoughts of Vanessa even though he didn't know her all that well yet, clouded his head. Focused his mind on R.J. and Vanessa to keep him calm.

Richard watched Santana pull the .9 millimeter from his dip pointing the nose at the ground with his right hand. Santana stood, fired two rounds blindly towards the Maxima. Three more return shots came from the open window of the car. Richard thought the short dude named Priest was crazy to just sit there in the open where everybody could see him, firing his gun like they were cowboys in the wild west. Santana and the Maxima traded shots for a few more rounds before the car left rubber on the street. Sirens could be heard approaching the block. Richard stood up from behind the car. Saw blood on the front of his jacket and felt his torso thinking he'd been hit. Put hand to face and realized then that he had a cut on his left cheek, probably from when he fell over the bottle. Looked at the crowd. Noticed that some people were jumping over something in their haste to get away from the violent scene. Richard looked a little closer. Put his head down when he saw what he saw. Alicia's blood spattered go-go boots—toes pointing skyward—extending from a short skirt.

* * *

Priest couldn't believe his luck. Seeing the same punk again in the same day? He had to take care of the situation. Show that he wasn't to be fucked with. Priest slowed down from a creep to a crawl, stopped right in front of them. Tapped the automatic button on the driver's side door to let the tinted window down just enough to shoot without being seen. He could hear some old school song with a lot of bass blasting from their direction. Priest watched the dude Geena had been talking to, go over to his buddy sitting on the hood with the bitch who had the big titties standing between his legs. Most likely the dude recognized the car. Priest hoped the chrome on the wheels caught the low light when he pulled up and stopped. He knew he was taking a chance by sitting there out in the open, but Priest thought he had a point to prove. Had to let them punks know that he didn't let nobody get the best of him, and if they did that he was going to be back to make them pay.

    Priest took the glock out of his dip, pointed the nose out of the window, squeezed off four from the clip. Damn the gun had a kick! Almost dropped it when he popped the shots. Priest stopped firing just long enough to see if the dude had been hit. Two shots were fired back in Priest's direction, one of them hitting the rear of the car. He could hear the impact when the bullet punctured the body of his ride. Priest felt a tingle in his gut, hoping that none of the bullets had hit the wheels. Paid near five grand for the damn things. Priest fired back three more shots before he heard some approaching sirens in the distance. Priest wanted to stick around a minute longer, see if one of the mothafuckas had caught a slug. But the sirens were getting closer. And in a minute cops were going to be all over the place. Priest floored the pedal hearing the screech from the front wheels against the asphalt. Tomorrow, Priest figured he'd check out the news on tv or read the Colver Star's early edition to see if he had made the headline.

Round Up

CHAPTER TWENTY-ONE

The cabin of the car was quiet as Santana drove south on MLK. Richard glanced at the digital clock in the dash, saw it was going on 2:30 in the morning. The radio was on but turned down low. Richard heard the Frankie Beverly and Maze cut Before I Let Go coming through the side speakers on the car door. It was an old song, but still popular in the clubs and use on mix tapes. The song helped to calm him down after what went down at the club. Reminded Richard of the innocent days of high school when his life was filled with girl chasing and house parties every weekend. Richard reached down to the dash, pushed the up arrow to increase the volume. Santana reached over and turned it back down.

"Why'd you do that?" Richard asked.

"It's my car ain't it?" Santana responded. Kept his eyes pointed straight ahead into the darkness. The city streets were buzzing with people like it was afternoon rush hour.

"You got a problem with me?" Richard turned in his seat, felt the soft leather under him, faced Santana.

"You goddamn right I got a problem! How you gonna leave me hanging like that back there?"

"What the hell made you think I was gonna shoot somebody?"

"I thought you had my back!"

"I'm past all that shit! I got my life together now, trying to make something out of myself!"

"Oh yeah, I forgot you're Mr. Executive at the bank," Santana responded sarcastically. He chuckled like someone had told him a corny joke.

"Better than hustling."

Santana mashed on the brakes. Stopped the car short. Caused Richard to lurch forward into the dash. "Wait a minute mothafucka! Just a few years ago you was doing the same shit! Don't act like you better than me just because you got a job! You forgot were you came from?"

"No, I didn't forget, but I know I'm not trying to go back either. Look man, I'm not knocking your hustle. You do what you gotta do. I'm just telling you that that's not me anymore. Something wrong with a man wanting to do something different with his life?" Richard noticed Santana's face softening up for a moment. Like he had actually given some thought to what Richard was saying. Then Santana's abrasive attitude came back. "Baltimore turned you into a pussy! You're weak Richie! It's like we're two totally different people now! I remember when you were fucking different girls every night! Remember that? Spending money like it wasn't nothing! Buying the best of everything. You was ready to fuck a nigga up just cause he looked at you wrong."

"That was an image. You gotta play hard or you ain't gonna make it out here. That's what I'm trying to tell you man. I'm tired of being angry for no reason. Carrying a gun when I wasn't even gonna pull the trigger."

"What?" Santana asked in disbelief.

"You heard me. I carried that .45 in my dip so people knew not to fuck with me. Everybody in the street knew I was strapped. But if it ever came down to me having to put a slug in somebody I wouldn't have done it."

"You fucking with me right?"

"No I'm not. You ever remember me pulling on somebody?"

"No. You was always trying to work shit out with a sit down."

"Damn right. That's because I knew that if I pulled, I was gonna have to use it. That's the first rule out here."

"So that's it huh?"

"Is what it?"

"So you just gonna let whoever killed Mark get away with it? Sit back and act like Martin Luther King with the nonviolence shit."

Richard didn't think about that. What was the purpose of looking for the shooter if he wasn't going to retaliate? Take out whoever took out his cousin. That's the way the streets worked.

Round Up

And everybody knew how close Mark and Richard were as cousins. "I don't know," Richard answered. "Just take me home. I wanna be there in case Ma wakes up. I don't want her worrying."

"I can't believe this shit," Santana whispered. The front wheels of the Audi screeched against the asphalt when Santana pulled off.

Santana pulled up in front of the Richard's mother's house. Richard stepped out of the heated Audi into the cold air.

"Catch you later man," Richard said.

"Peace," answered Santana. Richard watched Santana peel off down Lincoln Avenue, running the red light at the corner. Richard turned to walk up the steps. Looked up the block to see if Nico was at his post. Was glad to see that he wasn't. Richard took the first step up the stairs becoming cognizant of the extra weight in his jacket pocket. Richard knew what it was without thinking about it. He still had Santana's goddamn .38.

* * *

Richard sat on the bed in his room, the .38 in the shoebox in the closet weighing heavy on his mind like a ten-pound weight, thinking how fucked up life could be. He was gazing out of the window watching the black sky give way to the navy blue on the horizon. He reached into the pocket of his pants, pulled out Vansessa's number. He had carried it around since she'd given it to him. Looked at the phone wanting to hear her voice. Tell her what he'd been through earlier in the night. He looked at the clock on the bedside table. Saw that it was 4:30 in the morning. Shoved the torn and wrinkled piece of paper back into his pocket. Figured he'd wait until the sun was high in the sky. Besides, dudes didn't call for at least a couple of days after getting a chick's digits. Made a man seem desperate if he called too soon.

Richard hadn't slept yet and he wasn't even close to being sleepy. His chest was still fluttering with butterflies. Couldn't get the shootout at the club out of his mind. Yeah, he was lucky to come out of that whole thing alive. Thought that maybe the man upstairs was watching out for him, knowing that R.J. needed a Daddy in her life. Her real Daddy. Richard had never been a praying man. Didn't believe the church was good for anything except weddings and funerals. And that the church—no matter what religion or faith—was more of a haven for sinners than the streets were. Richard felt that he didn't need a middleman to talk to the big man upstairs. Richard had never told Ma how he felt. She'd have a heart attack. No, he kept those feelings to himself where they belonged. Sure Richard believed in God, he wasn't an atheist or anything like that. And Richard knew it wasn't his place to question why things happened. Things like Mark getting killed when he was in the prime of his life or that girl Alicia dying tonight when all she was looking for was some fun out on the town. And especially the big question of why Richard's father had to die when he did, leaving Ma all alone. No, it wasn't Richard's place to question things like that. He was just grateful when good things like tonight did happen. Richard looked into the darkness of the sky outside the bedroom window, and said a silent prayer, thankful that he was still alive to see his little girl.

Round Up

CHAPTER TWENTY-TWO

Detective Ryan looked through the smoke of the Winston's that was between his lips across the car at his partner. Ryan was starting to come down from the mental frustration in dealing with Sergeant Faith. Bastard acted like he was paying his goddamn paycheck. So what if he padded his timecard a little, Ryan was thinking. Faith had scrutinized Ryan's time so closely that Ryan was surprised that he was still able to pad his time with the three extra hours.

Ryan listened to Fields babbling on the cell in the driver's seat. He said some words for a couple of minutes then got silent for the same amount of time. Had the pen and pad out on the dash asking for names of streets. Fields' face was serious, stern. Ryan knew they were going to see a body. And it was somebody of color. Fields only got that "when is the violence going to stop" look on his face when one of his people—the African-Americans or Afro-Americans, whatever they were calling themselves now—got snuffed. Fields snapped the flip cell closed. Had a faraway look in his eyes like he was thinking really hard about something.

"So where is it?" Ryan asked.

"On Liberty."

"How bad is it?"

"Don't know 'til we get there."

Ryan hoped they weren't going to Liberty Homes, one of Colver City's five projects. He wasn't in the mood. "Where did dispatch say it was?"

"At the new club that just opened up."

"The Regal, some shit like that?"

"Retro. It's called the The Retro."

* * *

Detective Fields mashed the brakes of the Crown Vic in front of the club. Crowd control had done its job keeping the onlookers away from the scene. Though people were still breaking their necks to see the covered body on the ground. What was it that made people want to see something so gruesome? Fields was thinking. Fields stepped out of the car, grateful for the fresh air. The smell of cigarette smoke was all over Ryan like cheap cologne. Fields noticed the two uniformed officers standing by a girl who was sitting on the curb. She looked scared. She was shivering as she rocked back and forth. Fields didn't know if that was from the cold or from what she'd been through. From the light of the street lamp Fields could see the girl's eyes were swollen from crying. Ryan walked over to the where the body was laying on the ground. Fields made his way over to the girl. Knelt down on one knee so that he could see her face. Saw the ample cleavage from the low cut shirt she was wearing and diverted his eyes. Noticed a drop of mucus make it's way down the already moistened valley under her nose. Fields stood up, looked at the uniformed officer who looked no more than twenty-five. He had the bluest eyes Fields had ever seen. Fields glanced at his badge. Read Kimmel under the number 349.

"She see anything?" Fields asked..

"Said something about a gold car with chrome wheels and tinted windows."

Fields thought about Angelo's and the Gold Maxima that had been parked across the street. Wondered if it was one in the same. Had to be. Fields could almost see the short punk with the big mouth laughing at him. Besides, how many gold Maxima's with chrome rims were there in the city? Fields asked himself. "She know the vic?"

"Yeah. Said she was a friend of hers," said Kimmel.

"Name?"

"Rhonda."

"Rhonda what?"

"That's all she gave me."

Fields bent down by the girl again. "You okay Rhonda?" He asked. The girl didn't answer. Kept looking straight ahead. "Did you see anything that can help us get whoever did this?"

Rhonda started talking. "S-she was right beside me."

Fields didn't know if she was talking about the vic or the shooter. "Did you see what the person looked like?"

Round Up

"N-no. All I saw was the car pull up, then the window rolled down, then they just started shooting."

"They? You think there was more than one person who might have done this?"

"I d-don't k-know."

"Did your friend have a jealous boyfriend or something? Any enemies that you know of?"

"I said no! W-we just came out to have some fun! I don't even think they were after us!" Said Rhonda between sobs and sniffs.

"Why do you say that?"

"I was over here talking to a friend. I hadn't seen him in a long time. When the car rolled up, my friend acted kind of shook."

"Shook?"

"You know, scared."

"What's your friends name? I'm going to need to talk to him."

Rhonda paused for a moment before answering. "Richie. His name is Richie." She said his name quickly.

"His last name?"

"I don't know it. We weren't that close."

"Where does he live?"

"I dunno."

"I thought you said he was your friend."

"He was…I mean is," answered Rhonda. She dropped her face into her hands. "Can I go home now?"

Fields looked at the girl. Noticed the cracking in her voice when she answered him. Fields wanted to press a little further into the questioning, find out some more information, but he didn't want to upset her again. It was clear she was trying to protect somebody. "Yeah, you can go," Fields answered. "I'm going to need your full name and address so I can get in touch with you later. After that I'll get one of the officers to get you home." Fields looked up and saw Ryan crossing the street to where they were.

* * *

Ryan looked across the street at Fields trying to console some girl who was crying. Fields was probably falling for the innocent victim act she was giving, Ryan was thinking. Since Fields had a little girl himself, that made him an automatic target for some chick's tears softening Fields up. Ryan shook his head, continued

137

looking at the vic's body. The girl's eyes were still open. Ryan wasn't bothered by that. Had never had a problem looking at a body whether fresh or decomposed. It was part of the job. Besides, being a detective in Colver City gave a guy a crash course in seeing violence almost on a daily basis.

Ryan focused on the pretty face and swollen tits. A waste of a perfectly good piece of ass, Ryan thought. The pool of blood around her body had dried to the asphalt. From the impact of the slugs Ryan figured the shots had to come from around twenty to twenty-five feet away. Ryan looked up to the spot where the shots were fired then back at the girl. Spent bullet casings were scattered around the body. Figured either the vic or somebody near her had returned fire. Maybe she was just an innocent casualty. Or maybe she had something to do with her own death, thought Ryan. Ryan stood up. Looked across the street, locking eyes with his partner. Started walking over to where Fields and the girl were.

* * *

Fields met Ryan halfway across the street. "You find anything?" Fields asked.

"Casings around the body."

"So there was some return fire."

Ryan lifted his chin towards the girl. "What she have to say?"

"Didn't give me anything we could use. Said something about a friend named Richie. Doesn't know his last name or where he lives."

"Bullshit."

"I know that. She's protecting somebody."

Ryan thought of something. "You know what?"

"What?"

"That kid we talked to? Richard Anderson, Mark Anderson's cousin. When he hustled he went by the name Richie Rich on the streets."

"And didn't his mother call him Richie when we were over there?"

"Sure did."

"Think there's a connection?"

"Won't hurt to follow up on it now would it?"

"Guess not."

Round Up

 Ryan started walking back to the car, stopped in his tracks. "Aw shit."
 "What's up?"
 "Faith wants me to come back to the station to look over some of the open cases in the shitbox. He knows I hate being in the station."
 The shitbox was the nickname of the station file and evidence room. It was located right under the bathrooms and smelled liked waste. No one could stand being in there for more than a few minutes. Fields smiled. Knew that Faith was probably angry that he didn't find any padding in Ryan's overtime. "That's exactly why he gave it to you. I'll be right there too. I have some paperwork to knock off myself. We'll stop by Anderson's on the way home after shift is over."
 "Faith. What a goddamn asshole. Fucking 5 o'clock in the morning and I'm gonna be holed up in a room that smells like a backed up shitter," said Ryan right before he fired up a Winston's.
 Fields waved over one of the uniformed officers at the scene. Pointed to Rhonda. Told him to take her home. Fields watched as he escorted Rhonda to the marked vehicle. Kept watching as the marked vehicle drove south down Liberty until it was gone from his line of vision.

CHAPTER TWENTY-THREE

    Priest drove north on highway 307 in the darkness. He was beginning to wind down from the adrenaline rush of the shootout back at the club. Priest hoped that he plugged one of the punks. He'd have to wait and see what the paper said in the morning edition about the body count. Priest hadn't planned on going back out to the motel but now felt that he didn't have a choice. Fucking Torrio. Why couldn't he have just met Priest somewhere and given him the keys? Priest looked through the front windshield. The dark sky was beginning to turn that funny shade of blue when the sun was about to come up. Priest yawned feeling sleep starting to overcome him. He changed the radio station from some slow jam by Luther Vandross, that House Is Not A Home song that drove the chicks crazy to the twenty-four hour hip-hop station WRAP. When the bass from Eric B is President came through the speakers, he perked up, started bobbing his head to the beat.
    Priest drove for another mile when the red and blue lights from a cop car started flashing behind his ride. Dammit, Priest said under his breath. He turned the music down. Thought briefly about what he was going to do. No doubt a description had already went out over the wire about the Maxima with the chrome rims. Priest moved his foot over to the brakes. Started to spin the steering wheel to the side of the road. Then he remembered that he still had the Glock in between his legs. Priest wasn't trying to go to jail. Having the gun in his possession would get him no less than five years under the new mandatory illegal weapons law. He glanced in the rearview. Saw the knocker right behind him. Priest hit the accelerator. Made a sharp turn to the right back towards the road. He heard the wheels of the cop car spinning out on the gravel getting ready for the chase. 307 intersected with 40 about five miles ahead of him. Priest figured he'd take the turn, head out towards the Pennsylvania line that was about ten miles up. The

Round Up

cop would then be out of his Maryland jurisdiction. And most likely the Maryland knocker wouldn't call the Pennsylvania authorities wanting to collar Priest himself. Priest counted on that ego hawking to get his freedom.

Priest mashed the accelerator, increased his speed from 80 to 90 to 100. Felt like he was damn near flying from how loose the steering wheel felt in his grip. He couldn't even hear the siren behind him any longer. Hoped he had gotten away. Priest needed to go somewhere to think what the next move was going to be. His main focus right now was nailing the sharp turn when it came up. Priest kept his eyes locked on the road ahead of him. Saw the intersection, turned the wheel sharply to the right, smashed the brake, felt the back wheels leave the ground for a moment before hitting the street again with a thump. He'd done it! Priest glanced in the rear view mirror. Saw the cop was still on his tail. Priest left the main strip. Turned into a cornfield hoping to shake the knocker. His vision was littered with corn stalks flying by the windshield sounding like a violent rainstorm on the hood and top of the car. He hit the button to lower the driver's side window feeling the husks from the corn whipping painfully against his face. Priest reached into his lap, tossed the Glock out, hit the button to raise the window back up. He felt disorientated seeing nothing but green and darkness in front of him. Didn't know where to go and what to do next. And no matter how fast he seemed to be driving, the cop stayed right behind him.

Priest turned the steering wheel sharply to the left before whipping it back to the right. He finally emerged from the field and saw a road in the clearing. The car bounced in the valleys of the ground. Wondered briefly how much he'd have to put out to fix the alignment and have the rims cleaned. A deep dip in the ground made Priest bump his head against the ceiling. He turned to the left feeling the tires hugging the street under the car. Priest heard the cop car smashing against the ground with the wheels screeching on the street behind him. For the first time in a long time, Priest was scared. He hadn't felt like this since his mother left him when he was eight years old with his aunt for a month without calling to see how he was. Felt like she had deserted him. Like he was trapped in a place he didn't want to be. Alone to fend for himself. He couldn't shake that scared feeling even when she came back a week later. Priest found out later that she'd been tricking and living on the streets to support her habit. He was glad to see his mother when she walked through the door. And she got clean after that. Still, the abandoned feeling stayed with Priest like a permanent scar. Though he'd buried it deep inside him so that it didn't hurt so much. But now that trapped feeling was making itself known again. Like there was no way he was going to get out of this one. He saw another intersection just ahead of him with two trooper cars, flashing red and blue, parked nose to nose on the street. More cop cars were coming from the distance. Priest slammed on the brakes hearing the screech of the tires against the street. The feeling of defeat overcame him like a fever, shutting down his entire body. It was over.

* * *

Priest looked at the walls of the holding cell. For the past three hours he had been reading the jailhouse philosophies of the men who'd been there before him. He'd learned everything from who gave the best head in Colver City, complete with a phone number and an address, to how Allah could save him from the oppressors who had locked him up. Once the Belver County cops had arrested Priest for various traffic violations, the locals did a check and found an open warrant on him in Colver City. Belver County gave him a court date and transported him back to the city. They also confiscated his ride. A smart ass clerk told him he'd get it back when he came back to get it. The clerk chuckled. Even joked that they'd shine up his shiny wheels for him. Then he walked away. Priest wondered what the warrant was for. Sure, there was the shootout at Angelo's, but Colver City cops were too lax to put out a warrant on him so quickly. So Priest sat there in the cell waiting for somebody to tell him what the hell he was being held for. After that, he could bail out of the bullshit traffic violations that Belver County had on him. At least he was alone in the cell. Meant he didn't have to worry about playing the hard role to keep anyone from bothering him. Someone entered the corridor. Slammed the door. Caused the sound to boom like thunder throughout the hallway. A uniformed officer came into view walking towards the cell. Priest noticed how the cop kept averting his eyes from Priest when he tried to look at him. A rookie. Still had that fresh out of the academy look to him. Eager to protect

Round Up

and serve. Veteran cops who had some time on the force had this hard look to them, like their human sides were gone, leaving only emotionless machines. The cop opened the door, pulled Priest out of the cell, cuffed his wrists, and led him upstairs to be booked. Priest glanced at his nametag. Saw that the rookie's last name was Davis.

Priest decided to test him. "So where you taking me Officer Davis?" If the cop didn't say anything or acted like a smart ass, Priest would know how to assess him.

"Taking you to get processed. Just routine stuff," Officer Davis responded. His voice was pleasant, even toned like he just came on shift. Once they were upstairs Priest could see the sun shine in through the windows of the building. Officer Davis sat him down at a desk that had Christmas cards hanging on a string on the side, still handcuffed, and, said "good luck", and walked away. Priest looked around. Saw young dudes, old dudes, chicks wearing too much makeup, all types of people who had broken the city's laws during the night. Priest looked at the nameplate on the desk beside him. It read Detective Peter Hampton. Peter Hampton, Priest repeated to himself. Sounded like the perfect name for an uptight white dude. Cat probably graduated at the top of his class, had a smiling blonde haired wife and two blonde haired kids, a boy and a girl waiting for him to come home safely from his dangerous job as a cop. A man laughing wearing an undone blue tie and a white button down shirt made Priest turn around. The loud guy was laughing with another man before they parted ways.

The guy looked over at his desk, saw Priest sitting there and yelled out, "okay, who left the piece of shit sitting at my desk?" Priest heard a couple of people chuckle at the comment before the detective sat down. His piercing blue eyes reminded Priest of the picture of Jesus Christ that used to hang on the living room wall at his aunt's house. "Okay tough guy, you like shooting people?" Priest didn't answer. "I just wanna get your vitals then you can go on about your business. So do us both a favor and cooperate all right?" Priest didn't respond. "Don't answer me then. You got a warrant here and I'm going to see you on it whether you talk or not. There's a picture of your ugly face right on the front of the packet." Priest looked at the photo. It was a mug shot from a few years back when he caught a domestic charge against his girl at the time. Priest cracked a small grin, not big enough for the detective to see, thinking, I beat that charge and I'm gonna beat this one too. "Hmmm, Terrell Adams. Your mother named Mary by any chance?" The detective asked. Priest looked up into his blue eyes but didn't answer. "I was just wondering. There used to be a trick named Mary Adams who used to come through here a lot some years ago and you kinda look like her. Right up around the eyes there," the detective said, demonstrating on Terrell's face. The detective turned around to the computer keyboard, cracked his knuckles, and looked Priest directly in his eyes. "All right. Name." When Priest didn't answer, he said it again, louder. "I said name!"

"Terrell," answered Priest. Why was this dude asking for his name when he had already read it from the warrant?

"Terrell what?"

"Adams. Terrell Maurice Adams."

The detective spun around in his chair towards Priest. "Okay Terrell, we've got you on attempted murder here. And if the guy dies, it automatically gets bumped up to first degree."

Priest shrugged with indifference, said "I didn't have nothing to do with that."

"Well a shitload of witnesses in Angelo's say you did. And I'm inclined to believe them."

Priest sucked his teeth. He was scared as hell on the inside but he couldn't let the detective see his fear. "Believe what you want."

"Oh I do and I'll tell you what else Bishop or Reverend or whatever you call yourself, you're gonna fry in---"

A man with a bad case of acne, a cheap blue suit, and a red polyester tie yelled from across the room. "Pete hold it!"

"What is it?"

"Add kidnapping to the list of charges on the kid. They just found his girlfriend in a side of the road motel out in Belver County."

Detective Hampton turned towards Priest and smiled. Priest looked at the cuffs on his wrists then at the floor. That abandoned feeling was taking over his body again. Priest looked at the cop, trying not to have a defeated look on his face. Decided that if he was going down, that he was going to take a rogue cop with him.

Round Up

"You don't look so cool now reverend," Detective Hampton said. He was squinting at the computer screen like he needed glasses.

Priest jingled the cuffs on his wrists. "What if I make a deal or something, you know, tell you some valuable information that you might can use against somebody?"

"The final decision is up to the State's Attorney, but I'm willing to listen to whatever you put on the table." Priest started to spill all the information he knew about Ryan's shakedowns over the past few months then hesitated. Didn't know if he could trust a cop against a cop. Not with that blue wall where they watched each other's backs that Priest kept hearing about. No, he decided he'd wait until he talked to his lawyer. Detective Hampton was looking at Priest with an impatient look in his blue eyes. "Well, what is it?"

Priest leaned back in his chair. Jingled the handcuffs on his wrists like they were toys. "Nothing."

Detective Hampton chuckled. "Sure? Last chance before the train leaves the station."

Priest looked at him. Wondered why the hell he was talking about trains leaving stations.

CHAPTER TWENTY-FOUR

A barking dog in a yard two houses down the block woke Richard from his sleep. He rolled over; first facing the wall behind the bed, then back over facing the bedroom door before sitting up. Felt the splitting pain of the headache rising from the base of his neck up to his head. His left hand searched the bedside table for the bottle of ibuprofen. Richard struggled to twist off the childproof cap. Richard dropped three pills into the palm of his hand. Dry swallowed them and laid back down on the pillow with his left arm draped over his eyes. Images of that dead girl flashed through Richard's mind like a slideshow. Kept seeing the blood splattered go-go boots lying there in that crimson pool on the street. Made the thumping in his temples become more intense. Richard's chest felt hollow, and his mind was dizzy from what he'd seen. Made him remember the senseless killings from his hustling days on the streets of Colver City. Richard had seen it all. Drugs deals gone wrong, women selling themselves for the high, stealing, murders, judges handing out lifetime sentences like they were candy, all of it adding to his desire to walk away and do something different with his life. In thinking of the .38 that sat in a shoebox in his closet, Richard realized all ties had to be broken from his past before he could really consider himself a free and changed man. As long as he continued hanging around with Santana, Richard's hands would be just as dirty as Santana's was.

 Richard tried to remember what a cop had told him once when he got caught in a round up, what was it—guilt by association—that was it. Richard was guilty just by being friends with Santana. Fortunately, the cop knew Richard when he was a kid and let him go. But before he left, the cop grabbed Richard by his collar and told him that he was only as good as the company he kept. Richard didn't understand what those words meant back then. All he knew was that he wasn't going to be taking that ride to central booking. Now though, the words were becoming clear. Richard

Round Up

moved his head a little. The pain didn't feel as bad as it did before. The sharp stabbing feeling had subsided to a dull throbbing. Figured the pills must have started to kick in.

Richard looked at the phone again. His stomach had that tingling feeling from wanting to call Vanessa. He liked the feeling that thinking of her gave him. Hadn't felt that way since meeting Desiree at the mall a few years back. But he was scared too. Losing Desiree had hurt Richard like nothing else in his life had done. Yeah, Pop's death was painful but it was more sorrow than anything hurt. No, the hurt that came from losing someone that you were in love with, that was a whole different kind of feeling. Richard knew relationships were iffy, like shooting dice. But no matter how they ended, the beginnings were usually good. Moments when both people saw eyes to eye on things and when they were still getting to know each other. That's the part Richard liked. The newness and the excitement at the beginning of meeting someone new, that's what he was addicted to.

Richard stretched his arm across the bed. Grabbed for the cordless receiver. He picked up his pants from the floor, searched his pockets for the number, found it and dialed. His heart was pumping fast as the phone rang like he'd just finished running five blocks from the cops. When a female's voice answered, Richard stuttered his first word before getting himself together. Felt like he had a grade school crush.

"Vanessa there?" Richard asked.

"Speaking."

"Good morning. It's me Richard from the bank," he said. Thought he sounded a little corny.

"I know. I didn't expect you to call so soon," Vanessa responded.

Richard's leg started shaking. Thought he shouldn't have broken the first rule of trying to get to know somebody. "Naw, it's just that I had something to do and I was probably gonna be gone all day. Just wanted to see what you were up to that's all."

"Nothing much. Just getting ready to go back to school. Vacation went fast this year."

"Tell me about it."

"When you going back to Bmore?"

"Probably not until the day before school starts. I ain't in a rush to get back to the bank."

"That's one place I won't miss," Vanessa said. She laughed. Richard thought she sounded cute. They talked for fifteen more minutes. Their conversation was so natural, felt like he had known her longer than he did. Richard felt so comfortable that he had almost disclosed what had happened to him with the shooting last night. Still felt the anxiety clutching his chest like somebody had knocked the air out of him. But again, it was too much, too soon. Might have turned her against him, make her think he was just a common thug. So Richard kept his mouth shut. Knew it was time to cut the conversation short before they ran out of things to say to each other, even though it felt like they could talk for hours.

"Well I'd better get outta here. I don't wanna be out there all day," Richard said.

"Okay, I'm glad you called," Vanessa said.

Richard wanted to say more, maybe something corny like, I'm glad I did too, but he decided against that. "Alright, I'll talk to you later."

"Okay. Be careful out there," Vanessa said.

Richard felt like she knew what his life was about, the things he had been involved in his past, and the people he knew, when Vanessa said those words to him. But that was impossible, thought it was probably something she said to everybody. Figured he was reading more into the words than he should have. "I will," Richard said. He hung up. Insides felt light now, like the weight in his chest was gone.

Richard got out of bed, the smell of bacon filling his nose. He put on some black sweat pants, a Raiders tee shirt-when they were still in L.A., and some slippers and walked towards the door. His stomach wasn't up for anything heavy, so Richard decided on a simple bowl of corn flakes.

Richard brushed his teeth, washed up, and started down the stairs. Realized before reaching the bottom that the stereo was turned off. He could hear the voices of the detectives who had stopped by the other day talking to his mother. His insides fluttered like a nest of butterflies had been disturbed. Richard hesitated in the middle of the staircase before coming all the way down. He killed the butterflies in his stomach. Looked at them

Round Up

nonchalantly and said, "Back again? You find out who killed my cousin yet?" The black Detective addressed him. Richard tried to remember his name, Fielding—no Fields—yeah, that was it. Richard couldn't forget Fields' partner Detective Ryan if he wanted to. The room smelled of his presence. Ryan was leaning against the wall near the Christmas tree just like he did on his last visit. He was chewing loudly on some gum like a cow chewing on cud.

"No unfortunately not yet. I just wanted to ask you some questions," asked the Detective.

Richard sat down on the love seat. The Detective remained standing. "About what?" Richard asked.

"There was a shooting last night. A person we talked to this morning said a friend of hers named Richie was talking to her when it went down."

Richard snickered. Knew that chick Santana was pushing up on had given his name. "So? You know how many Richie's there are out there?"

Fields turned to his partner. "I figured it was a long shot." He turned back towards Richard. "So if you don't mind telling me where you were last night/early morning?"

"Here...sleep."

"Did anybody see you?"

Richard chin nodded in his mother's direction. "She did. I went to bed after I ate."

Fields turned towards Richard's mother. "This true?"

"Yes. I heard him watching television up in his room when I went to bed."

Fields scribbled something on the notepad in his left hand. "And what time was that?"

"About eight o'clock."

"Would you have heard him if he went back out?"

Richard was getting tired of the detective. He interrupted the Q &A. Felt it was bordering on harassment of his mother. "No she wouldn't have because I was here all night." Detective Ryan continued chewing loudly on the gum in his mouth. "People get killed in this city everyday and you over here asking us these stupid questions, like I had something to do with it. You still haven't found out who killed my cousin and now you've got another body that you're asking around about." Ryan stepped forward, looked like he wanted to say something. Fields turned around and Ryan receded.

"Just doing my job," Fields answered. His voice was calm and unmoved. "Don't get so defensive. I just figured that this might lead to some information about your cousin."

"Well too bad because I wasn't there," Richard answered.

"That's a nasty gash on your cheek. Where'd it come from?" Fields asked.

Richard had forgotten about the cut. He rubbed his face and answered, "Shaving."

"You should put something on that before it gets infected."

"Thanks, I will," Richard responded. He watched Fields signal Ryan towards the front door.

"We'll be in touch," Fields said. Both men exited the room, Detective Fields going first. Richard followed them down the hallway to the vestibule. He opened the door feeling the cool air rush into the house and watched them get into the Crown Vic. Detective Ryan waved at Richard before the car pulled off into traffic. When Richard returned to the living room, his mother was standing there looking at him.

Richard averted his eyes from hers and said, "Don't worry Ma, they'll find out who did it."

"Were you here last night?" Ma asked.

"C'mon Ma. Are you gonna let them mess with your head?"

"Answer me."

Richard took a deep breath and answered, "Yes I was here." Then he went into the kitchen to fix a bowl of cereal.

An hour later Richard was listening to the radio. The news at noon reported on the shootout at the club the night before. Richard clicked it off not wanting to hear the details since he was there. He hated lying to his mother, but what other choice did he have? Richard knew his mother. She didn't believe the cut came from shaving. He could see the disbelief in her face. But mothers for some reason were born with built in denial when it came to their children. She may have thought Richard was lying but she didn't press him for the real story. Richard got up from his bed. Twisted his head around on his shoulders still feeling a small throbbing in his neck. But it wasn't anywhere near the pain that he had felt earlier.

Round Up

Richard looked out of the window over the alley towards the playground. A couple of kids were jumping on an old mattress in the empty lot. Thought it was a damn shame how they didn't have the same types of recreational equipment that kids in the suburbs took for granted like swings, see-saws, and sliding boards. Saw some girls and boys chasing each other around the lot. Reminded Richard of his daughter. Remembered that he hadn't talked to R.J. in damn near two weeks. She was in day care about now. He picked up the phone dialed Ms. Jackie, the day care provider's house. The phone rang once before she picked up. Richard heard Barney the Dinosaur singing his trademark I love you, you love me, song in the background and smiled.

"Hello," a woman's voice answered.

"Ms. Jackie?"

"Yes."

"This is Regina Anderson's father, Richard Anderson. Is she there?"

"Regina? No, she's gone. Her mother gave permission for someone to pick her up."

"Who?"

"Don't know Mr. Anderson. I'm not allowed to give out that kind of information."

Richard had an idea who it was. "That's okay. Thanks." Richard hung up and dialed Desiree's house. The phone rang three times before Antoine picked up. "Who's this?"

"Regina's father. Let me talk to her."

"I'm getting tired of this shit! Look punk I told you not to call my goddamn house! Don't let me tell you again!" Antoine yelled. Then he clicked off. Richard threw on his coat. He'd had enough of this shit. He was going to see his little girl.

CHAPTER TWENTY-FIVE

Richard grabbed his leather coat, ran through the hallway and out the door before Ma could ask him any questions. He jumped the steps, landed on the sidewalk, ran to the car and unlocked the door to the Tercel. Richard slid into the cold cabin pushing the key into the ignition. He turned it. Heard the engine struggle to turn over. "Dammit!" He yelled. Richard turned the key again, heard the same grinding sound of the engine. He looked out the window and saw Santana walking down the street. Richard got out of the car, ran up to meet him in the middle of the block. "Where's your ride?"

Santana looked at Richard with concern in his face. "It's parked. What's up?"

"I need to go to Baltimore."

"Let's go."

An hour later, Richard and Santana were on 95 heading south. Richard was glad Santana hadn't held a grudge from the night before. The rap group EPMD's cut Strictly Business, which sampled Eric Clapton's cover of Bob Marley's I Shot The Sheriff was coming in through the car's speakers.

"So what are you gonna do?" Santana asked. His eyes were pinned straightaway through the windshield.

"I just wanna see my kid. I can't believe her mother is letting this whole thing happen. Acting like I'm not her father."

"That's how females are. They meet a new dude and wanna erase everything from their old life. Always trying to get that happy family," Santana said.

"Yeah well she could have had that. Matter of fact she did have it."

"Must not have been enough if she's with that dude."

"The funny thing is that me and Desiree, we were tight at one time. I loved her to death. Still do."

Round Up

"So what happened?"

"I dunno. Maybe she wanted something else. But she helped me. Made me a different person."

"How's that?"

"This new hustle I'm doing working nine to five at the bank, that wasn't me. That was all Desiree's doing. She said I could make something out of myself if I wanted to. At first I didn't feel what she wanted me to do. Felt like she was trying to change me and shit. I thought she always gonna be there for me. Then one day, I came home and she was gone." Richard could see Santana shaking his head out of the corner of his right eye. He kept talking. "Guess I didn't change fast enough for her."

"You should have just fucked her and left."

"What about my daughter?"

"What about her? The mother obviously thought she didn't need you. Now she's gone off and got herself another father for your kid."

"But he's not her father. I am."

"Don't tell me, tell your baby's momma."

"I plan to."

"Who is this cat anyway?"

"Some dude she met after we broke up. Then she turns around and has a kid with him too."

"That's why I'm glad I did what I did."

"What?"

"Got myself fixed. Can't have no kids."

Richard turned his head sharply towards Santana. "Seriously?"

"Why would I be joking about something like that? I'm waiting for a chick to tell me that she's knocked up with my kid. I'm just gonna laugh in her face."

Richard looked up, saw the exit for Baltimore about a mile ahead of them. "Take the next exit after we get out of the Fort McHenry tunnel," he said. Once they were coming out of the tunnel, Richard looked out the window at the scenery in downtown Baltimore, thinking how much money went into the baseball and football stadiums when just past them were some of the poorest neighborhoods in the city. Back when Richard hustled, most of the money he made came from the streets of Baltimore. A pang of guilt went through Richard's chest when he thought of how much he had contributed to the drug problem. Santana interrupted Richard's thoughts.

"So where's the spot at?" Santana asked.

"Few more blocks."

"Remind me to stop off at one of these sub shops to get me some lake trout before we leave."

"What kind of fish is lake trout anyway?" Richard asked.

"Hell if I know. Baltimore is the only city I know that's got it. I went to New York and asked for some, they looked at me like I was crazy."

Richard chuckled, saw the corner where they were supposed to turn, and said, "make a right onto Pennsylvania Avenue." They drove in silence for a few blocks. Then Richard said, "pull over here." They were in front of an apartment building where four guys were shooting craps. One was kneeling while the remaining three were standing around in front of the double glass doors. His jacket was unzipped revealing the platinum chain and diamond encrusted charm hanging down to his stomach. All of them looked at Santana's Audi as it pulled over to the curb. From their youthful faces, Richard figured them to be around 16 or 17.

"Want me to go in with you?" Santana asked.

"Naw I'm cool. These are young cats."

"Those are the ones you gotta worry about. They don't give a shit about themselves or nobody else. Anyway, you know I got your back," Santana said. Richard watched Santana tap his dip, touching the .9 millimeter he knew was there.

"Just keep cool." Richard opened the car door, stepped onto the sidewalk. Closed the door feeling the security of Santana's presence giving him courage. The dude who was kneeling stood up blocking the doors. Eyeballed Richard as he walked towards them. "Excuse me," Richard said. The kid moved out of the way as Richard walked through the doors. He could still feel their eyes looking at him as he walked up the steps to the third door on the left towards the back. Apartment 2C. Richard could hear the music from some cartoon playing on the other side of the door. He knocked and took two steps back. Heavy footsteps made their way to the door. The peephole blackened before the door swung wide open. Antoine was standing there dressed in blue basketball

Round Up

shorts and a white tee shirt. Hair was half plaited in cornrows. His facial expression twisted into a grimace when he saw Richard.

Antoine leaned against the frame of the door, said "What the fuck you doing here?"

"I came to see my daughter. Where is she?" Richard asked. He kept his eyes fixed to Antoine's. Richard readied his body to come to blows if he had to. Clenched his fists and put his weight on his right leg.

Antoine grinned, like somebody told a joke that he found half funny. "Man you'd better get the fuck outta here!" Started to close the door. Richard used his left foot to block it.

"I said where is she?" Richard asked again. Antoine flung the door open causing Richard to fall inside the apartment. He tried to recover but Antoine started hitting him with a flurry of punches. Richard curled up, rolled over near the Christmas tree in the corner of the room when Antoine reloaded for his next round of hits. When Antoine raised his leg to kick, Richard grabbed Antoine's ankle and threw him off balance. Antoine crashed into a glass table. Broke some toys that were lying on the ground upon impact. Richard looked around and saw the boys that were standing in front of the building at the doorway. The one who eyeballed Richard on the way in ran through the door.

"What's up punk?" The boy asked. He rushed into Richard's body pushing him into a wall. Richard felt the air from his lungs escape him before he recovered throwing punches into the kid's back. Richard put leg to the kid's face feeling the impact against his kneecap. He heard the kid scream in pain before seeing a flash of red spill on the beige carpet. Richard looked towards Antoine who was coming towards him followed by the other kids who were outside. Richard continued throwing punches into the kid's back trying to break his grip from around his torso. In the next moment Richard heard a child's voice. He looked towards the hallway and saw R.J. standing there wearing the pink Barbie pajamas that he'd gotten her for Christmas. Her hair was done in two ponytails on each side of her head. Her baby brother was standing beside R.J., clutching tightly onto her legs.

"Daddy!" She called out over her little brother's crying. Richard wanted to run over to her. Pick her up and hug her like he used to do before Antoine came into her life. But the kid was still holding tightly onto his waist. Felt like a vice grip was squeezing the air out of Richard's body. Richard saw Antoine loading up to throw a punch. He braced himself to take the hit. Then Santana yelled into the room.

"Step the fuck back now!" Santana yelled. Richard looked towards the door where Santana was standing pointing the .9 millimeter towards Antoine who'd stopped moving. "I said step the fuck back!" Santana yelled again. Antoine moved back. Richard let the kid who was clutching his waist fall to the floor. The kid stood up, his cheek and nose bloody. R.J. saw the mess and started screaming.

Richard ran over to her, picked her up in his arms, said, "It's okay baby, it's okay." He cradled her head into the nape of his neck, feeling her tears against his skin. Noticed her brother from another father looking at him. Richard turned away from the child. Felt guilty that all this had happened in front of him.

Santana shook the nose of the gun from side to side at the boys. Motioned for the kid wearing the chain to come closer to him. When he moved close enough, Santana snatched the chain off of his neck. "Now get the fuck outta here!" They scrambled out of the door and down the stairs. Antoine stood silently in one spot looking at Richard. Richard could feel his glare but ignored him focusing on comforting his daughter. "I hate to break this up man, but we'd better get outta here." Richard knew Santana was right, but he didn't want to leave his daughter. A pain stabbed at his heart from seeing her, knowing that because of this incident he probably wouldn't be seeing her again for another few months. "Let's go Richie!" Santana said. He started moving towards the steps. "I'm gonna get the car started." Santana looked at Antoine. "Don't fuck with them hear me?" Antoine didn't answer, but Richard knew he wouldn't bother them. He figured Antoine to be one those punks who talked a good fight but couldn't back it up. He heard Santana jump the stairs and run out the glass doors. Richard put R.J. down and looked at her, then gave her another hug. She was the one good thing in his life.

"You okay now baby?" Richard asked. R.J. responded with a nod of her head. "Daddy's got to go now but I'm going to call you later okay?" R.J. nodded again. Richard stood up, mugged Antoine who was still standing in the same spot. He heard police sirens outside. Richard turned around and jumped the stairs hearing R.J. calling 'daddy' after him. He ran outside and saw that Santana was gone. Three blue and white cruisers pulled up to the front of the building. An elderly woman dressed in a flowered housecoat was standing on the sidewalk pointing at Richard.

"That's him! He just burst right into the apartment! And he had a gun!" She yelled. Two cops jumped out of each car with their guns drawn cautiously at him. Richard put up his hands indicating that he wasn't going to resist. Two male cops one white and one black rushed towards Richard, threw him on his stomach and cuffed him. They pulled him off the ground with force. Walked Richard towards the car, past the crowd of people that had collected on the sidewalk to see the show. Richard looked behind him. Saw R.J. standing in the doorway looking at him as they pushed his head into the car.

CHAPTER TWENTY-SIX

Detective Fields slid into the Crown Vic. Looked across the car at his partner Ryan who expressed what Fields was thinking after the interview with Ms. Anderson a few minutes before.

"Bullshit. I seem to remember the mother saying how sound of a sleeper she was the last time we were there. She wouldn't have known if the kid left to go back out or not," Ryan said.

Fields flipped back through the pocket-sized notebook that he carried inside his jacket to verify what he already knew the answer to. "Yeah. Says it right here." Fields put the notebook back into his jacket. Keyed the engine and merged into traffic, going south on Lincoln Avenue. Flipped the switch for the wipers to clear of window of the specks of rain that had begun to fall.

"My instincts tell me the Richie kid was there. And my instincts have never failed me yet. Remember how I broke open the Burns drug case a few years back?" Ryan asked.

"How could I not? You remind me every chance you get. Anyway, even if the kid was there, that still doesn't necessarily tie him into his cousin's killing," Fields responded.

"I'm thinking retaliation. The shells were in one spot, like the shooter stopped the car and started blasting like he could give a damn about getting caught. That was personal. The girl just happened to be at the wrong place at the wrong time," Ryan said.

Fields thought about the short big mouth kid's confrontational attitude when Fields was trying to talk to the girl and agreed. "Makes sense to me." Fifteen minutes later Fields pulled into Ryan's apartment complex. Saw the trash littered all over the parking lot. Looked like a parade just ended. "I don't know how you can live in this dump."

Ryan chuckled. "Better than paying that small fortune that you call a mortgage every month."

Round Up

Fields ignored the comment. "And don't be yanking your dick to those porno's when you get in there either. Get lots of shut eye for our shift tonight. You look beat."

"I'm tired. Shit's starting to wear me out."

"What the case? It's no harder than anything else we've---"

"No it's not just the case. It's all of it. The job, the killing, this whole fucking dump of a city. It's like they never learn."

Fields raised his left eyebrow. "They?"

"Yeah they. The fucks in the street who wanna put us six feet under for getting in the way of their cash flow. It's a fucked up cycle of life and death out here and it's taking more and more of my soul everyday. I'm telling you Fields, there's a beat calling my name on a quiet street somewhere in Pennsylvania."

"I figured as much. You haven't been the same lately."

"Wasn't that hard to notice."

"So when do you think you're gonna make a move?"

"Right after this case is over. I've gotta do something or I'm gonna lose my fucking mind."

"Get some sleep man. And like I said, no yanking your dick."

"Why not? It's mine ain't it?" Ryan winked and got out of the car. Fields watched him climb the steps and go into his apartment before pulling off.

Fields arrived at his own house twenty minutes after dropping off Ryan. The rain was falling steady now. He pulled into his wet driveway feeling his stomach starting to turn. Felt like somebody had drilled him in the stomach with a hard right hand. Fields stepped out of the car, walked towards his house thinking this is how inmates on death row must feel walking the last mile. He crouched down, picked up the paper from the walkway. Saw that the girl's shooting had made the front page. Fields opened his front door expecting to hear the big screen blaring a cartoon but it was silent. Closed the front door behind him figuring the kids were probably still asleep. Fields glanced at his watch. Saw that it was only five after nine. He was grateful for the quiet. He clicked on the tube and saw the tail end of the shooting scene on the morning news. Fields was glad that he missed it. He walked through to the kitchen, saw that it was spotless. He opened the fridge, poured himself a glass of apple juice. Took a swig and sat the glass on the counter. He looked towards the ceiling for sounds that Charlene was awake, like her heavy footsteps across the floor. Nothing. Fields started thinking that something didn't feel right. He walked up the back staircase from the kitchen towards the bedrooms. Stopped at Brian's room first. He opened the door. Saw that the bed was made, like it hadn't been slept in the night before. Figured Charlene had gotten the kids up and went to an early function or something.

Fields stepped over to Brian's walk in closet, opened the door and saw that both sides were empty of clothes. He backed up, left, and went into Jennifer's room. The bed was made just like Brian's. Fields went straight to her walk in, flung open the door and saw that it was empty too. He rushed out and went to his own bedroom. The king-sized bed he shared with Charlene was neatly made. He started to go to the closet until he saw Charlene's two-carat rock and platinum band on her white nightstand. Fields stood in the same spot on the beige carpeted floor for what felt like hours. His insides were empty, like someone had siphoned the blood out of him leaving only the shell of his body. Fields sat down on the paisley comforter on the bed, with the realization that Charlene and the kids being gone sinking into his psyche. Sure, he wished they were gone out of frustration sometimes but that was based on anger and hurt from when they ignored him. He never thought that Charlene would actually take off with them. Fields felt tightness in his chest, like his lungs were starting to constrict. Made him take deep breaths. Then came an array of confusing emotions. First anger. The bitch had taken off with his kids. What gave her that right? Then sorrow. His family served as his rock. As badly as they treated him, thinking about them got him through the hard nights out in the streets of Colver City. Like a constant reminder that there was something for Fields to look forward to after the hell of the shift was over. Fields got up from the bed. Paced the floor before searching Charlene's side of the chest of drawers for some kind of final confirmation that she was really gone.

Fields frantically pulled out the drawers seeing that each one was empty. No panties, tee shirts, socks, bras, nothing. When the phone rang, Fields ran over to it, snatched it up in the middle of the second ring. It had to be Charlene, or rather he hoped it was. There was a pause before a recording kicked in saying something about long distance service. Fields slammed the phone down and sat back down on the bed. He felt alone. Wanted more than anything to talk to somebody. He couldn't call Ryan. He wouldn't have an understanding ear for a situation like this one. Hell, Ryan never even had a steady girlfriend let alone a wife. Just the steady line of hookers that he called whenever he wanted to get what Ryan called intimacy. Fields picked up the receiver again, dialed Monica's cell, letting it ring twice before hanging up. A minute later the phone rang. Fields snatched it up.

"Monica I need to see you."

She paused before answering. "What's wrong? You sound scared or something."

"I need to see you at the spot. Is it a bad time?"

"What's with the urgency? I just got in to work."

Fields took a breath, then spoke. "S-she left me. Took the kids with her."

"Aww wow. Think she found out about us?"

"Naw, I-I don't think that was it." Fields figured that even if she did know, that it wasn't the only reason.

"I'm so sorry baby."

"So can you?"

Monica chuckled. Fields knew that wasn't meant for him. She had sounded preoccupied ever since she had gotten on the phone. Said something to one of her co-workers in the background before answering. "How about noon? Lunchtime?"

Noon felt like a lifetime away from right now. He needed to be doing something to take his mind off of Charlene. "What's wrong with now?"

"Baby, I just got to work."

"I need to see you Monica."

Monica paused, answered, "okay, go to the spot. I'll meet you there."

Fields hung up. Grabbed his keys and ran to the undercover car. It would take Monica about an hour before she arrived at the hotel. Fields didn't care though. He'd just wait there until she came. Just as long as he wasn't alone in that house.

Fields turned the usual half-hour ride from the house to the spot into a ten-minute excursion. He checked into a room and curled up under the cheap comforter to wait for Monica to come.

Didn't even take the time to open the curtains to allow some natural light into the room. He heard a light tapping at the door some time after getting into the bed. Fields got up, went to the door, looked out the curtain and saw Monica standing on the other side dressed in a beige pantsuit. He cracked the door, started walking back to the bed. Fields slid under the covers hearing Monica come in closing the door behind her. He felt Monica sitting on the bed.

"You okay baby?" Monica asked.

"I'm cool. Just can't believe she did this. She took my life."

"I don't mean to be cruel but from what you told me, you two didn't exactly have a good marriage."

"It was bearable."

"Obviously not to her. You have any idea where she might have taken the kids?"

"Not until she calls."

"You checked the answering machine yet?"

"No. I'll wait until later. Maybe after I get off tonight."

Monica climbed into the bed. Spooned up to Fields' back. "You still going in to work tonight?"

"Can't sit home with this on my mind. Got another body I have to deal with anyway to keep me busy."

"The one at that new club on Liberty? I read about that in this morning's paper. Waste of a promising young life."

"Story of this city."

"Any leads?" Monica asked. Fields liked the fact that Monica showed an interest in his job. But he couldn't tell her anything. Not even if he had something to tell her.

"Nope."

"Guess everything seems like it's coming down on you right now huh?"

"No more than usual," Fields answered. He allowed himself to drift off to sleep remembering the moments when Charlene had been the one cuddled up to him.

Round Up

CHAPTER TWENTY-SEVEN

Detective Ryan opened the door to his apartment. Felt the chilly air from the place even before he stepped inside. Realized that he'd forgotten to turn on the heat before leaving for work. He hated coming home to a cold apartment. Ryan picked up the remote, clicked on the television. Saw the news cameras panning the scene around the club where that chick had been clipped. Watched the reporter give a few details about the shooting before going to the head to take a leak. Ryan walked past the combination phone and digital answering machine and noticed the number in the message indicator read an crimson number two. He released the liquid that filled his bladder first before coming back and hitting the message button. The first one was from some telemarketer selling timeshares in Jersey. Ryan had a friend who'd fell for that too-good-be-true shit. Five years later and the guy was still trying to get his money back from the scam. The second message was a woman's voice, a civilian named Jenna Mays, who served as the timekeeper for their precinct. She was a black chick with huge tits that Ryan kept telling Fields to fuck. She said that Faith noticed some inconsistencies on the time card and to fix them before the time went in. Ryan figured Faith must have found the padded three hours that he had claimed. Well he wasn't coming all the way back down to the precinct just to sign some goddamn piece of paper. Ryan picked up the phone receiver, dialed the station. He'd have Petey H, one of the only guys Ryan liked at the station fix the shit for him. Petey minded his own business. He was loud sometimes, but a cool guy nonetheless. Petey answered the phone on the first ring.
"Detective Hampton."
"Petey, Ryan here."
"Hey Ryan, how they hanging?"

Ryan ignored the greeting. If he didn't cut him off now, Pete would've talked forever about his family. "I need you to do me one."

"Whassat?"

"Need you to fix my timecard for me. Your handwriting kinda looks like mine. Just sign it and give it to Jenna."

"I gotcha. Just gotta take care of this intake and I'll get on it."

Ryan figured he owed the guy at least some small talk since he was doing him a favor. He'd just be careful not to get in any familial subjects. "Yeah, paper works a bitch ain't it."

"You know it is, and the fuck even has the nerve to give me attitude."

"What can you do?" Ryan asked rhetorically.

"And then when he saw his little girlfriend come through here, he clammed up on me."

"Domestic?"

"Kidnapping. Had her holed up in some hotel like a caged animal."

"Crazy fuck. Anyone I know?"

"Kid named Adams. Terrell Adams. Calls himself Bishop, or Reverend or something on the street. You remember how we used to bust his mother like once a week when she was tricking?"

All Ryan heard was the name Terrell Adams before he zoned out of the conversation. They had Priest. Ryan wondered if the punk had started making any deals yet to save his skin. Ryan figured that at least he had the leverage of the kidnapping on his side in case he had to bargain. "Pete, never mind about the favor. I have some errands to run. I'm just gonna stop by the precinct and take care of the card myself." Ryan hung up before Pete Hampton had a chance to respond.

Ryan pulled into the parking two hours after ending the conversation with Pete Hampton. Wanted to make it look like he'd been really running errands all day rather than sitting at home waiting for the time to pass. Ryan tried catching some shuteye but sleep wouldn't come. He was too wired from wondering if the Priest kid was going to open his mouth about Ryan's extortion activities. Ryan, still dressed in the clothes he ended his shift in, walked through the glass doors. Immediately his stomach turned from seeing the assholes he couldn't stand on day shift. Jerks like

Nate Jackson who was talking on the phone at his desk. And his sidekick, Mark Kelly who Ryan thought of as the bastard who somehow broke into Ryan's locker and filled it with a bunch of air freshener trees as some kind of sick fucking joke. Ryan knew Jackson was in on it too, but he claimed ignorance. Jackson saw Ryan and grinned like he was thinking of a new insult about Ryan's body odor. Fortunately Kelly wasn't anywhere around right now so that left one less asshole Ryan had to deal with. Ryan figured Kelly was out in the street somewhere on a case and hoped he wouldn't see the asshole either while he was there.

Ryan walked through the building feeling as if every eye in the place was on him. Reminded him of the days back in high school when he got teased by the other kids because of the way he smelled. He saw Pete in the back at his desk typing into the computer and the back of some kid's head. Ryan walked up to the desk, eyeballed Priest who was sitting in a chair on the side of the desk. Kid looked serious, like someone had played a joke on him that he didn't like. Ryan didn't say anything to the kid as he leaned against the front of Pete's desk. Noticed the kid avert his eyes to the floor.

"Hey buddy," Pete said.

"How's it going?" Ryan asked.

"It's not. I'm gonna throw this punk in the lockup until he's ready to talk. All I got is his fucking name."

"Let me take him," Ryan said. Noticed the Priest kid look up with concern on his face when Ryan said that. His eyes were hard and cold. No feeling behind them.

"Knock yourself out." Pete rose from his chair. "I'm gonna get a bite to eat from the sub joint across the street. Want something?"

"Naw I'm good."

"Suit yourself," Pete said. He walked towards the door, then turned around. "Oh, and he said something about having some kind of valuable information. See if you can find out what that's about would you?"

Ryan looked at Priest who looked away. "Sure will." Ryan watched Pete wink his eye at the kid before leaving. Ryan looked at Priest again who was sitting in the wooden chair with the iron bracelets around his wrists. He was twiddling with his fingers still looking down at the floor. "You want those off?"

"Whatever you wanna do," Priest answered. He straightened up, slouched in his chair. Ryan leaned over to Pete's drawer, pulled out a ring with three keys on it. Unlocked the cuffs and watched the kid rub his wrists.

"Aren't you gonna thank me?" Ryan asked.

"They shouldn't be have been on me in the first place."

Ryan rose off the desk. Grabbed the kid's file folder as he walked to the other side of the room. Decided that he wasn't going to chance the kid dropping a dime on him. Ryan was going to make sure the kid went down on the kidnapping plus whatever else he could find. But Ryan wanted to play with the kid a little first. Bat him around like a cat did with a toy mouse. He gripped the kid by the shoulders, escorted him to down the hallway to the interrogation room. Priest pulled away from his grip. Ryan grabbed him, slammed the kid into some lockers as they walked. They came to white door numbered 426 and stopped. Ryan opened it, sat the kid down in a chair with the back against a dirty wall scrawled with scratches and marks. Ryan sat down on the other side of the room facing him. Clasped his hands together on the top of the metal table with chipped white paint like a child in first grade. Ryan looked the kid directly in the eyes. The kid didn't look scared or intimidated. Just sat there waiting to see what was going to happen next. The kid's smug attitude was making Ryan angry.

"I guess you know you're in a lot of trouble," Ryan said. He flipped through the folder looking at the kid's eyes following the turning pages.

"Am I? For what? I didn't do nothing."

"Looking at a lot of time on this one."

"Oh really? I figure when the court hears what I have to say, my time will come down."

"Yeah? And what do you have to say?" Ryan watch the kid sit there with a grin on his face. "Let's cut the bullshit," Ryan said.

Priest sucked his teeth. "Let's."

Ryan leaned in closer to the kid in case any hidden mics were picking up the conversation. "They've got your girl out there saying you kidnapped her. Held her against her will. That's a

Round Up

felony in this state. And when I get through typing up the narrative to give to Hampton you'll be lucky if they don't give you the death penalty." Ryan watched the kid lean forward in his chair. His thick left eyebrow was raised in anger.

"What? That's some bitch's word against mine. They ain't got no proof about none of that shit she's talking about!"

"Look I don't know what happened and frankly I don't give a shit. But I think you're rolling the dice with this one kid. Let's say you crap out and get a woman judge on her period and a racist ass bitch of a States Attorney? You know those white women don't play when it comes to another woman, black or white. They're like pit bulls with tits. Then once the girl gets up on that stand and starts the flood of tears, there's nothing you can say that's gonna keep your ass from going to the pen."

Ryan noticed the kid start to show some emotion. Fear invaded his face before confusion came. "So what are you trying to say?" Priest asked.

"You're gone. That's all there is to it. I couldn't give a fuck what happens to you now. Whatever you're planning to do with your supposedly valuable piece of information, you're gonna take it right to the pen with your ass." Ryan smiled, then got up from his chair.

Priest had a disbelieving look in his face. "Look I got something you might wanna hear."

"What, more valuable information? Who are you planning on screwing now to save your ass?"

"For real. I got something you can use."

"Let me hear it then."

"If I tell you, you gotta promise me that you'll try to get me outta this."

"I'll see what I can do, that is, if whatever information you've got is worth anything."

Priest eyeballed Ryan. Like he'd heard empty promises too many times before to take the words seriously. "First what can you do to help me?"

Ryan smiled. Showcased his teeth. "Let's just say I can make the charges go away."

Priest shrugged. "What happens if I think you're fucking with me and I change my mind?"

"Stop wasting my goddamn time kid. You can go through this on your own and get fucked by the Judge and the States Attorney, then you'll still have me to deal with. And if you try to make some bullshit deal with the court on the side and set me up, I'll make it so you won't wanna close your eyes even for a second in the joint."

Priest shrugged with indifference again. "Whatever you say boss man."

Ryan winked at the kid. "Just so long as we understand each other."

Priest got up, eyeballed Ryan when he stood. "What made you think I was gonna snitch on you? I ain't no pussy." He said.

"Maybe because you're blabbing to save your ass now," Ryan answered. Ryan knew that once punks like this kid were facing a block of years ahead of them, their hard hearts turned to mush and they sang like they were in a choir. "Now cut the bullshit. What do you have for me?"

Round Up

CHAPTER TWENTY-EIGHT

The smell of vomit, courtesy of the intoxicated man that was passed out in the corner of the room made it hard for Richard to breathe. He breathed through his mouth while he sat on a wooden bench in the holding area of Baltimore's central booking facility. And he could feel the dull throbbing in his temples starting to grow into a more serious pain. It scared him. Knew that here nobody gave a damn about some pills to make him feel better.

Richard along with ten other men were waiting to see a District Court Commissioner who would give them a bail. He had no idea how long he'd been there since there were no clocks on the wall and no windows to see if it was light or dark outside. Richard looked around the room. All of the men had been stripped of any fancy jewelry they might have had when they came in. Richard had never heard of a Commissioner. He was only familiar with the judges in Colver City who handed out high bails like they were giving out candy on Halloween. The horror stories that floated around the holding area about how tough the Commissioners in Baltimore were scared the hell out of Richard. He really got shook when he heard about a story about a young girl who got a million-dollar bail for a simple possession. That was usually a recognizable offense. Then when she tried to explain how the drugs weren't hers; that she was holding it for her boyfriend, the commissioner ignored her tearful story and called the next person waiting in line to be seen. Richard had never been arrested before, not even when he was hustling, so he didn't know what to expect. He maintained his cool, though his insides were bubbling with fear. Made him want to relieve himself of the digested food in his stomach. But with the toilet that sat out in the open in the corner, the absence of privacy made Richard clench his ass cheeks together tightly to avoid any accidents. But a conversation in the back of the room really took his mind off of his problem. Two dudes were talking about some cat that was running Colver City with an iron fist. He had a hit put out on anybody who he felt was a threat to him. Said he even had this guy shot to death in his car and two slugs put into the dude's girl, one bullet in each eye. Added that the dude had to be making loads of money, a clear fact from the midnight black Benz with the chrome wheels that he drove around town to check on his corners. Richard remembered how that stripper Janell said the same thing. His stomach sank like he'd just taken the first drop on a roller coaster ride. They had to be talking about Mark and Monique! So now it was clear that whoever drove that car had put the hit out on them. He hoped they would give up a name or say something that would lead to the shooter but the conversation ended when keys were inserted into the door of the holding cell.

Richard watched a female correctional officer dressed in a blue uniform with a shiny badge on just above her left breast come through the bolted doors. He could see that she was fairly attractive even with her hair clipped up in a bun. Didn't look like she belonged in the building full of criminals. Her navy blue uniform hugged her upper body so that the shape of her breasts was clearly determinable though the matching pants hung loosely off of her legs. Wearing her nametag on her right side just above her breast made her an easy target for the catcalls from all the men. Richard didn't even bother to look up when she passed by the cell where he was. The other dudes yelled and screamed at her like they'd been in a twenty-year bid when it had only been a few hours since they came in from the street. The dudes stopped when she opened the cell where they were. Meant it was their time to be seen. The men, with the exception of the drunk passed out in the corner filed out of the room clomping along the floor like cattle. Their shoes hung loosely on their feet since the strings had been taken as a precaution to keep any suicides from happening. The CO closed the door behind them after the last man was out.

"This way," she said with authority. Sounded liked she was talking to a class full of kindergartners. Reminded Richard of his hustling days and the degrading way the dealers talked to the addicts when it was time to get served. They followed her as ordered walking through the taunts of the men still in the cells. Richard was third from the end, behind a white boy with long stringy blonde hair. He smelled of stale alcohol. And from the way

Round Up

his shirt was ripped and stained with blood, Richard guessed he had been in a fight. The CO led them to small room where a chair and a desk sat on the other side of a plastic shield. Richard ended up near the entrance. He watched the CO close the door, lock it, before walking back towards the holding area. A portly white man with a bulging beer gut came into the room on the other side of the protective window. What was left of his black hair was combed over to hide the baldness. His red tie was undone at the neck. Contrasted the blue dress shirt that was rolled up at the sleeves to his elbows. He was chewing on a piece of chicken that he put down on his desk before sitting down. Everyone in the little room's eyes was planted on the man waiting to see what he was going to do next. The different body odors in the confined space made Richard sick. Almost to the point of throwing up. The man picked up the phone on his desk, made two calls, then addressed them as a group. Richard listened intently as the man explained the procedure of their civil rights—some shit about right to trial and all that—before telling them that he was the commissioner. The man sat down in the chair, shuffled through the folders on the desk, pulled one out. Looked towards his computer monitor, hit a button and faced them. The men in the room held their breath hoping they weren't going to be the first one on deck.

"Wilson...Steven Wilson," the man called. The men shuffled around the confined space of the room to allow a man wearing a red velour warmup suit to come to the window. He sat in the steel chair that was bolted to the floor under a ledge. Richard stayed near the back, listening intently to the exchange between the two men. The Commissioner opened the folder. Read the crimes that Steven had been accused of like he was reading the items off of a grocery list. Included first degree rape, second degree assault, and trespassing. Said the most serious charged of rape carried a life sentence. Richard winced at hearing the list. Steven was unfazed. The man on the other side of the glass then got quiet as he read the officer's report. Richard could feel the tension emanating from the other men in the room. The Commissioner then looked up. Eyeballed Steven for a moment like he'd already passed a guilty verdict before addressing him.

"Full name," the Commissioner said.
"Steven James Wilson."

The Commissioner punched the information into the computer, then asked, "address?"

"17 Belton Terrace. Over on the west side of town."

More punching into the computer. "How long you lived there?"

"3 years."

"Where'd you live before that?"

"With my moms."

"Where?"

"21 Park Towne Way."

"How long there?"

"Since I was born."

More punching, then, "employment?"

"None."

"How long?"

"Two, three years."

"Birthdate?"

"March 6."

"Year?"

"'78."

More punching, then, "says here that you're pending trial for second degree assault. Court date is set for two weeks from now, correct?"

"Yeah."

More punching into the computer, then a grin, before he said, "lucky that you got a fast trial coming up."

"Why's that?"

"Because I'm denying you a bail. Next person have a seat."

Richard's heart thumped faster and harder. The dull pain in his neck had been upgraded to a full headache. He watched Steven stand up from the metal chair and bang his fist against the plastic window. "I didn't do nothing to that bitch! She set me up! She should be the one in here not me!" Steven yelled. The CO that put the men in the booth opened the door accompanied by two other male CO's built like football players. They made their way into the booth, pushing the men to the side, and snatched Steven out of the cell. The CO's slammed the door as the men focused their attention back to the man in charge on the other side of the window.

Round Up

"Next person, name of Anderson...Richard Anderson."

Richard stepped forward from the back of the room, sat in the seat in front of the window. "I'm Richard." The man repeated the same procedure step for step as he did with Steven. Ten minutes later, Richard had a $1000 bail. With the ten percent he had to pay, it was only one hundred dollars. He had the money in his pant's pocket. Right now he was waiting to be released from holding. Richard watched as another man was seen on his charges as he leaned against the steel door.

The commissioner shuffled some papers, picked up a bright yellow folder, examined it closely and called out another name. "Last name of Adams. I don't know if I'm pronouncing this right Tee wan." A man with dark hairy eyebrows, thin mustache, and neatly braided hair made his way to the front of the booth. The other men moved out of his way. The commissioner looked the man in his eyes, asked, "are you Tee Wan Adams?"

The man paused, interlocked his fingers together on top of the table and answered, "It's Twan Adams."

Richard listened as the commissioner chuckled in a condescending tone. "Oh, my mistake." The commissioner looked over the folder. "Let me see, you're in here for assault." The commissioner asked the same questions that he asked the previous man. Twan answered every question with a tone of indifference in his voice as if he didn't care what his fate was going to be. When it was over, Twan had a bond of $5,000. He stood up and made his way to the back of the cell next to Richard.

The female CO was escorting Richard and Twan out of the cell and down a cement hallway to a cell even smaller than the first one. The smell was indescribable, a mix of piss and vomit due to the clogged up toilet in the corner. Twan went in first and stood with his back against the wall and his head down. She led Richard inside and was getting ready to shut the door behind him. "Do I get to make a phone call to try and make bail?" Richard asked.

She smiled and responded, "I'll come back to get you in a half-hour." Richard sat down on the cement floor across from Twan. The CO closed the steel bars and turned the key.

"Could you get me some aspirin or something? My head is killing me," Richard asked.

"I'll see what I can do," she answered, and left.

Richard rested his head against the bricks. Looked over at the man sharing the cell with him. Wasn't sure whether to say anything or not. Twan broke the silence between them. Richard was surprised.

"Ain't you Richie Rich?"

"Used to be."

"What's that mean?"

"I don't hustle no more."

"That's good man. Found something else to pay the bills huh?"

"Got a nine to five."

"Good move." Twan got quiet when two CO's walked by their cell, looking at them like they were caged animals in a zoo. "That kid who got shot, name was Mark, he was your cousin right?"

"Yeah."

"Used to see ya'll hanging around the way. I heard what happened to him. That must've fucked you up."

"Yeah, " Richard answered. He felt a tugging at his heart. Hoped his face didn't display his pain. Alumni of the streets were supposed to keep feelings hidden.

"No disrespect but I heard your cousin was off the hook lately."

Richard wondered what else his cousin had gotten into. Who else he had made an enemy. "How?"

"Heard he was creeping with a bunch of young chicks who belonged to some big time people."

"I've been hearing a lot of that."

"I don't know if it's true or not. I don't spread rumors. Just thought you'd like to know what's being said about your cousin, you being his blood and all."

"I hear you." Richard leaned his head against the wall. Felt his eyes beginning to close against his will.

Jingling keys turning in a lock awakened Richard from a cautious sleep. A different CO was at the door, a small chocolate colored man of about five seven with a muscular build was standing on the other side. Richard stretched, stood up from the cement bed and said, "am I getting my phone call now?"

Round Up

The CO shook his head. Made Richard's stomach jump at the thought of being held any longer inside the cell. "You got bail."

"What? Who posted it?"

"Dunno. All they said was to come and get you. Oh yeah, these are for you," said the CO. He reached into his pocket, pulled out a sealed white packet, handed it to Richard. Richard saw the word "ibuprofen" written across the front in black letters, and smiled.

The CO led Richard outside of the cell. He chin nodded to Twan who returned the gesture. The CO led him back down the hallway. The horrible funk was still present in the corridor and seemed to have gotten worse. After being outprocessed, Richard walked on the other side of the metal detector for visitors and saw Santana sitting on one of the chairs in the waiting room. A full moon against a black sky was on the other side of the glass doors of the building. Richard eyeballed Santana on the way out like he wanted to take a swing.

Santana chuckled and said, "Oh, so that's how you thank me for bailing your ass out of jail?"

Richard heard the remark but didn't comment. He stood outside, breathed in the cold city air that was a gift to his nose after smelling the stink of the booking facility for all those hours. He put on his jacket. Looked for a cab to take him uptown back to his mother's house. Santana came out a minute later. Grabbed Richard by the shoulders, led him down the steps towards the public parking lot across the street. Richard moved away from Santana's grasp. He knew he had to relent to a ride from Santana. The chances of catching a cab downtown at the late hour were nonexistent. Too many cabees had been robbed by dudes who'd just released so they weren't taking any fares. Richard walked over to the car in silence. Stood on the passenger side of Santana's car. Santana reached the car with a smile on his face. Richard felt a burning anger rising from deep in his gut. "What the fuck is so damn funny?" Richard yelled.

Santana straightened his demeanor for a moment then started laughing again. Harder this time. After a few minutes Santana said, "My fault Richie. But I know you don't blame me for what happened. I told your ass to get outta there. What, you wanted me to wait outside so the cops could lock me up too?"

Richard knew Santana had a point. He just didn't want to admit it. "Just take me home."

Santana disarmed the alarm and started laughing again. Hit the button on the CD player. DMX's raspy voice boomed through the car's speakers. "Alright, we'll be back in Colver in a little bit."

They had been driving for about a mile before Richard said anything. "I overheard these two dudes talking about who killed Mark." Santana turned the music down.

"Oh yeah? What you hear?"

"Whoever did it drives a chromed up black Mercedes. He has to be a dealer if he has a ride like that. Anybody you know making serious bank?" Richard asked.

Santana thought for a minute, said, "not that I know of."

"Well I know he's gonna come out sooner or later."

"How do you know?"

"He's gonna want to show off with a car like that."

Santana nodded his head, responded "true," then turned the music back up.

Richard looked out of the passenger window into the darkness. Hoped his mother hadn't worried much since she hadn't seen him since the early afternoon. But he knew his mother, she was probably sick from wondering where he was. He'd make up something to tell her to explain where he had been. Richard hated to lie to his mother again but what was he gonna do, tell her that he'd been in jail all night?

Round Up

CHAPTER TWENTY-NINE

Richard woke up when Santana jerked the car to a stop. He had drifted off to sleep on the highway coming back from Baltimore. He woke up with his mind on R.J. and the sad look in her eyes when he left. He hadn't meant for his little girl to see her Daddy fighting and acting like a criminal. And Richard was sure that the only way Desiree was going to let him see her again would be through a court order. Figured if he called Desiree later, maybe explain the pressure that he was going through, she would understand. Richard looked towards the house and saw a light on in the front window.

"Looks like your mom is awake," Santana said.

"I see that."

"You gonna be okay later on?"

Richard turned to Santana, said, "why wouldn't I?"

"Mark's funeral."

Richard did a quick assessment of the days that had passed. With everything that happened he had forgotten about the funeral. It was New Year's Eve already. Never in his life had time passed by so fast. "Dammit!"

"What, you forgot?" Santana asked.

"Naw. I just thought I would be okay by now."

"It's gonna take time to get over something like that."

Richard only heard half of what Santana said. His mind was on the grief he was going to be experiencing later in seeing his aunt and mother crying. He answered, "yeah, I guess."

"You know I didn't mean to leave you like that, but like I said, if they had locked me up too I wouldn't have been able to bail you out."

"It's cool. Least you did that."

"You'd better get in there and face the music. I'll catch you later alright?"

Tony Cheatham

Richard opened the car door, felt a cool blast of morning city air hit him in the face. Put foot to concrete and got out. "Yeah." He started the walk up the steps to go into the house. Turned around when Santana yelled from the open window of the car.

"You okay for a ride?"

Richard looked at the Tercel parked by the curb. This wasn't a day to be dealing with car problems. "I'll call you if I need you." He watched Santana nod his head before pulling off. Richard made his way up the steps, keyed the lock, and opened the door. He turned around to close it and caught sight of Nico sitting on the steps of an abandoned house across the street. Richard wondered if he ever got off the streets and went home.

* * *

The moment the door to the vestibule shut, Richard's mother appeared at the end of the hallway, hands on hips. She yelled, "Boy what the hell is wrong with you?"

"Ma I---"

"You think you can just go and stay out all night without calling me to say that you're alright?"

"Ma---"

"I'll tell you one damn thing, you may be grown and on your own, but when you're in my house you respect me, you understand?" Richard nodded his head without looking at her. Answered yeah under his breath. "Boy look at me when I'm talking to you. And I didn't hear you, I said do you understand me?"

Richard cleared his throat, answered "yes" in an audible tone.

"Where were you all this time?"

Richard wanted his mother's sympathy, and even though he knew it was wrong, he used the forthcoming events of the day to his advantage. "Just doing some thinking. Getting myself together for today." He noticed his mother's angry façade change to one of understanding.

"We're gonna get through this. Just trust in the Lord and everything will be okay," said his mother. She walked over to him, arms outstretched, and hugged him. "You alright now?"

"I guess."

Round Up

"Your aunt is upstairs sleep in your bed. I didn't want her sleeping on the couch when she has the funeral ahead of her today."

"That's cool. I just need to get a quick sleep before all of this. What time is the funeral again?"

"The wake is at ten thirty. After that the limo's are going to take us to the funeral site."

"Where's that?"

"Meadowfield."

"Out in Eldersburg in Baltimore County?"

"That's the one."

"Why all the way out there?"

"Because that's where his father is buried."

Richard was surprised to hear that information. Mark had never talked about his father. Not even when Richard talked about his own. "His father's dead? How?"

"Got shot in an argument a week after Mark was born. She ain't been right in her head since. Shelly didn't always wear that tight stuff. She used to be in the church. Then after her husband got killed she stopped believing in the Lord. Then just when I was starting to get her to come back to church, Marky gets taken away from her too." Ma shook her head, like she was beginning to question the Lord's ways herself. "You'd better get some sleep. I'll wake you up when it's time to get ready. You got three hours." She kissed Richard on the cheek and went upstairs. Richard sat down on the couch, closed his eyes. He was asleep in a few minutes.

* * *

Ma's voice woke Richard from his deep sleep telling him to get up. Three hours felt more like three minutes. He remained on the couch for a few more minutes until his mother came midway down the stairs dressed in a black skirt and matching blouse fiddling with her left ear. "Get up Richard and get dressed!" She yelled. It was dark in the living room and rain was pitter pattering against the roof of the house. Richard stood up from the couch, made his way up the stairs to his room. The bed was made and his aunt was gone. Figured she was in Ma's room getting ready. He hoped she would be composed when the time came to see Mark in the casket. Hell, Richard didn't even know if he would be okay after seeing that. He clicked on the stereo. Listened to the morning radio shows talking about all the parties happening around town for New Years Eve. Then he listened to the DJ pleading for a night without violence. Richard thought the pleas were falling on deaf ears. In a city where the murder rate was always over two hundred at the end of every year, it would be a miracle just to get through the night with less with than two bodies. Richard showered, dressed in the suit that he'd bought, and slipped into his black shoes. He looked in the mirror, thought he looked good, but for the wrong occasion. He grabbed his black full-length leather coat and made his way down the steps where Aunt Shelly and Ma were waiting for him. His aunt looked solemn like she was doped up on something to help her cope with the situation. Shirley Caesar's sad voice was coming from the stereo. Dictated the mood of the room. Richard sat down next to his aunt. Put his hand on top of hers. Richard listened to rain pounding harder on the roof hoping it would clear up before they went to the burial site. A horn blew outside. Richard helped his aunt up from the couch and followed his mother down the hallway to the car.

When the limo pulled up to the church, Richard could see the parking lot was packed full of cars. He helped his aunt out of the car and inside the building. The pews were filled with people. Richard escorted his aunt down the aisle as Ma walked behind them. Caught sight of Santana who was sitting in the back pew wearing a black suit. As Richard got closer to the front, he could see Mark's body in the white casket with gold trim. He looked unnatural. Looked more like a wax dummy was lying inside the box. Though Richard's legs were wobbly, he kept his steady pace. His aunt fell limp in his arms. He stopped, let her have her grieving moment and continued walking. Felt every eye in the place on them until they sat down in the front. The three of them were the only ones sitting in the reserved section. With the exception of the woman playing the organ beside the casket, the church was quiet. Flashbacks of the childhood years with Mark went through Richard's mind. He felt his chest welling up with emotion. Knew he'd be crying soon if he didn't get himself together. But it was hard. It was so goddamn hard to see his cousin in that box. And these people that were here to mourn his memory. They didn't know him, not like Richard did. Found

Round Up

himself getting angry with them then caught himself. Knew he was displacing his anger from whoever took Mark out of Richard's life. The woman playing the organ bought the song to an end when a man entered the front of the church from a side door. He was dressed in a black robe with gold embroidered crosses on the left and right side. The preacher. The low murmur among the attendees turned quiet when he raised his left arm in the air.

"Brothers and sisters, family and friends, we're here today to send Mark Anderson, who left his us much, much too soon, home to our Father…"

He was interrupted by a woman's outburst of tears that echoed throughout the church.

* * *

Richard watched the procession of vehicles leave for the burial grounds under the sheet of rain pouring from gray sky. After carrying the casket and loading it into the hearse, Richard couldn't bring himself to see Mark being dropped into the ground. Mark asked Joe, one of Mark's friends to stand in for him at the burial ground. This was truly it. Mark really wasn't coming back. Richard heard his Aunt Shelly's sniffles as someone helped her into the limo. He tried to hold off from crying as long as he could. And he was fine right up until the choir did a cover of Donny Hathaway's "Someday We'll All Be Free", Mark's favorite song during the benediction. Richard lost it after that. Remembered how many times they had dreamed of making something out of themselves while they listened to that song. Richard felt a tapping on his back. Turned around to see it was Santana.

Santana gave a weak smile, asked, "You okay?"

"I got to get outta here," Richard responded.

"Let's go," Santana answered.

Richard led the way up the carpeted aisle and through the glass doors to the street. The cool air outside felt good.

CHAPTER THIRTY

Detective Fields awoke to the steady rhythm of rain falling on the roof of the hotel room. Took him a minute to realize that he was alone now. Fields wondered when Monica had sneaked out. He looked at the clock that was chain wired to the top of the nightstand. Face read one-fifteen. Still had fifteen minutes to check out of the room. He picked up the phone, dialed the voice mail to his house, listened to the lady telling him that he had no new messages. Meant Charlene hadn't called. Or maybe she did and just hadn't left a message. He'd check the caller ID when he went home. Fields got up, showered, left the room. The rain had slowed to a steady drizzle. His head was spinning and his heart felt heavy. Knew it was because he was disorientated by Charlene's absence. Where the hell was she and when was she going to call him? And what about the kids? They were on winter break now but what about when it was time to go back to school? Figured seeing Monica would make him feel better but it only made him feel worse. Since she had left him to go back to work, Fields truly felt alone.

Fields crept south on Ross Boulevard doing twenty in a thirty-five. He ignored the cars blowing their horns behind him. Watched the angry drivers as they sped around his car giving him hard stares and profane gestures as they passed. Fields was unaware of the elderly woman making her way across the busy intersection. Slammed on his brakes to keep from hitting her. He noticed the woman's terrified look and watched as a dark haired man eyeballed him as he helped her the rest of the way across. Fields pulled over to the curb. He needed to clear his head. Decided to go to a coffee shop, maybe cop a booth and a cup of cappuccino and think. He got out, made his way across the street to a mom and pop joint and went inside. Saw that mom and pop were two male dark colored male foreigners, like from Egypt or

Round Up

Pakistan. When the shorter of the two men asked Richard what he wanted, the accent confirmed Pakistan. Fields ordered coffee with sugar and cream, and a bear's claw pastry. Handed the man five on a four-dollar check and copped a booth near the back of the place in front of a window. He sipped the coffee and thought it was too sweet. He took a bite of the pastry and sat it back down on the plate. The hard crust almost made him spit it back out. Decided to forgo the snack and gazed out of the window at all the cars driving by.

An emerald green Volvo stopped in front of the office building across the street. Fields watched a woman open the passenger door, giving the man in the driver's seat a peck on the lips. She shut the door, waved once more at the driver, and mouthed him a kiss before going into the building. Fields watched the car pull into traffic going north on the boulevard. He wondered what their story was. Maybe they had just gotten together and hadn't really had the chance to experience the ups and downs that come with a serious relationship. Maybe he just had a one nighter with her and was gentleman enough to drop her off at work. Or maybe they had been married for a shitload of years and knew how to keep the passion in their relationship. Something Fields wished he had done with Charlene. Kept thinking that maybe if he had taken a little less time off the street and a little more time at home, she wouldn't have left. But he had to do what was necessary to give Charlene the life that her and the kids deserved. And if he had it to do all over again, he wouldn't change a goddamn thing.

A man standing in an alley next to the office building diverted Fields attention from thoughts of the couple. The blue denim jacket, jeans, and gray ski hat looked familiar. He was holding a brown bag in his left hand. It was the same man that he and Ryan had talked to the other day. Since that day Fields had felt that the man was holding back something. But with Ryan's presence, there was no way that man was going to talk. Fields got up, walked out the door, and across the street. Fields saw that the man recognized him. Noticed his face drop before he was all the way across. Fields held up both hands like he was throwing up the white flag.

The man greeted Fields with a crooked grin. "Came back for another round?"

"No. But I do want to talk to you."

Tony Cheatham

The man raised the brown bag to his lips. Looked at Fields before he took a drink. Fields eyes signaled that it was okay. Noticed that the man was still fiddling with the fake diamond stud from the last time he had seen him. Figured it must have been his lucky charm or something. The man took a swig and said, "about what?"

"More about what you saw that day."

"I don't have nothing else to say about that man. If it gets back to the wrong people that I was even talking to you, that's it. I'm dead. Next place you'll be talking to me is in the city morgue. Shit, I left my other spot because I was getting dirty looks."

"From who?"

The man took another swig then said, "doesn't matter. You weren't there to protect and serve me when I needed you."

"Just run it by me again. You heard some shots. From what direction?"

"I dunno."

"Did you see anybody in the area?"

"Naw man. I didn't see nothing like that. Like I told you before, I heard some shots. The car crashed, then I saw this black car with them fancy shiny wheels pull up next to them then---"

"Hold up," Fields said.

"What?"

"You said a black car pulled up. You didn't say anything about a black car before."

"I didn't?"

"No."

"Must've forgot. My fault."

"Did you see anybody get out?"

"Naw I went to take a piss. Then some Chinese dude started yelling at me to get out of the alley or he was going to call the cops. When I came back out, the black car was gone."

"You didn't hear anything while you were in the alley, like shots or something?"

"Just the ones I told you about before. Couldn't hear anything else over that dudes big mouth."

"Well can you remember anything else that you forgot?"

"Nope."

Round Up

Fields wondered how the shooter could have killed the guy and put two slugs into the girl without it clearly being heard. There was a chance that the guy was lying but what other information did he have to go on? Witnesses weren't jumping at the opportunity to come forward. Figured that the shooter used a silencer. "Thanks."

The man took another swig from the brown bag. Fields watched the man tip the bottle to empty its contents. He wiped his mouth with the sleeve of his jacket and said, "Just don't tell nobody I talked to you."

Fields raised his left hand, said, "I won't." Spun around and made the short trip in the direction of his car on the other side of the street.

CHAPTER THIRTY-ONE

Priest sat in the metal chair feeling the needles stinging his ass. He had been in the station coming up on three hours with no offers of food or something to drink, like they did on those television cop shows. Just a smelly ass white man who was talking some bullshit about getting his case thrown out. Hell, Priest knew that Detective Ryan didn't have enough clout to help him. Priest had listened to the other cops, including that one who Ryan thought was his buddy, Pete Hampton, talking about Ryan's stinking ass when he was sitting at the desk. Said how awful his ass smelled and how he was always fucking up cases. Priest even heard the sergeant say a negative word or two about Ryan, something to do with a time sheet or some shit. Priest didn't know anything about that other stuff, but Ryan's ass sure did stink. Like piss with a side order of dog shit. And here was Ryan, breathing in Priest's face, trying to make him cop to a kidnapping. Like he was actually going to admit to that shit with no witnesses or at least another officer in the room. If Priest knew Ryan, he'd twist the statement around so much that the confession would sound like he shot the President of the United States. But Terell told the man that he had some information. Priest knew Ryan wanted the name of who put slugs into that dude and chick a few days before. Figured he could use that to his advantage. Sure, Priest knew who pulled the trigger. But he wasn't about to give up a name to this cracker for nothing.

"So what you gotta say kid?" Detective Ryan asked.

"You'd better not be fucking around. I want them charges dropped or reduced. I can't go to jail after this."

Ryan sighed deeply. "Okay, okay. Whatever you want, now talk."

Priest opened his mouth to start the first words of his statement. A knock at the door and the rookie, Officer Davis

Round Up

poking his head into the room interrupted him. "Faith wants to see you Detective."

Ryan turned his head sharply at the uniformed cop. "What?"

Officer David repeated himself, his voice still pleasant in spite of the fact that Ryan had just yelled at him. "Sergeant Faith wants to see you."

"Tell him I'm with a suspect!"

"He said now, and he sounded serious."

"What the fuck does he want?"

Officer Davis shrugged. "Don't know, I'm just the messenger."

"Dammit, how in the hell does he expect me to do my job if he keeps fucking with me?" Ryan rose out of his chair. Addressed Officer Davis. "Watch him until I get back!"

"Yes sir." Ryan stormed out of the room as Officer Davis closed the door behind him.

Priest sat back in the chair. Looked around the room thinking twice on what he was about to do. He wasn't a snitch. It wasn't in him to punk out like he was about to do. Still, he had to give something to Ryan. Priest figured that maybe if he copped some information about another body, Ryan would take it easy on him. Priest knew in the back of his mind that the cracker wouldn't do that. Priest thought hard about what to do. Backtracked through his mind from the moment he got arrested. He needed a weak link, something or someone that he could manipulate to get the odds in his favor. After a few minutes, Priest smiled.

Priest stood up, knocked on the door to the interrogation room. Officer Davis came to the window; opened the door as Priest hoped. "What's up?" Officer Davis asked.

"When's Ryan coming back?" Priest asked.

"Why?"

"I gotta take a leak real bad," Priest said.

"Dunno. He might be awhile from the way the sergeant sounded." Priest started doing the piss dance, like he was doing his best to hold it. Then the cop said what Priest hoped he'd say. The words of an inexperienced rookie who wasn't schooled in the ways of a criminal. "I'll take you."

"I'd appreciate it."

"Turn around so I can cuff you." Priest did it, still doing the dance. Officer Davis led Priest out of the room and down the hall to a bathroom. Priest knew from when Paco—one of his workers—had been arrested, that there was a window in there. Heard him joke about wanting to jump through there to escape but that he didn't have the heart. Priest did though. When they reached the door, Priest held up his wrists for the cuffs to be taken off. Officer Davis whistled a tune and reciprocated.

"Thanks Officer Davis," Priest said. Did the dance one last time to add to his act. Priest opened the door and saw the window. Figured that it had to be a cop's bathroom since there were no bars or anything. And the opening was just wide enough for him to fit through. Priest ran the water in the sink to cover his sounds and climbed up on the toilet. He looked out of the window and saw that the back was facing an alley. He used his foot to flush the toilet, opened the window and hang jumped from the ledge. His ankles stung once he hit the ground after the seven-foot drop. He dropped and rolled into a puddle of dirty rainwater. Smelled stale, like somebody had taken a leak in it. He stood up, pulled the clinging wet clothes from his arms and legs. Felt like pins were pricking his ankles. Once Priest recovered he ran towards the opening of the alley and blended in with the busy afternoon crowd on the street gearing up for the New Years Eve celebrations that night. He knew the cops were going to catch him, but before they did, he was going to take care of their main witness. What kind of case would the state have against him after Geena was gone?

Round Up

CHAPTER THIRTY-TWO

Detective Ryan walked out of Sergeant Faith's office fuming with anger. Faith wrote him up for conduct unbecoming an officer for padding his time. Ryan felt he deserved more time. Hell, if he wasn't officially working the case on the street, he was thinking about it when he was sleep, watching television, or taking a shit. So technically, he was still on duty. Screw Faith, Ryan thought. He had bigger things to worry about like getting the information out of that kid. When Ryan got what he wanted then he'd hold the kid over in the booking facility downtown. Once the kid was in the joint awaiting trial, Ryan would call this guy, an inmate named Robby Fox, and have the kid clipped. Fox owed Ryan a favor for knocking down a drug charge from a felony that would have gotten him life, down to a simple possession, a misdemeanor. Ryan hated to do it but it was better not to have anything that could be held over his head later. Especially when he wanted to transfer out of Colver.

Ryan walked back towards the interrogation room and saw a commotion. Uniforms were running all over the place, like chickens with their heads cut off. He grabbed one of the officers, asked what the hell was going on. Found out that the kid had escaped out of the window from the officer's bathroom. Ryan fumed. Felt his heart pumping faster, feeling the pulse of his temples. He saw the uniform that he asked to watch the door. Grabbed him by the front of his shirt.

"How the fuck did he get out of your custody you prick?" Ryan asked. Saw the terrified look in the young cop's eyes but Ryan didn't give a damn.

"I-I let him got to the bathroom. I d-didn't know there was a window in there. I swear! I was right outside the door the whole time!" Officer Davis answered.

Tony Cheatham

"I don't give a fuck if you held his goddamn dick for him while he took a leak! I told you to watch him, in the interrogation room, until I came back! He could have pissed on himself for all I care! You were not supposed to move him!" Ryan screamed. He threw the kid cop to the floor and walked back to his desk. Figured he was gonna have to find the kid now or his career was over. Ryan went to his desk, shuffled through some papers looking for some paperwork on the kid. Looked up and saw his partner Fields walking in through the door. What the hell was he doing here?

* * *

Fields watched the streets of Colver with apprehension as he drove south on Bingham Avenue. He made a right on Connelly Avenue then a sharp left heading north on Rosemont Street towards the precinct. Figured he might as well get in some overtime. Besides, it wasn't like there was anything to go home to anyway. Fields ran over some facts of the case in his mind. So the shooter might possibly be driving a black Mercedes Benz with chrome rims. Something fancy like that would be easy to spot in this city. Meant whoever was driving it was a high roller. He'd leave the drug part to the Narcotics Unit. Fields' goal was to catch the killer of that young couple. Put the bastard away that was blackhearted enough to put two bullets into a woman's head at point blank range. Someone that evil didn't need to be on the streets. Someone like that was a potential threat to anyone who looked at him wrong or asked the wrong question. Most importantly, Fields felt it was his duty as an officer of the law to put that animal under the jail. Fields parked in the gated lot reserved for cops across the street from the station. He opened the car door, put foot to ground and made his way through the busy oncoming traffic. He trotted up the steps, walked through the glass doors of the building and immediately noticed the confusion. Saw Ryan at his desk shuffling through some papers until he caught sight of Fields. Noticed Ryan avert his eyes in another direction when Fields saw him. Fields walked over to the area in the back of the building where they shared desk space. Saw Ryan's look of frustration and knew whatever was wrong in the station had something to do with him.

* * *

Round Up

Detective Ryan thought there couldn't have been a worse time for his partner to show up. The truth was, Ryan felt embarrassed. No, he wasn't the one who let the suspect climb out of a bathroom window, but Ryan knew he would feel the heat from Faith for leaving the kid in the hands of a rookie. A mistake Ryan knew Fields would never have made. Honestly, Ryan had always been a little intimidated by Fields. He didn't know why. It was just something that happened ever since they had become partners. From the first day out together, Fields seem to know how to handle the street. Seemed cool with the derelicts and how to handle them. Knew how to talk to them to get any whatever information he was looking for. Like with that drunk a few days ago. Hell, if Ryan had been there alone, he would have probably beaten the crap out of the guy. Especially if Ryan thought he was holding out. Coupled with Fields' damn near mansion size house and picture perfect family, he was the man everybody respected. That rare cop who could balance his personal life and work and still keep his sanity. The only fucked up part was that Fields' wife had stopped sleeping with him, and even then he got a mistress to make up for the lack of intimacy. Yup, the guy had it all together. That cool demeanor, that confidence that he exhibited in doing his work, that's what made Ryan feel like he could never measure up to the kind of man that he felt Fields was and what everybody in the precinct saw him to be. Not that Ryan gave a damn, but still, to get that same level of respect could lift a guy's spirit sometimes. Ryan looked away when Fields approached. Didn't give his partner eye contact until Fields was in Ryan's three feet of personal space.

Fields threw up his hands, asked, "what the hell's going on around here?"

"Fucking suspect escaped from custody."

"How?"

"A rookie took him to our bathroom to take a leak."

"Let me guess, out the window right?"

"How else?"

"Who turned the perp over to a rookie?"

Ryan plopped down in the wooden chair at his desk. "What the hell was I supposed to do? Faith called me into his office for my daily dose of bullshit. My mind was on getting Faith off my ass. Anyway uniforms are out combing the streets for him now."

Fields sat down at his desk. Rummaged through some papers, then leaned back in his chair. "What was he in for anyway?"

"Kidnapping. Possibly some other shit too."

"Like?"

"He didn't come out and say it but I suspect he knew something about the shooting at that club."

"What gives you that idea?"

"He was just about to bargain when Faith called me in."

"Does he know someone that drives a black Benz?"

"Didn't get that far in questioning. Why?"

"Cause it was at the scene. And I figure whoever was driving it is who we're looking for."

"How'd you find that out?"

Fields cleared his throat. "I went back over some of the facts."

Ryan knew that meant Fields had talked to someone they had already spoken to. Figured it was probably the drunk. "Anyway, I sent some uniforms over to the house of the girl he kidnapped. Something tells me he's gonna head straight over there."

"Glad to see you're using some common sense again."

Ryan felt a familiar pang of inadequacy. He didn't like that. "Fuck you."

Fields chuckled. "Let's go over to the girl's house, see if we can find this punk ourselves."

Ryan rose from the chair, glanced at his partner. Walked down the corridor ahead of Fields and out the front door.

* * *

The cabin of the Crown Vic was quiet riding down Penance Avenue. Detective Fields kept his hands at the ten and two o'clock position on the steering wheel. His eyes were staring ahead through the windshield, perusing the scenery of the corner hustlers and dwellers in the streets. Fields glanced over at his partner Ryan. Knew that Ryan's feelings had been hurt with the 'common sense' remark back at the station. Fields hadn't meant to insult his partner's intelligence but Ryan was a veteran cop. He knew better than to make a bonehead mistake like leaving a suspect with a novice. Fields hadn't figured Ryan to be the sensitive type. He seemed impervious to insults from Sargent Faith. And he never said anything when the other cops cracked on his odor. But then again, none of them were close to Ryan like Fields was so Ryan

Round Up

wouldn't give a damn what they thought. Fields knew Ryan respected him, maybe even felt intimidated by him. Fields wasn't sure but he got that vibe sometimes. Like when they would be out on a case, Ryan would wait for Fields to give his input before adding his take on the situation. And during questionings Ryan always let Fields take the lead, like at the Anderson kid's house. Fields took his eyes off the road towards Ryan again, asked, "you okay? You're kind of quiet over there."

"Why wouldn't I be?" Ryan responded. Fields knew then that Ryan was okay. Simply inquiring about Ryan's state of mind was the only form of an apology that Ryan would accept. Nothing emotional or sensitive sounding, like a woman would get.

"Did you get the girl's address?" Fields asked.

Ryan pulled out a folder, flipped through a couple of pages. "Yeah, make a right at this next corner. Keep going until the end of the block." Fields cut a sharp right onto Fitzhugh Avenue. Saw a black Mercedes with chrome rims pass by them and leave out of the mouth of the street, making a left on Penance.

"Son of a bitch! There's the car!" Fields slammed the brakes, hit the flashers and did a U, almost hitting a parked car. The tint on the windows was too dark for him to see who was driving. He made a call for backup, gave the location, and made the same left as the Mercedes. Fields rolled up on the rear of the ride with his lights flashing. The Mercedes didn't slow down or pull over. Two police cars pulled out on the street ahead of the Mercedes. The car slowed to a stop in the middle of the street like a cornered rat. Three other cop cars arrived with flashing lights coming from the side streets on both sides of Penance blocking the black car in. All of the officers got out of the cars with guns drawn at the vehicle. Fields and Ryan did the same. Fields walked around to the uniforms blocking the Mercedes from the front. Saw two uniforms approaching the driver's side from the rear. A crowd had gathered on the sidewalk to watch the scene. An officer was handling crowd control telling everyone to clear the scene. With the exception of a few stragglers, the crowd did as they were ordered. Fields kept his cool. He didn't even know if the person driving the car had anything to do with what happened at the Retro, but it was in his training to be ready. He watched as the two uniforms crept closer to the vehicle. The car lurched forward unexpectedly, like a runner making a false start at a track meet. Fields could see the officers he was standing near were caught off guard. Both fired their Glocks in unison at the car. Fields yelled out not to shoot but not before both officers let off at least three rounds apiece. Fields watched the slugs shatter the windshield and puncture the shiny black hood.

Fields and Ryan gingerly approached the car arriving the same time as the officers coming from the rear. Ryan pointed his .9 millimeter at the tinted driver's side window, barking profane commands for the occupants to come out. After thirty seconds and no response, Ryan opened the door as Fields backed him up. Fields watched as Ryan stepped back from the car, dropping the hand holding the Glock to his side. Fields moved closer to the vehicle. When he looked inside his insides dropped like the first dip on a roller coaster ride. He saw the young girl that he had talked to in Angelo's, sitting in the leather seat with her head turned slightly to the left side. Her eyes were wide open as blood poured from the two bullet holes in her face.

Round Up

CHAPTER THIRTY-THREE

Richard looked out of his bedroom window at the light drops of rain falling from the dark sky. The funeral was over hours ago but Richard was just starting to get control of his grief. Ma was probably over Aunt Shelly's with the rest of the mourners and family, remembering Mark and Richard's childhood, and how close they were. Richard was glad he had left. There was no way he could have been able to withstand the memories the family would have talked about. Things like all the awards they won for the sports they played in school. And how sharp Richard and Mark looked for the senior prom they went to together, pulling up in front of the school in a white limousine. Richard felt his eyes tearing up. He was tired of feeling that weight pulling on his heart, but he knew it would take time and patience to get over Mark.

Richard glanced at the clock on the table next to his bed. Saw that it was a quarter to five. The new year was almost seven hours away yet Richard could've cared less. So what that it was the start of a new millennium. People in this city would still have the same problems. Violence without a solution. No end to the senseless killings that kept most people who lived in poor neighborhoods scared to come out unless they had to. And the violence was mainly attributed to the heavy demand for drugs, which caused serious competition for the corners. There may have been hope and excitement in the New Year for the rich people who lived uptown, but here in downtown Colver things would continue to be like they always were. Hopeless. Richard closed his eyes. Allowed the music of Mozart to penetrate his mind. Piano Concerto Number Two made him feel like he was in a symphony hall sitting directly in front of the orchestra pit. The fantasy ended when a stray gunshot in the streets bought Richard back to Colver City. He looked at Santana asleep on the bed. He had gone home and changed from the dressy clothes that he had worn to the funeral.

Tony Cheatham

When Santana came back a few hours later he was decked out in some baggy blue jeans, a heavy red sweatshirt with Indiana University scrawled across the front and some tan colored construction boots. Santana suggested on the ride home that they go out that night to the New Years celebration that the city held every year, get a couple of freaks to help them deal with the funeral. Richard nodded in agreement but didn't really feel like going. Still, Richard knew he needed to do something to get his mind off of how he was feeling. Maybe a meaningless screw with some chick might do just that. Richard looked at Santana moving around on the bed like he was about to wake up then focused his attention back out of the window. A minute later Santana was stretching and looking around the room like he had forgotten where he was.

"You still listening to that classical shit?" Santana asked.

Richard kept his eyes pinned to the city, answered, "I told you, it relaxes me."

"Violins and shit relaxes you?"

"It put you to sleep didn't it?"

"That's 'cause the shit's so boring."

Richard had enough of listening to Santana berating his taste in music. If it wasn't hip hop, Santana wasn't interested in it. "Whatever."

Santana rose off the bed. Asked, "you still going out tonight right?"

Richard shrugged. "I dunno."

"What you mean you don't know? I already called some freaks to hang out with us!"

"How can you even think about partying when Mark just got put into the ground a few hours ago? Plus I'm still fucked up from the last time we went out."

"Look you ain't gotta worry about nothing happening tonight. Everybody's gonna be too busy having fun to worry about getting into something."

"I just ain't feeling it."

Santana sighed out of frustration. "Believe me, I'm upset but sitting in the house staring at the four fucking walls ain't gonna bring him back! You the one that said this were supposed to be a celebration of Mark going home and shit! It's bad enough we didn't

Round Up

go to your aunt's house after the funeral for the food. I'm not trying to miss out on the biggest party night of the year too! You know many freaks are gonna be downtown tonight?"

"Why don't you go out by yourself?" Richard asked.

"If it was a chance that I could get both of these chicks in bed without you, believe me I would! But the chick I talked to wants me to hook somebody up with her cousin."

"I'll think about it," Richard answered. He was tiring of the conversation. Maybe he'd feel like going out the closer it got to midnight, but right now, his mind wasn't in the partying mood. He clicked off the stereo, pointed and clicked the remote at the television. Saw the five o'clock news flash something about a breaking report across the screen. A female reporter said something about the police shooting a young woman on Penance Avenue. She had been driving a black Mercedes Benz when the police began tailing her. The car stopped at a blockade and as the officers approached the vehicle lunged forward causing the officers to fire at the car, instantly killing the girl. Also said that she had been wanted for questioning in the murder of a couple that happened a week earlier. Richard knew that she was talking about Mark and Monique. She finished by saying that police were not releasing the victim's name because she was a minor.

Santana focused his attention to the television, said, "oh shit," before sitting down on the bed next to Richard. Richard didn't hear what Santana had said. Had he heard her right? A young woman was driving the Benz? Maybe she had borrowed it from her boyfriend or something. Yeah, that had to be it. But if her boyfriend or whoever's car it was knew it was hot, why would he let her drive it? Santana interrupted Richard's thoughts. "I can't believe it."

Richard turned towards Santana. "What?"

"You know who that is?"

"Who?"

"They talking about Geena."

"Geena?"

"Yeah. For the past few days I saw her wheeling a black Benz up and down the street. Probably belonged to one of her new tricks."

Richard calmed his heart that was beating hard like it was about to burst through his chest. "Naw, it can't be her."

"What are you talking about?"

"That same car was there when Mark and Monique were shot."

"Forreal? You think she did it?"

"It don't sound right. Why would that young girl shoot two people like she was a cold-blooded killer? She didn't even have the heart to stand up to that dude that was loud talking her in Angelo's."

"Mark was fucking Geena and still with Monique. He probably filled her head with empty promises of taking care of her or something. Then when he didn't come through she probably got jealous and went after both of them."

"How do you know that?" Richard asked.

"That's the same game all the dudes she's been with ran on her."

Richard thought about it. Even if it was true that Mark was sleeping with that young girl, the female usually got mad with the dude's girlfriend, not him. He wasn't buying Santana's version of what might have happened. "Let's wait and see what they find out," Richard responded.

Santana stood up, doubled over laughing. "You think the cops are gonna look for what really happened? They don't wanna know the real story, only the one they made up to make it sound like they solved the case. Something they can give to the newspapers and tv stations to make the Mayor and Police Chief happy. Face it man, even if she didn't do it, they're gonna say she did."

Richard clicked off the tube in the middle of the reporter recapping of the breaking news, thinking that maybe Santana just might know what he was talking about.

CHAPTER THIRTY-FOUR

Priest hobbled to the nearest corner through the crowds of people hanging out in front of the bars gearing up for the New Years celebrations. He was glad the rain had slowed down to a misty drizzle, especially since he didn't have a jacket. Priest waited under the cover of a newsstand looking for a cab. Caught sight of the afternoon paper on the counter. Headline on the front page mentioned the shooting of a young woman at a club. Priest smiled. He had made the news. He hoped that his boys saw his name, saw that he was important now. But he knew better. They hadn't read anything except the menu at Angelo's since he'd known them. Maybe they would see him on the tv news instead. They watched the tube for hours when they weren't sleeping for messing around.

Priest stepped off the curb, raised his right hand to signal for a taxi or hack, whoever would stop for him. Four cabs drove by before a hack pulled over. Priest stepped into the street almost falling in a puddle of rainwater as he got inside. Pain was shooting up his left leg from the drop out of the window. Landed on his ankle wrong when he hit the ground. Figured it was broken. He'd go to the hospital when the heat died down a little. Priest opened the door to the mud brown Ford Taurus and got in. Priest told the driver where he wanted to go. In a few minutes, he'd be at Geena's house. Figured he would try to talk to her first. Play it cool and find out where her head was at as far as testifying against him. If she already had her mind made up, Priest knew he'd have to do what was in his best interest. Sure, it would be hard. Hell, he still cared about her, especially that tight young pussy she had. But chicks like her came a dime a fucking dozen. And he wasn't about to do time for some young girl who had decided that she didn't want to be with him anymore. The cops took his gun, but he figured he could cop another one easy. Guns were easy to get in this city.

Tony Cheatham

Priest watched the driver make a right on Percel Boulevard before going north on Penance Avenue. He noticed a bunch of cops huddled around a black Benz. The area was sectioned off with that yellow tape that identified a crime scene. It was always a body turning up in this town, Priest thought. Figured somebody got taken out in a deal gone bad or something. That was always the case. People were always trying to get over on each other. If they just did business honestly the way they were supposed to, there wouldn't be so many killings. But people were always trying to get over. Somebody always wanted to be greedy and try to get something for nothing. Nobody liked to be disrespected. So if you were, if someone took you for bad, you had to make that person an example. Show everyone that you weren't to be fucked with. And that's exactly what Priest did to make a name for himself. He'd never forget it.

It was his first day in juvie for a car theft he'd done when he was fourteen. A seventeen-year old kid named Rock kept taking the personal articles out of the care package that Priest's mother sent every week. Shit like toothpaste, soap, and floss. So the next week when mail was delivered Priest waited for Rock to come over to his table. Priest looked at Rock snatch up the box and search through it. Priest waited until Rock's eyes were in the box, then he sliced into Rock's face with a razorblade embedded into a toothbrush. Rock screamed, hollered, and rolled around on the floor with blood gushing from his face. The paramedics took Rock away to the hospital. Gave him sixty stitches. Rock never did say anything about who sliced him, which let Priest know that he had gotten his respect. And most important, everybody in juvie knew who had done it. Nobody bothered Priest after that.

The car was detoured around the scene. Priest looked out the window. Saw the body lying under the sheet on the street. Saw reporters from three different tv stations talking into their microphones, reporting the newest incident of violence going on in the city. When Priest caught sight of Detective Ryan, he ducked down into the seat until they further down the street. Priest sat up, looked out of the rear window, and chuckled. Pictured Ryan's face turning red with anger at the thought of Priest's escaping out of a window. He would have paid anything to see that. Hopefully

Round Up

whatever was happening in the street took away some of the heat of his escape.

Priest saw they were nearing Geena's house on Blanchard Avenue. He told the driver to pull over a block away from the spot just in case the dude went talking to the cops. Gave the driver a ten on what was probably a five-dollar ride. Priest got out, watched the car pull off. He stood on the corner, looked up and down the block. The area was familiar to him. He used to do his business around there. Matter of fact that's where he met Geena. He saw her coming out of her house and decided before the end of the day that he was going to get that ass. He signaled her over, flashed some loot, promised to buy her an outfit if she went out with him to a movie. After that, he took her back to his crib and knocked it out for a whole afternoon. Her pussy was good, better than most of the chicks his own age. Priest decided he wanted to keep her around for awhile, at least until he got tired of her.

Priest felt his dip, remembering that he didn't have anything on him, which was dangerous for someone like him. He made his way through the traffic across Blanchard. Knew a dude over there that dealt in guns. It had been awhile since Priest had been there. He hoped the dude still lived there and remembered him. He bounced up the steps, knocked twice on the door. Priest looked at the pane glass on the left at the top of the door. Noticed the curtain move to the side. A woman opened the door. Her skin was tough looking like a baseball glove and her eyes were red. She cracked the door, looked him up and down, and asked, "what you want?"

"I'm looking for Jay, he here?"

She raised her chin. "Who asking?"

"Priest."

"Hold on." Priest watched her close the door, hearing the locks click into place. She came back after a few minutes, opened the door, said, "come on."

Priest walked into the house, waited for the chick to walk him to where he had to go. She started down the hallway and he followed. She came to room in the back. Saw Jay laid back on a green leather sofa playing a video game on a big screen television. He was wearing a red tee shirt with a pocket on the left side and some matching shorts. The woman plopped down into the matching love seat, and fired up a Newport cigarette. Priest could see that the girl wasn't wearing a bra underneath the blue half shirt that she had on. Could tell by the way her titties jiggled when she moved. Jay kept playing for a few minutes, his concentration heavy on the game. When the sound indicated that Jay was out of lives, he focused on Priest. Jay got off the couch walked over to him. Chin nodded his greetings. "Been awhile. How you been?"

Priest kept his eyes planted to Jay's. "You know how it is."

"What you need?" Jay asked. Priest looked over at the woman in the couch then back at Jay to make sure it was safe to talk around her. Her attentions were focused on a soap opera on the tube. "I hear you. Let's go into another room." Priest followed Jay into the kitchen. Once there, Jay lifted his chin, said, "now what's up?"

"I need a tool."

"What you looking for?"

"Something small with no history on it. Like a .22 or .25."

"Auto?"

"That's cool," Priest responded. Jay went to a door. Opened it and went downstairs. Priest looked around the kitchen. Saw the white microwave over the electric range stove. Noticed the white marble counter and the matching dinette set that went with it. It looked nice. He doubted that the chick in the living room did any real cooking in there though. It looked too clean, like none of the stuff had ever been used. Jay came back upstairs with a black container the size of a lunch box. He sat it on the counter. Opened it gingerly like it was glass. Priest looked inside and saw a silver .25 and a black .22 fit snugly into molded black velvet.

Jay reached into his shirt pocket, took out a pack of Newports. Fired up a smoke from one of the range eyes. He took a deep draw, said, "take your pick."

Priest reached for the .25. Held it. "Is it loaded?" He asked.

Jay responded through squinted eyes from the smoke. "Naw."

Priest dry fired the weapon. He had always liked the .25. It was small and easy to use. A .22 was a kid's toy. Didn't do any real damage. "This one's cool."

Jay closed the box. Locked the latch. "That's clean. Never been used. It's gonna run you two twenty five."

"That's cool. I'm gonna need you to do me one."

"What's that?"

Round Up

"Like I told you, I just got out. You let me take this, I'll give you back three hundred."

Jay looked Priest in the eyes. They never had beef with each other, even when Priest had done business on his block. Priest even did right by Jay by giving him a cut of his take out of respect. "That's cool. After all, a man needs protection out there."

Priest smiled. "Tell me about it."

"So what you been up to since you left the block?"

"Had to get off the corner man. That's small change."

"Moving up gets you bigger risks."

"Gotta take chances to make real cash," Priest said. They slapped hands in agreement.

"Once you moved out some other dude moved in. Goes by the name Santa Claus or something. No, Santana, that's it."

Priest recalled that name from Angelo's. Remembered him as one of the dudes who jumped him. "Yeah? I ain't surprised. It was a good spot."

"Thinks he's big time and shit, driving around town in that Audi. He was even fucking with Geena last I heard."

Priest fingered the gun, thinking of the dude having sex with Geena. The dude was probably running his mouth all over the city about creeping with Priest's girl. Priest couldn't have that. Then everybody would think they could get over on him. Now he had two scores to settle with the dude. First the scrap in Angelo's and now this. Priest was going to find the dude and take care of him before the police put him back on lockdown. "Oh yeah?"

"Yeah. I used to see his ride parked across the street at her house for hours sometimes. With Geena's fast ass, you know she was giving up that young pussy."

Priest tried not to respond even though the comment hurt a little. He still cared about the girl. Knew it was going to be harder to kill her than he had thought. He acted like the news didn't phase him. "Forreal?"

"Yeah. Shame what happened to her."

"What happened?"

Jay walked back towards the living room. Said over his shoulder, "you didn't hear? It's been on the news all day." Priest slid the .25 into his dip, covered it with his shirt, and followed him. Jay grabbed the remote from the girl sitting on the couch. Priest noticed the angry look she gave him. He clicked through the local stations until he found something on the tube. Priest listened to a reporter talking about the police shooting a minor driving a black Benz.

"How do you know it was her? They didn't give any names." Priest said.

"I saw her driving that car all the time. Figured it belonged to one of the hustlers she was messing with. It was her, trust me." Priest felt his insides sink but at the same time there was feeling of relief. The police had done what he wasn't sure he could have. Now Priest had to go pay the dude Santana a visit.

"You know where this cat hangs out at?" Priest asked.

"Naw, I haven't seen him lately. But check downtown tonight at the celebration. He should be down there somewhere flexing his wealth."

Priest was thinking that was exactly where he was going to be.

Round Up

CHAPTER THIRTY-FIVE

Richard moved around his room in slow motion. It was going on a quarter to nine and Richard still didn't feel like going out. Especially downtown as crowded as it was going to be for the celebration. After eating some of his mother's spaghetti and meat sauce and showering, his level of excitement still remained tepid. Even the club music coming from the speakers didn't do anything to jolt Richard's mood. He couldn't believe Geena was dead. Cops lived by the shoot first, ask questions later rule so it wasn't hard to believe the cops had killed her. Still, she didn't deserve to be bought down like some animal. Things had changed so much in the years since Richard had left. People respected each other's territory. Sure, he'd heard about the killings in the other part of the Colver, but where Richard did his hustle, people respected who he was. And that was because he gave respect to the people he dealt with. And nobody had thought to fuck with little girls. Now Colver City was a new town with new rules. Felt like he was a first time visitor rather than somebody who'd lived in the city for almost his entire life. Richard thought briefly about Vanessa. Wished he was out at some fancy restaurant looking at her pretty face while they talked about the interesting things in each other's lives. Getting to know each other a little more, feeling out the common ties of their likes and dislikes. He wondered what she was doing right now.

Santana was looking out of the bedroom window into the alley. He hadn't said anything for a few minutes. Richard figured a hooker was out there doing her business for Santana's attention to be held that long. He thought about Mark screwing Geena and wondered how he could have done it. She was a little girl not to mention that he had Monique who should have been enough to satisfy any man's sex drive. Maybe Santana had it wrong. But Santana had his ear to the streets. Most likely the story was very true. Richard clicked off the irritating music taking Santana out of his trance. Santana turned from the window, said, "I hope you're not putting the classical music back on."

Richard turned the music back on to a lower volume that was barely audible through the speakers, said, "what difference does it make? You're not listening to the radio anyway."

Santana chuckled, said, "I was listening. I was just checking out this freak down here in the alley. Shit, I should come over here instead of watching my tapes. You almost ready?"

"Yeah. Pass me the cologne over there on my dresser," Richard said.

Santana tossed the clear bottle with the brown liquid. "What is that?"

"I dunno. It smells good. That's why I wear it."

"Hurry up, I still gotta get dressed. You're worse than a chick."

Richard pulled on his jacket, readying to leave. He looked over at Santana who was still standing by the window, said, "tell me something."

"What's up?"

"What are you gonna do about that dude who fired off at us at the club?"

Santana looked back out of the window, answered, "what you think I should do?"

"I know what we're supposed to do. It is all about keeping your name clean in the streets ain't it? You can't have somebody trying to kill you without some type of retaliation right?"

"You answered your own question."

"What if he catches you off guard? Finds you before you find him?"

Santana shrugged, answered, "didn't think about that."

"Don't you get tired of this shit?"

"I didn't start it."

"That really make a difference?"

"Does to me."

Richard didn't realize how much of a cycle he had been caught in when he hustled. The you kill one of mine, I kill one of yours mentality. "What if you just let this one go and walked away?"

Santana turned his body towards Richard, looked at him with intensity in his eyes that Richard had never seen before. "You

Round Up

know how it is out here Richie, or should I be calling you Richard now since you acting all brand new and shit. Look, I appreciate you trying to open my eyes to things I haven't seen before, but this is it for me. I'm was born to hustle and die right here in Colver City. I ain't meant to do nothing else."

It hurt Richard to hear Santana so down on himself. His lack of self esteem became clearly evident for the first time in all the years that he had known him. "Why you say that?"

"Look at me, my momma's dead and my Pop raised me. If God had meant for me to be something different, he would have had me born with a silver spoon in my mouth to some white family uptown. But no, I'm a mixed breed half nigger half spic who don't know nothing else but how to hustle to survive. I got my cards, now I'm gonna play them. I'm not mad, I just gotta do what I gotta do to stay alive and be happy. And hustling makes me happy," Santana said. Richard thought he saw a tear come to Santana's left eye but he turned around to the window before the drop could fall. Richard knew that was all bullshit. Santana wanted a regular life just like everybody else did. He, Mark, and Richard used to daydream when they were little about what they were going to have when they grew up. Santana didn't dream of a mansion and cars like Richard and Mark. Santana's dream was simple and always the same. All he wanted was a house big enough to keep a wife and two kids happy and enough money to spoil them all for the rest of their lives. Richard didn't know when or where Santana's simple dreams had changed, but he definitely wasn't the same person as before Richard left for Baltimore. Richard clicked the remote, turned the radio off. Santana turned back around, and said, "so I guess you're ready to go." Richard nodded, said, "I ain't playing. No bullshit out there."

"Swear on my grandmother's grave," said Santana. He smiled like a mischievous kid. Richard walked out of his bedroom door. Santana followed.

CHAPTER THIRTY-SIX

Detective Fields sat in the Crown Vic waiting for his partner Detective Ryan to finish talking to the uniforms around the shooting scene. The sun had set a half-hour before at five-fifteen. The street was illuminated by streetlights and car beams. Fields had watched the ambulance take the girl to the hospital knowing the media was going to have a field day reporting on this one every five minutes. How were they going to justify shooting a teenage girl? Even if they had a justifiable reason, being the car jumping like it did, the public would still hate them. A riot could possibly start from this one. But what was she doing behind the wheel of that Benz in the first place? The same car that witnesses said they saw at the scene of the shootings. Fields knew a boyfriend had let her drive the car. He bet that when he ran the tags and registration, they would come back to somebody who had been paid to sign the paperwork and disappear. Fields would run the tags anyway because it was what he was supposed to do as part of an investigation but he wasn't hopeful that it would get him any leads.

Fields watched Ryan shake hands with a couple of uniforms before he made his way over to the car. Ryan opened the door and slid into the passenger seat. It wasn't long before his smell filled up the cabin. Fields cracked his window a few inches for some fresh air. Ryan began shaking his head, said, "we're fucked."

Fields looked at Ryan. "Why? We didn't pull the trigger."

"I meant cops as a whole. You are still a cop right?"

Fields ignored the question. "This'll die down after a few days. The next killing will take this out of the spotlight. What we need to worry about is Faith."

Ryan chuckled. Dug into his jacket pocket, pulled out a pack of Malboro's. He noticed Fields glaring at him and put them away.

Round Up

"He's always on my ass anyway. What difference will one more thing make?"

"Cause now my ass is in it with you. As senior officers we should have taken control of the situation. We might as well had pulled the trigger ourselves."

"I ain't taking the heat for some inept cops who don't have any control. I tell you with all these new cops they got out here on the street, I'm not surprised this happened. Most of them can't even control their dicks. How are they supposed to handle a gun?" Ryan asked.

Fields mentally agreed but didn't want to get into any further discussion about something he couldn't change. He keyed the ignition, heard the roar of the engine. "Well that's something for the department to deal with. All I know is that now we don't even have the girl to talk to see how this connects to the Anderson case."

Ryan looked across the car at Fields. "Where we going?"

"Over to Ross Boulevard."

"Ross? That's not in our district."

"I know that. When we get there I want you to do two simple things."

"What?"

"Keep your mouth shut and sit in the car." A half-hour later Fields pulled the undercover ride over to the curb by the coffee shop. Looked across the street for the man with the brown bag. When Field didn't see him, he sat back in the driver's seat wondering what his next move was going to be. He hoped talking to the witness once more would get him some new information.

After a few minutes, Ryan said, "You can sit here if you want to. I'm going over to the coffee shop." Ryan got out of the car, jogged across the street to the diner where Fields had cappuccino and the stale pastry. Fields knew Faith was going to want to talk with him and Ryan once they got back to the station, something he wasn't looking forward to. Images of the dead girl with the two holes in her head kept flashing into Fields' head. Made him think of his own daughter and how selfish it was for Charlene to have taken her and his son out of his life without at least trying to talk about it. Wondered how she was going to raise them by herself without him. Fields knew she was going to get in touch with him sooner or later. Charlene needed him and what his money could provide. Fields had seen too many kids without the strong presence of a father around to make sure they stayed on the right track. The kids didn't respect him, that was clear, but if they had ever stepped out of line like talking back to an adult or stealing, he'd be on their asses so fast they would ever think about doing it again. They were Charlene's babies but Fields was their father and he was damn sure going to act like one. There was no way in hell that he was going to see his little girl hanging around with some loser whose only ambition was to get some respect in the streets. And his son wasn't going to end up in juvie before graduating to the pen. No, those were not in the plans for his kids. If only his wife would call him! They didn't have to talk about them getting back together, but at least she should consider their children's welfare.

Fields reached for the cell inside his jacket. Dialed his voicemail to see if anyone—particularly Charlene—had left any messages. Fields entered his code at the woman's prompting. Listened as the automated voice said there was one new message. He felt his heart thumping like he was running in a marathon at the hope that it was his wife. Fields hit the button to get the message. Found it was from some telemarketing service peddling a free carpet cleaning. He erased the message. Felt his heart rate going back to normal as Ryan opened the door of the car and slid into the passenger seat.

Ryan sipped on the steaming cup of coffee and shook his head. "Damn shame what this city has turned into. I remember when I first started walking the beat here, everybody knew everybody. Reported anything that was suspicious without hesitation. Now everybody wants to mind their own business, scared that somebody is gonna come get them if they talk."

Fields looked across the car, said, "what are you babbling about?"

"A man was killed, was shot right over there. Said somebody rolled right up on the guy, plugged him with five shots," said Ryan, pointing at the spot where Fields had talked to the man with the brown bag. "Nobody called in anything for hours, meanwhile the poor guy is bleeding his guts out in the street. By the time some kid flags down a cop, and an ambulance comes out, the guy is D.O.A."

Round Up

Fields knew who Ryan was talking about. That's why the guy wasn't over there now. "Who told you about this?"

Ryan took a sip from the cup, nodded his head towards the diner. "Those guys in there did."

"They see who did it?"

"I asked them that too. Said they didn't see anybody. I looked into their eyes though. They know something, they just don't wanna say what it is."

Fields felt his chest filling with frustration like a balloon expanding with air. "Fuck it," he said. He floored the gas pedal of the Crown Vic to the floor, screeching off into traffic.

"What the hell's wrong with you?" Ryan asked. He was steadying the paper cup of coffee in his hands from spilling. Fields didn't answer. His eyes stared straight ahead through the windshield for the next few blocks. He knew the more time that passed the more of a chance that whoever killed those two kids would get away. Just like the rest of the two hundred ninety six people who'd died in the city earlier in the year. And more than half of that number's killer's still hadn't been bought to justice. One more body and Colver would pass the number of bodies for the previous year. This being the eve of the New Year, Fields figured they would beat that number by at least five before the night was over. Fields was starting to understand why Ryan wanted to transfer now. Doing a job like his in an urban city sucked the life out of you. Made you hard and emotionless so that friends and family were disregarded like broken toys. Maybe that's why Charlene and the kids treated him the way they did. Maybe that's why she left him. Figured if he could talk to her, explain to her that he understood what his problem was that maybe she would give him another chance. At least it would show he was making a sincere effort to save his family.

Fields approached the intersection of Jackson Avenue and Francis Street, made a sharp left on Jackson. The streets were beginning to fill with people looking for a good time going into the New Year. Continued north for a couple of miles and did a double take when he passed a kid on the corner wearing a red ski hat, black leather coat, and sagging jeans surrounded by a two others dressed in the same style. The kid looked like any other corner hustler except that when he smiled, Fields noticed the space in his mouth where a tooth should have been. His cop reflexes made him take in the kid's features, flashing through a mental file of recent events that caused the kid to look so familiar. The scene at Angelo's came to Field's mind. When he was trying to talk to that young girl and the short kid and his sidekick with the missing tooth acted like her chaperones. Fields kept driving and rounded the block so that he wouldn't tip the kid off. The car sat on a side street across from where the kid was standing. Field's bet anything that talking to this kid would lead them to the short kid. Ever since Fields saw the short dude in Angelo's he couldn't shake the feeling that somehow he had something to do with the killing of that young couple. Field just had to connect the dots. He looked across the car at Ryan who was still fuming over almost spilling the coffee in his lap then back out of the window.

"I'm gonna talk to the kid over there on the corner," Fields said.

Ryan looked over out of the window on Field's side. "Why? Think he knows something?"

"I'm about to find out." Field opened the door. Stepped onto the asphalt and made his way across the street. The kid with the missing tooth glanced at Fields heading towards him. When their eyes met, the kid broke into a run down the street. Fields started running after him. The accomplices took off in opposite directions. Fields wasn't concerned about them. He wanted that kid. The kid ran south on Jackson and ducked into an alley with Fields right behind him. The kid jumped a wire fence and cut a sharp right onto another street. Fields slowed down, backtracked, ran towards the fence feeling his legs turn to rubber upon impact with the cement. It had been years since he had to run after anybody. He could see the kid about a half block in front of him. Fields could feel the burn in his chest as he kept up the steady pace. The kid rounded the corner on Belvedere Avenue disappearing from Fields line of vision. He started to slow down thinking the kid had gotten away until hearing a woman scream. He forced himself to run the few extra yards feeling disgusted with his age and the way his body had let him down. When Fields got around the corner, he saw a woman on the ground with the contents of her purse scattered on the sidewalk. A husky man wearing a dirty green garbage uniform

Round Up

was holding the kid in an "L" hold. The kid was struggling to get loose but the man held tight with little effort.

The man called out, "Somebody call a cop!"

Fields reached for his badge, said, "Officer right here!"

The woman on the ground was screaming about how the kid had attacked her and tried to take her purse. Ryan came around the corner a moment later with the red and blues flashing in the grill of the Crown Vic. He jumped out of the car, ran towards the kid, threw him against the wall with his hands behind his back.

The kid continued to struggle, yelling, "what I do? What I do?"

"You like running huh? You like making cops chase you?" Ryan yelled. Fields walked over to the lady who was still visibly shaken from the incident. Told her that she could file charges for assault if she wanted. Then walked back towards Ryan and the kid. Fields could see in the kid's face that he was scared. After Ryan frisked him and pulled out a wad of cash—tightly bundled—and a .32, Fields could see why. "We got a gangster Mr. Rockfeller here!" Ryan chuckled before cuffing him. He turned the kid around, did miranda from memory.

The kid continued to yell, "What you taking me in for? What did I do?" Ryan shoved him into the back of the car. Closed the door behind him and got into the passenger seat. Fields got into the driver's seat. The kid was still yelling. "What did I do?"

Ryan mocked him. "What did I do? What did I do? Sounds like a goddamn parrot."

Fields looked up in the rearview at the kid. "Right now, I'm thinking first degree murder."

The kid jerked forward in the seat. Mashed his face against the metal partition that divided the car. "Murder! What the fuck you talking about? I didn't kill nobody!"

"Angelo's a couple days ago. That security guard," Fields said.

"Angelo's? I wasn't in no Angelo's a couple days ago!"

"We'll see what the witnesses say when they see you in a lineup," Ryan said.

"That wasn't me!"

Fields looked up in the rearview again, asked "Then who was it?" The kid leaned back in the seat. Didn't answer the question.

"I'll tell you what. How about if I give you some information on another shooting? What about that? Will that take some of the flack off of me?"

Ryan turned around, looked at the kid. "Depends on what it is."

"That double killing a week ago. Mark Anderson. I know who did it."

Fields pulled over so that he could look into the kid's eyes. See if he was telling the truth. "Who was it?"

"And you'd better not be making this shit up," Ryan added.

"A dude named Santana. He runs the business in the neighborhood."

Fields remembered hearing that name at Richard Anderson's house during the interview. So they're friends, he thought. "How do I know that you're not just telling us this to get the competition off the street?" Fields asked. He felt his insides swelling with anxiousness that this case might get solved.

"Cause I was there."

"Then tell us something that the press doesn't know," Ryan said.

"He snatched the platinum chains after he put bullets in both the chick's eyes," said the kid. Fields noticed the second of hesitation before he answered.

Ryan asked, "You know where he is right now?"

"Not at this second but I'll bet he's gonna be somewhere downtown for the city New Year's celebration tonight."

Ryan looked at Fields. Fields turned around in his seat, looked out the front windshield into the city's darkness. He was smiling.

CHAPTER THIRTY-SEVEN

Richard leaned back in the soft leather seats of Santana's Audi, listening to Santana's favorite rapper, Biggie Smalls, telling stories of hustlers, fancy cars, and chicks. The six block strip downtown between Central Avenue and Philadelphia Boulevard was filled with people waiting to bring in the new year which was in a couple of hours. Traffic was at a standstill. The flashing lights in the street and shiny cars fueled the excitement of the evening. Honestly, Richard would much rather had been home listening to some Mozart in the comfort of his room, reminiscing about the good times that he and Mark had during their childhood days.

At one point in his life, Richard could identify with the street lifestyle that Biggie described in his music. But now, it all seemed trite and phony. Aestheticism and materialism were the forefronts of the life as a dealer. Dudes bedded women who had the biggest titties and the phatest asses. Women went after men who had the fanciest rides and the flashiest jewelry. Just like the two girls in the back seat of the car. Santana had called them at the last minute to come with them. They cancelled whatever plans they had just to come along with him. Being with Santana meant a night of luxury and celebrity status. And they both knew that more than likely Santana was going to want to sleep with them before the night was over. He had already reserved a room at the Marriott when they said they were going to come. Richard wasn't in the mood for whatever freaky things that were going to happen afterwards. He simply wanted to go home and climb into bed. It was all like some sick cycle. Kids like Geena grew up looking at the hustlers and the rappers in videos using them as role models, thinking that the lives they portrayed were real. Richard knew firsthand that it was all a front. But he couldn't convey that message to the kids without sounding like he was trying to preach to them. Richard looked across the car at Santana. He was perfectly comfortable with the fast life of hustling that he lived. Sadly realized that his friend would probably die doing it. Richard thought briefly about R.J. Damn he missed his little girl. He wanted to call and wish her a happy New Year. But Desiree hadn't even called yet to say anything about the fight at the apartment. Richard decided to wait a few more days before he would try to make any contact. She was probably still cooling off.

Richard looked across the car at Santana. The blue Kentucky Wildcats skull hat that he was wearing was pulled down over his head and perfectly complimented the white and blue velour sweatsuit he had bought on his last shopping excursion. The gleaming silver metal watch on his left wrist hung loosely and jingled whenever he lifted his hand. They sat under a brightly lit streetlight waiting for traffic to move. Richard noticed for the first time that Santana had an extra hole for an earring under the diamond stud in his right earlobe. Richard wondered what happened to the earring in that ear. Knew Santana would have an ice stud for every hole in his body if he could.

Santana's deep voice mouthing the lyrics to the song pulled Richard from his thoughts. Santana had enough energy for the both of them. He was waving his fist and yelling out of his open window every few minutes at different people that he knew.

"Ain't you glad you came with me tonight?" Santana asked over the loud music. The girls screamed happily in unison from the back of the car. The car sat still in traffic as onlookers maneuvered through the streets. Several people kept coming up to the car, slapping hands with Santana. A few looked over at Richard, chin nodded their greetings, and disappeared back into the crowd. Richard knew that he was yesterday's news, a name from the past. Nobody knew who Richie Rich was anymore. But it wasn't like the honor was something Richard wanted to be remembered for anyway. Richard continued watching people come up to the car for another few minutes. Then a dude staggered towards the car. Richard could see he was drunk. The dude clumsily reached his hand into the car to shake Santana's hand.

The dude spoke with slurred words. "Come out to party yo?"
Santana slapped his hand away from touching him. "Yeah."
"Why you ain't return my calls?"
"I been busy."

Round Up

The dude chuckled, looked the car over and reached his hand into the Audi again. "Why you driving this piece of shit? Where's your black Benz at? I haven't seen you driving it around the way in awhile." Richard leaned forward hoping he hadn't heard what he thought he had heard. His insides lit up like a Christmas tree. Santana had a black Mercedes? Where had he kept it? Santana immediately got angry like someone had turned a switch on in his head. He threw open the door of the car, started throwing a barrage of punches at the dude. The girls in the back started screaming. The dude fell to the ground begging Santana to stop hitting him. Santana started kicking the dude once he hit the asphalt. Richard got out of the car, pulled Santana back in as a crowd gathered around the scene. Santana turned down an alley off of the street to avoid getting stuck in traffic. The girls were still screaming until Santana told them to shut up. The car entered Allen Street and stopped. There weren't as many people and nearly no traffic since all the action was taking place on the main strip.

Richard looked across the car, turned down the music, listening to the girls in the back breathing heavily and whimpering.

"I wanna go home," one of them yelled.

Santana looked at them through the rearview, yelled, "Ain't nobody going nowhere!"

"What the fuck was all that about?" Richard asked.

"Punk owed me some money. He's been ducking me for the past few months," answered Santana. Richard knew the story was a lie. If the cat owed Santana money, why would he make his presence known by coming up to the car and speaking? No, Santana was trying to shut him up. Didn't want him saying anything else about the black Mercedes. Richard knew at this point that Santana had something to do with what happened to Mark and Monique. Richard wasn't going to say anything just yet. Knew Santana was still carrying his gun. Didn't want Santana to know that he knew. And if Santana was crazy enough to kill Mark—when they were as close as brothers—he could kill Richard just as easy. Richard felt the familiar pounding in his head coming back again. Knew it was from the tension and pressure of the moment. If Santana did indeed have anything to do with what happened to Mark, Richard was going to kill him. A sharp stabbing pain caused Richard to rub his temples. The pain was worse than he had felt in a long time. And he didn't have his pills. Richard held in the pain, maintaining his composure.

The cabin of the car was quiet until Richard broke the silence. "So we going back to the strip or what?" Santana gassed the pedal, drove around the block until they were at the end of the slow moving line of cars. Richard pulled down the visor to look in the mirror. Noticed the girls in the back were clinging to each other, like two scared little children. He pushed the mirror back up, looked across the car at Santana. Could see that his mood was serious as he stared straight ahead out of the front window. Richard looked behind them. Noticed a car with its high beams on following them out of the alley.

* * *

Priest crept along behind a car in front of him down the strip. He glanced at his watch. Saw that it was a couple minutes after ten. Another couple of hours and it was going to be 2000. People were all excited about a new Millennium and shit. Changes in years and centuries didn't make Priest a bit of damn difference though. Why would he worry about the future when his existence was in jeopardy on a daily basis? Any day that he stepped outside could very well be his last. New Year's was just another day for him. Priest was happy to have a car though. For another hundred, in addition to the three for the .25, Jay hooked him up with a connection to get an unmarked car, a midnight blue '82 Dodge Shadow. It wasn't the luxury of his Maxima but it served its purpose of getting him around. Only problem with it was that the right headlight didn't work. He had to keep the high beams on to keep both lights working. Otherwise the car was perfect since nobody would give a second look at the piece of shit. It would allow Priest to get inside the crowd without any attention, hopefully finding that punk Santana. Then once he saw him, Priest was going to put a cap in his ass; two shots, one to the chest and the other to the head. Priest wasn't doing it because he killed Geena. No, he was doing it because Santana disrespected him by fucking Geena when she was Priest's girl. Now the punk was probably running around the streets acting like he had gotten away with something. There was no way Priest could let anything like that mess up his street reputation. Yeah, Priest knew he was going to do some time once the cops caught up with him, but not before

Round Up

he set things right. He pressed on the horn out of frustration of the slow moving traffic. They were barely going five miles per hour. A crowd gathering on a side street caught Priest's attention. He looked out of the window, saw a dude wailing on some cat on the ground. Then he saw another guy pull the guy who was fighting back into the car before they pulled off. His insides jumped at seeing them get into a cream colored Audi. Priest tapped on the gas when he saw the car cut across traffic into an alley. Knew it was that Santana punk he was looking for. He followed the car, seeing it stop for a moment before going back around the block over to Allen Street. He made a sharp right and followed behind him. Turned up the radio blasting LL Cool J's I'm Bad from the speakers. Pulled the .25 in his dip and sped up beside the Audi.

* * *

Detective Fields approached Allen Street to avoid the strip. Made the turn up an alley towards the traffic jam. The same thing happened every year, usually with minimal altercations. Yeah, there were the usual drunks and nuisances but nothing really serious. Fields remembered the loneliness he felt from the year before. He requested off of work to be with his wife and the kids. Charlene apparently had other plans. Said that she thought he had to work so she made a date with some girlfriends and was going to take the kids to her mother's. When he had told her that he was off, she refused to change her plans. So he sat in alone in the house watching the downtown festivities on television. Even Ryan was spending time with somebody. Granted she was nothing more than one of his "arrangements" but at least Ryan wasn't alone. Fields wondered briefly if the kids were over at his mother-in-law's again and if Charlene was out with anyone. Ryan caught his attention with his usual complaints about the city.

"All this for a goddamn New Year. People should be home in bed this time of night," Ryan said.

"Sure would make our jobs easier if they were," added Fields. He leaned closer to look out of the windshield, pointed towards a crowd that was gathering in the street. "Looks like a problem."

Ryan sucked his teeth, said, "Let the uniforms handle it."

Tony Cheatham

Fields kept looking at the scene, saw a familiar face. "Isn't that Anderson right there?" He pointed towards the scene. Richard Anderson was pulling some guy into an Audi. Then they sped off down an alley towards Allen Street.

"Damn we should've stayed back there," Fields said.

"I'll bet that's his buddy Santana," Ryan said. He put the blue light on the dash, hit the red and blues in the grill. "Cut through the goddamn traffic!"

* * *

Richard saw a beat up blue Dodge pull up beside them on his side. He immediately saw the short dude from Angelo's pointing a gun at them through his open window with a scowl on his face. Santana looked across and saw the dude too.

"Drive!" Richard yelled to Santana. The car jerked forward with the tires screeching in the street. The girls started screaming again.

Santana yelled to the back, "I said shut the hell up!" The red and blue lights from a knocker car came towards them from across the street. Santana hit the gas pedal, made a sharp left, and drove up on the sidewalk causing people to jump out of the way to avoid getting hit. Two shots shattered the glass in the back of the car. Made one of the girls cry uncontrollably, sobbing repeatedly that she wanted to go home. The blue Dodge followed them onto the sidewalk still firing shots at the Audi. Richard ducked low into the seat. Mouthed a silent prayer that he didn't get hit. "Who is that?" Santana asked the car. He turned to look intermittently out of the back window and the front while still trying to maneuver on the sidewalk.

Richard saw that they were past the traffic. Yelled, "get back into the street!"

"Can't do that, the cops are over there! I'm gonna turn down this next block!" Santana yelled. He made a sharp turn down a dark alley. Lost control of the car and crashed into a parked Honda Accord. Richard jerked forward into the dash feeling a gash opening on his forehead upon impact. Felt the girl sitting behind him bumping into the back of his seat. The car was silent for a moment until the rattling of the Dodge could be heard coming down the street. Santana shook his head, opened the car door and ran north down the sidewalk. Richard cleared his head and did the same except he ran in the other direction. He jumped two metal fences and hid in the backyard of a dark rowhouse.

* * *

Priest pulled beside the Audi. Saw the pretty boy who'd been fucking Geena. Priest retrieved the .25 from his dip, pointed the nose at the car ready to pull the trigger. The other dude saw him before he could get off a shot. The Audi sped off turning onto the sidewalk. Priest didn't care where the punk went; he was going to follow. Priest turned the steering wheel sharply, hit the gas pedal, and drove on the sidewalk behind the Audi. Saw that they were right in front of him. He cocked the .25 automatic, let off a round from the clip, saw the back window of the Audi shatter from the slug. Watched the crowd scatter in confusion and fear. Priest smiled, hoping he hit the punk. He looked to his right, saw the red and blue lights of an undercover car joining in the chase. Priest saw the unmistakable face of Detective Ryan in the passenger seat. Then he noticed the Audi turn down a dark street. Priest rounded the block knowing that they would come out on the other side. He'd be there to meet them when they did.

* * *

Detective Fields slammed on the brakes to avoid hitting the car full of teens in front of him. He'd heard a shot fired into the night air. Saw the crowd react in confusion to the danger. Caught sight of the blue Dodge chasing the Audi down a side street. He alternated between hitting the horn and screaming out of the window to the crowd to move out of the way. But the traffic blocked the cops from getting to where the Audi was. Calling backup wouldn't have helped either. Simply would have made the situation even more confusing than it was once the uniforms and patrol cars hit the scene. Ryan hit the dashboard with his fist out of frustration. "Goddammit!" Ryan yelled. "They got away!"

CHAPTER THIRTY-EIGHT

Richard sat still on the cold cement of the backyard feeling the chilly air beginning to penetrate his jacket. Dogs barked at each other from other yards around him. Sounded like somebody was giving a New Years party in one of the houses along the row. Could hear music and lots of laughing in the air. His head was throbbing. The pain made him double over to relieve the stress in his temples. Sometimes that helped. He rubbed his face, stood up and left the yard. Walked at a staggering pace up the street, oblivious to the crowds of people around him. Thoughts of Santana dying at the hands of Mark filled Richard's head like a clogged drain. Caused a pang to his head. Richard doubled over, continued to move. Walked a half block to a bus stop where he plopped down on a bench. Richard looked around. Saw stragglers heading south towards the excitement over on Allen. Richard looked up the block, saw the headlights making their way down the street. The high beams blinded him. Made him shield his eyes with his right arm. Richard rose off of the bench to run but the worsening pain slowed his steps. The car pulled up to the curb next to him. Heard Santana's voice coming from the car.

"You okay Richie?"

Richard turned around. Looked up the street like he was waiting for a hack. "I'm cool. Where'd you get the car? I thought you crashed the Audi."

"You look bad man, you should let me take you to Colver General."

"I just need to lay down that's all. I'm gonna catch a hack back my mother's house."

"I'll take you."

"Naw that's cool." Richard said. He watched Santana cut the ignition, get out of the car and walk over to where he was standing.

Round Up

Santana sat down on the bench. Shoved both hands into his jacket pocket. He looked at Richard, said, "You know don't you?"

Richard played dumb. "Know what?"

"I killed Mark and his girl."

"How you figure I know?"

"See it in your eyes. Look like you want to beat me down, but you're being cautious."

"I'm always cautious."

Santana stood up, said, "Get in the car."

"For what?"

"Cause I said so," Santana responded. He pulled a .32 out of his pocket, pointed it at Richard.

Richard felt a stabbing pain in his head. But that was the least of his problems. Richard knew Santana wasn't going to pull the trigger. Would have been too hard to make a clean escape with the crowds so close by. "I ain't getting in that car. If you're gonna do it, you're gonna have to do it right here."

Santana raised the gun, aiming it at Richard's head. "Don't make me do that Rich."

Richard looked past the nose of the .32 directly at Santana. "Just tell me…why'd you do it?"

Santana lowered the gun, raised it again, and let his arm drop to his side, like he wanted to talk. To clear his head of all the secrets that he'd kept. "Things wasn't the same after you left. We weren't tight like before. Mark got real distant, started acting like he didn't know me. Then he got into a new hustle, that promotion thing. I was jealous. I'm man enough admit that. He had the money, got it honestly too. Got out the game, then started looking down on me, the same way you did when you got back just cause he didn't have to hustle anymore. Like he was better than me or something. I didn't worry about it though. I was still making loot; that's all that mattered. I just kept doing my thing, minding my business. Pretty soon, we would see each other around the way and wouldn't even speak. I was like fuck it. Then I started messing with this young chick…"

"Geena?" Richard interrupted.

"Yeah. The funny thing is that I was really liking her. Then I found out that Mark was fucking with her too. She told me he was saying things about me."

"You believed some hearsay from a chick?"

Santana looked at Richard as a siren passed by on the street over from where they were standing. Richard thought Santana would leave, but he didn't. He started talking again. "She wasn't the only one telling me that. Plus it sounded like the kinds of things Mark would say."

"Like what?"

"Like that I was a low life street hustler, a corner boy, shit like that. So I had her set him up. Told her to tell him that this singer wanted to talk to him about doing a show. Mark believed it like I knew he would. I sent Geena there to meet him, she called me on the cell, then I rolled up and blasted him."

Hearing the words caused a shooting pain to go through Richard's head, more painful than all of the other times put together. "So why Monique?"

"Her? I didn't know he was going to bring her. But I was glad that he did. See, after Mark pushed up on my girl, I made a move on her. It was easy, especially since they were having problems."

"You're foul Santana," Richard said. He remembered what Janell had said about Monique meeting some dude with a chromed out black Benz. Thought it made sense now.

"Wasn't no more foul than him fucking Geena now was it? Besides, it wasn't no big thing. We fucked a few times but she wouldn't leave that punk. Even after I told her that I could take better care of her than he could. She just kept saying that she was paying him back for fucking around on her. Made up my mind right then that she was a throwaway. Seemed like I could never win when it came to Mark. Anyway bringing Monique just made it better for me. I plugged her first while he watched. You should've seen him crying when I put a bullet into her eyes. Made him cry like a bitch. Then it all started coming apart."

"What you talking about?"

"Geena? I found out she was fucking with that dude we were fighting in Angelo's a few days back. Then the cops picked her up. It was just a matter of time before she talked. And besides that, I left my diamond stud somewhere around there when I clipped them. The cops would've got me sooner or later."

"So getting rid of Geena was the last part?"

Round Up

"Damn right. I knew the cops were looking for the Mercedes and Colver cops always shoot first and asked questions later, so I sent her out on an errand in my ride in the middle of all that heat. Then the cops got rid of her for me."

Richard shook his head thinking how this whole thing sounded like it was from some television show. "You're crazy."

Santana raised the .32 at his head again. "I gotta take you out Rich. It ain't personal man, but you know too much now. Just a matter of time before they flip you or you turn me in."

Richard ignored the pain in his head that was spreading to his neck. "You ain't gotta do this Santana. I'm going back to Baltimore tomorrow. I won't say nothing."

"Can't take that chance Richie. You know how the business works. No witnesses or have you forgotten that too?"

"Somebody's gonna hear the gun Santana."

Santana looked at his watch. "It's a couple minutes to midnight. I'll do it when everybody else starts popping shots in the air to celebrate the New Year."

Richard thought about his mother having to experience the loss of another family member. But this time it would be her only son. Thought about how his name was going to end up in the Metro section of the Colver Star, the city's newspaper. "You really gonna do this?"

"I have to Rich."

Richard heard some pre celebration shots in the background. Knew his time was almost up. Santana looked at his watch, then looked in the direction of a rattling car making its way down the street. Richard ducked under a car when Santana used his free hand to shade his eyes from the blinding highbeams. Santana turned back around, shot two from the chamber in Richard's direction. Richard heard the slugs penetrate the car door. Heard Santana cursing. Then Richard heard two more blasts from what sounded like across the street before Santana returned fire. Three more shots from across the street before Richard heard a thump against the car, and the rattling noise getting fainter as it moved further down the block and out of earshot. Midnight was signaled by a barrage of gunshots into the air around the city. Richard moved from under the car after a few moments. Stood up and saw Santana struggling to breathe. He was lying in a pool of blood on the ground and his chest was heaving in and out. Sure, Richard knew he could have called somebody. Instead he started running down the block.

CHAPTER THIRTY-NINE

Priest mashed pedal of the Dodge making the rattling sound in the engine louder. He drove north, made a right on Arlington Avenue, and continued a few blocks. Priest watched the people popping champagne and hugging and kissing in the street, happy that the New Year had come. The millennium was five minutes old, and Priest had already contributed the first body to the city's murder rate. He was smiling, happy that he had accomplished what he had set out to do. Priest stayed long enough to watch the punk that he'd shot fall against the car to the ground. His heart beat hard and fast like a drummer at a rock concert when he pulled the trigger. Felt like he'd hit the goddamn lottery when the dude dropped.

Priest made a left on Rancher Boulevard and drove south towards 95. Figured he'd head to Virginia. Maybe hide out in one of the small towns near the North Carolina line for a few months. Priest looked up in his rear view when red and blue lights flashed behind him. Dammit, he thought. Knew that had to be Ryan and his partner. They weren't going to take him back alive though. He mashed on the pedal, saw four cars with flashing lights blocking the street in front of him. Looked in the rearview and saw two more cop cars in addition to the undercover. Priest turned the steering wheel sharply to the left, mashed on the brakes, feeling the car's momentum make him swerve to the side. He braced himself, felt his body being thrown against the car door as the vehicle smashed into the cop car in front of him. The glass exploded from the door in what felt like slow motion. Priest felt pieces cutting into his face until a sharp pain in his chest caused him to look down. A long steel bar was poking through his chest. Noticed it tore a big hole in his Baltimore Ravens Jersey. He struggled to take short breaths. Darkness faded in and out like the flickering lights in a club. Felt like he was leaving his body in some weird kind of

Tony Cheatham

way. Before he blacked out, saw cops approaching the car cautiously with their guns drawn on him. It was funny, Priest thought, even though he was lying there dying with a pole stuck through his gut, they still thought he was dangerous.

Round Up

CHAPTER FORTY

Detective Fields watched Colver City's fire department use the jaws of life to free that kid Priest from the wreckage. The kid was dead; Fields knew that. There was no way that he could've survived that crash. Why the hell didn't the kid just stop? And on top of everything else, another body turned a few miles away from the crime scene. Figured this tally of bodies in the first few moments of 2000 would put the city on a fast track to surpassing the number of killings for the previous year. Ballistics hadn't come back yet on the bullets but Fields bet anything that the gun that was found on the ground near the crash matched the one they would find in the body of that friend of the Anderson kid, Santana, yeah that was it. Fields began piecing together the pieces of what probably happened after that girl was killed joyriding in the Mercedes Benz. The car wasn't hers; there was no doubt about that. Most likely it belonged to one of her hustler boyfriends. And as soon as he got back to the station, Fields placed another bet with himself that the prints wouldn't match the kid in this crash. That fancy car was too high end for this nickel and dime hustler. No, it had to belong to somebody who was making lots of money but had to keep the amount that was spent to a controlled level. Buying things that had prestige but wasn't showy.

The final piece of the puzzle came when Fields noticed the broken piece of silver five on the floor of the kid named Santana's Audi. The same piece that the only witness who could tie it all together was rolling between his fingers had before somebody put a slug in him. Santana must have taken it from the guy after killing him as some kind of homage to himself and what he had done. The question now was where was the Anderson kid? Fields was taken from his thoughts when Ryan came over to where he was standing.

"Hell of a way to start off the New Year ain't it?" Ryan yelled. A twisted grin was embedded in his face like the ones in the stone gargoyles at the library downtown.

Fields ignored the comment. "We have to go see the Anderson kid. I'll bet talking to him will tie all of this nonsense together."

Ryan continued his evil smile. "You figured it out huh? The body down the block is that friend of Anderson's."

"Yeah. All this happened to cover up that very first incident with Anderson's cousin and his girlfriend. I don't need to talk to Anderson to know what happened. I just want him to confirm it. I'd feel better that way."

Ryan shrugged. "Doesn't make me a nevermind. I just want to get this over with."

Fields looked directly into his partner's eyes. Noticed the dead and indifferent tone in Ryan's voice. "And what does that mean?"

"I've had it. This is my last case in this hellhole. Got a call from a buddy in York yesterday. All I gotta do is put in the paperwork and I'm there."

Fields hesitated before speaking. Ryan had his problems but he was a good partner. "So you're gonna make the move huh?"

"Have to. This place is making me sick."

"Don't have to explain to me. I work here too remember?" Fields responded. He grabbed Ryan by the shoulders. Ignored the smell and guided him towards the undercover. "Think the Anderson kid is home?"

Ryan opened the passenger side and slid into the car. "Only one way to find out."

* * *

Fields and Ryan sat across from Richard Anderson's house waiting for him to come home. Fields had knocked on the door a half-hour earlier knowing the disruption would upset Richard's mother. She cautiously opened the door, surprised to see the detectives standing there. She immediately broke down. Fields asked if she knew the whereabouts of her son without giving an explanation of why he wanted to see him. After she closed the door, Fields suggested they wait across the street for Richard to come home. It was three hours into the New Year. Fields figured the Anderson kid would be coming home sooner or later. He had that kind of relationship with his mother that

Round Up

he wouldn't want to worry her by staying out all night. An hour later, Fields noticed Richard Anderson trotting down the block. Fields shook Ryan awake. They both stepped out of the car, walked across the street. Richard stopped in his tracks when he saw the men coming towards him.

"Richard, I need to talk to you for a sec," Fields said.

"About what?"

"Your friend? Santana? You know he was found shot to death near his car a few hours ago?"

Richard shrugged his shoulders. "Didn't know that. Know who did it?"

"We got leads."

"Just like my cousin right?"

Ryan jumped into Richard's face. Fields pulled him back a few feet. "You don't seem too upset that your best friend was whacked smart ass. Why not?"

"You learn to deal with loss living here. I got no more tears to cry for everybody that I lose that's close to me."

Fields looked at the young man. Knew the look from years of experience in dealing with criminals. The Anderson kid knew Santana was dead. But Fields wouldn't push it. Didn't want to give Ryan any ammunition to blow up about the incident. Besides, the prime suspect was dead now, on his way to the city morgue. Sure, Sargent Faith would want the lose ends tied up for the media and the Mayor and would probably try to force some kind of crazy theory for why those two kids were killed, but as far as Fields was concerned, the case was closed. He turned around to walk back towards the car. "Stick around in case we need to get in touch with you. We may need you to answer some questions later."

"Well you'll have to call me in Baltimore, cause I'm going back home tonight," Fields answered. Richard made his way up the steps of the house.

Fields stopped in the middle of the street, turned around towards Richard, and said, "Then call my office and leave your number before you leave."

"No problem," Richard responded. Fields crossed the street, got into the car. Noticed Ryan's face was full of questions when he opened the door.

"So that's it? You aren't gonna grill him about his friend?"

Ryan watched the Anderson kid go into the house before pulling off. "For what? No need to keep the kid here with a bunch of red tape. Sure, he might know something but so what? If he didn't pull the trigger—which I'm sure he didn't—there's no need to have him involved."

"How are you so sure about that?"

"This whole thing was about jealousy. Somebody had something that somebody else didn't. Somebody killed because of it, and this crazy kind of street justice corrected things."

"So that's it?"

"What are you so worried about it for? You're leaving this place. I still have to be here. That's how things work in this city. You could never figure it out."

"I guess you're right. These are your people. You deal with the headache."

Fields looked across the car at his partner Ryan, his eyes questioning his last statement. "Meaning?"

"I didn't mean it like that. Stop being so fucking uptight."

"Have to be. It's the only way to deal with you," Fields responded. He glanced at his partner then looked away taking in Ryan's image for what was now a limited time. When he thought about Ryan leaving, Fields knew he would miss him. Smelly ass and all.

* * *

Fields walked into his house after shift was over. The sun gleaming in the sky was uplifting after the events of the past few hours. He half expected to hear cartoons coming from the television in the living room and the smell of eggs and sausages in the air. He looked at the caller ID, saw Charlene hadn't called. Knew that he wouldn't hear from her for another couple of days at least. She wasn't cold hearted enough to simply run away with his kids and never let him see them again. Knew more than likely that she and the kids were with her mother. But he wouldn't call there. He'd give her the space that she needed. She stayed away because she wanted him to suffer. The same way that she suffered in feeling like she was alone in their marriage. And he was pretty sure that Charlene knew about his affair with Monica. That's why she was so cold towards him both emotionally and physically. Thought briefly about calling Monica to talk and maybe meet up then

Round Up

decided against it. He liked her but he wasn't in love with her, and right now he wanted to talk to the woman he was in love with.

Fields went into the bathroom, let loose some of the liquid waste that he'd been holding for a couple of hours. When the phone rang, he stopped pissing in mid stream and ran to the kitchen, looked at the caller ID. It read "PRIVATE CALLER". He answered the horn anyway. There was a pause before a woman spoke.

"Hey," she said. His heart jumped with excitement when he heard Charlene's voice. Knew she had blocked out her phone number from where she was.

Fields calmed his anxiousness, responded with a monotone, "hey."

"Ron, first let me say I'm sorry for leaving like I did and taking so long to call you."

"That's okay. Least I know you're alright now."

"Yeah, I'm good."

"And the kids?"

"They're good. They miss you."

Fields couldn't believe his ears. Those two ungrateful monsters of his had thought about him? "I miss them too. So when are you coming back?"

"I'm not. At least not right now."

"Charlene you can't just disrupt my life like this. You and the kids are the only thing keeping me straight with my crazy job."

"Well that's not my problem."

Fields couldn't hold back his anger any longer. The lackadaisical tone in her voice like she couldn't give a damn mixed with everything else he had been through in the last couple of days in the streets had made him mad. Made his insides heated with frustration in the fact that he couldn't manage any aspect of his own life. He had allowed Charlene to have control long enough. "Oh it's your goddamn problem alright, because if I don't get the kids back you can expect to be fighting me in court!" Fields was surprised when she started laughing, but not in the way as if she had heard a joke. "What the hell you laughing at?"

Charlene spoke in between chuckles. "You think a judge is going to give the kids to a cop with an irregular schedule who cheats on his wife?"

"What?"

"That right. I know about your little girlfriend."

Fields should have been surprised that she had known about the affair but he wasn't. And besides, he was at the point where he didn't even care anymore. "So you know, big damn deal."

"That's what I'm talking about right there."

"I'm not gonna beg your ass Charlene. Either you want us to work it out or you don't."

"I don't."

"Fuck you then!" Fields surprised himself with the choice of words he used to express his feelings.

"Excuse me?"

"You heard me! We'll just fight the rest of this out in court!" Fields yelled. It felt good to hear his wife express some concern for once instead of acting nonchalant like she usually did.

"Then that's what we're gonna have to do! That's the main reason why I can't stand it there, why I haven't been able to for months but you didn't notice that did you?"

"Yeah I did. I just thought it was something that you needed to work through by yourself."

"Well I haven't worked through it. I'm doing it all alone Ron. You're never there and the kids barely respect you! I can't come back to that."

"Bye Charlene!" He yelled and slammed down the phone. A pain of regret stabbed at his heart. But he felt good, like he had finally gotten her foot out of his back. Fields knew he had done the right thing. No amount of talking in the world would have made her come back home. He needed to clear his head.

Fields went to the living room and sat in the chair in front of the television. Pointed the remote and clicked on the tube. Saw a news report about the first killings of the New Year and how the previous year had surpassed the year before. Fields shut off the television. He didn't have to look at the reports. Seemed like he had investigated every one of them.

CHAPTER FORTY-ONE

Richard was awakened by the radio alarm playing a symphony from Vivaldi. He didn't get up though. Instead, Richard just stayed in bed with his eyes pinned to the ceiling listening to the soft music. The morning sun was peeking through the window blinds. He rolled over to avoid the light. Richard was still trying to cope with the thought that Santana was the one who had killed Mark and Monique. And he had a young girl set up to be killed by the cops. None of it seemed real. But it was real. There was a headstone with Mark's name on it in the cemetery to remind him that it had all happened. Things were different and had been since he'd left. The good times that Richard remembered back when he, Santana, and Mark were like brothers were just a good memory.

Richard glanced over at the suitcase on the floor. Felt the beginnings of some tiny pangs of pain in his stomach. He picked up the bottle of ibuprofen from the bedside table and popped two pills. Made up his mind that he was going to see a doctor about the pain as soon as he got back to Baltimore. Sure, he was scared of whatever the doctor was going to tell him was wrong with him but it was better to know. Might even save his life or something. And if it was one thing Richard had learned from Mark's death, it was that life had to be lived to the fullest. One day you're here and the next you're not. So he was going to try to do as much as he could with his before it was too late.

Richard had packed just before going to bed. His mother was right there waiting for him when he came home. She screamed at him about policemen coming to the house and getting her upset, especially after what happened to Mark. Richard apologized and lied about them probably wanting to question if he saw anything related to some shootings that happened earlier that night during the New Years celebration. She bought the lie, gave Richard a hug, and went upstairs to bed. Richard knew then that the detectives had knocked on the door. That's why they were waiting for him across the street when he pulled up. Richard could see that they knew he had information about what happened to Santana, especially Detective Fields. He acted like the undercover cops who tried to do buys back when he used to hustle. Had this authoritative way of speaking that was a dead giveaway, like they were playing a role in a movie. Richard expected the detective to take him to the station for questioning, interrogate him until he collapsed under pressure. Was surprised when he didn't. Sure, Richard would leave the number for the detective like he'd asked. He had nothing to hide.

Richard got up, showered, dressed in a pair of tan khakis, brown sweater, and some tan construction boots. He went to the window, looked down into the alley and saw the back of a pro giving some john head in the alley. Richard watched for a moment feeling himself getting hard. Realized that he hadn't been with a female in almost three months. He thought about Vanessa, couldn't wait to talk to her again. Looked at the phone then at his watch. It was too early to call her. Didn't want to seem too anxious to talk to her again even though he was. Her pretty face and curvaceous body kept popping into his head. Richard missed being in a one on one with a woman. Still carried the mental chest of good memories of the good times between him and Desiree. But all he had were the memories he shared with her. It was time to make some new ones with someone else. Hopefully that someone would be Vanessa.

The smell of bacon and eggs cooking filtered into Richard's room from the vent. He picked up his suitcase, opened the door and made his way downstairs. Decided he'd skip breakfast to get an early start on 95 north back to Baltimore. Even though there wouldn't be any traffic since it was a holiday, felt like he couldn't get out of Colver City fast enough. The next time he would be coming through town was for his court date and that was a month away. Besides, he wanted to get back home to see his little girl. He hoped Desiree wasn't mad at him for what happened at the apartment, but since she hadn't called to talk about the incident, she probably still was. Figured he'd straighten things out when he got back. His mother was sitting at the table when Richard walked into the kitchen. He dropped his suitcase in the living room and

Round Up

sat down in front of her, eyeing the food on the stovetop. Richard placed both of his hands on top of hers on the top of the red and white checkerboard tablecloth. She looked sad, like a child whose favorite pet just died.

Richard gazed into her eyes, said, "I'm about to go Ma."

His mother squeezed turned her palms up and squeezed Richard's hand, responded, "You know, you look just like your father."

"I know, you always tell me that."

"I miss him."

"Me too Ma."

"But God thought it was time to call him home, so I have to be thankful with the time that I spent with him, and that he gave me you to remember him by. I tried to get Shelly to understand that the good Lord was calling Mark to a better place too. But she wasn't trying to hear that. All she knows is that her son is gone, taken away like some wild animal killed in a hunt, and that no God who was worth believing in would've let him die like that."

"What'd she say?"

"Nothing. But I could see from the deadness in her eyes that her soul was gone. That any faith that she had had been buried with her only child. Death is a part of this life. We just have to trust in the Lord to get us through our sorrow."

Richard squeezed his mother's hands listening to her blind faith. He'd lost two people who were close to him in the span of a week. Richard may not have renounced the higher power like his aunt did, but his faith wasn't nearly as strong as his mother's right now. He got up from the table. Walked around to where his mother was sitting and hugged her from behind, whispered, "I love you Ma," and left the kitchen. Richard could feel her eyes on him as he walked into the living room. He pulled the plug to the blinking lights on the Christmas tree in the corner of the room before picking up his suitcase and walking down the hall. Richard put on his jacket and walked out of the door. The air outside was cold and frigid. Richard looked at the Tercel parked in front of the house and prayed that it would start. Figured he'd call his mother in a few days to make sure she was okay. Richard started down the stairs. Heard a familiar voice call out to him from down the block. Richard looked in the direction and saw Nico coming towards him.

Tony Cheatham

"I heard about your man Santana."

"Oh yeah?"

He smiled, showcased his gold tooth. "Guess you know whose going to take over right?" Richard didn't respond. Walked down the steps to his car. That was in another life when the words would have started a war. But that was behind all behind him now. Had been for awhile. Richard opened the door to the ride, threw his suitcase in the back seat. Went around to the other side and slid into the driver's seat. Before he closed the door, he heard the dude yell out, "Just don't forget who runs things when you come back around here punk!" Richard keyed the ignition, felt the engine sputter before turning over. He mashed the accelerator while in park to gun the engine. In the rearview he could see Nico still staring at the car. Richard clicked on the radio, heard the strings from Beethoven's fourth symphony coming through the speakers. He pulled off into traffic with screeching tires. That surprised him. Didn't think the Tercel had enough juice left to do something like that. He felt a throbbing pain in the back of his neck making its way to his head. Remembered he had packed the bottle of ibuprofen with his clothes in the back trunk. He'd unpack his medicine when he was sitting in his apartment back in Baltimore. Hopefully he and Vanessa could hook up later after he was settled. Maybe she could massage the pain away. But then again, that would be expecting too much, too soon.

Printed in the United States
30226LVS00004B/106-144